CRITICAL
MICHAEL L
THE NAR

"A terrific thriller debut. The action is nonstop and very authoritative."

—Peter Maas, author of *Serpico* and *Underboss*

"THE NARROWBACK is a thriller with real sweat on its brow and dirt under its nails. Michael Ledwidge can make the pages fly when he wants to, but he can also make you stop and admire the grace in his prose and the edge in his dialogue. A superb and hard-bitten New York noir."

—Peter Blauner, author of *Man of the Hour* and *Slow Motion Riot*

"Not only are all the elements of successful crime fiction present and accounted for—colorful characters, keen dialogue, sharp sociology, but *THE NARROWBACK* also sparks and sizzles like a wick burning shorter and shorter, until its explosive conclusion."

—*Irish Voice*

"Preaching like a street-corner prophet, Ledwidge writes with a wicked sure-handedness and cooks up a novel that's the love child of authenticity and savage creativity. Hard, tough, and undeniable, the pages fly by just as fast as your fingers can turn them."

—John Ridley, author of *Everybody Smokes in Hell* and *Love Is a Racket*

"As powerful and important a debut as Richard Price's *The Wanderers* or Vincent Patrick's *The Pope of Greenwich Village*. Michael Ledwidge writes with a haunting, disturbing precision which is at once lyrical, literary, and street-smart. His guided tour through the netherworld of New York would make Martin Scorsese shudder."

—Denis Hamill, author of *Fork in the Road*

"A taut crime thriller . . . [with] an easy, fluid style; a quick-moving plot; and dialogue that goes down as smoothly as Jameson's. . . . A gangbusters first novel reminiscent of Jim Thompson and David Goodis."

—*Library Journal*

"*Odd Man Out* meets *Reservoir Dogs*. . . . Ledwidge has produced a model postmodern caper."

—*Kirkus Reviews*

"[An] alcohol- and cocaine-fueled noir page-turner. . . . Ledwidge's too-cool characters are, like his prose, lean and mean, and their inability to distinguish the difference between loyalty to a cause and senseless violence on its behalf creates an aura of futility and hopelessness that pulses through this well-executed debut."

—*Publishers Weekly* (starred review)

"Gritty, violent. . . . Ledwidge's noir world is as grim and bloody as they come."

—*The New York Times Book Review*

"A most promising debut. . . . A new twist to the crime-that-went-wrong situation."

—*The Times* (London)

"A sharp, focused thriller, a tension-packed venture into a world of barbaric violence motivated by depression. . . . It's not often one reads a tale of carnage written this poetically. Ledwidge has raised the bar for crime fiction with *THE NARROWBACK*; fans of the genre will eagerly devour his first effort and wait hungrily for more."

—*In Pittsburgh*

"The fun in this fast-paced yarn is watching Farrell, like a terrified mouse, skitter through the New York underworld, darting here and there, hoping to find a safe hole he can crawl into. . . . Readers will enjoy the chase."

—*Booklist*

"Michael Ledwidge's excellent first novel [is] just about as fine a debut as you'll find in a month of Sundays."

—*The Independent on Sunday* (London)

"This remarkably shrewd first novel debuts a formidable talent for crafty plotting; warm, mortal, charismatic players; and a lucid prose style."

—Maggie Griffin, *Partners & Crime Mystery Booksellers*

For orders other than by individual consumers, Pocket Books grants a discount on the purchase of **10 or more** copies of single titles for special markets or premium use. For further details, please write to the Vice President of Special Markets, Pocket Books, 1230 Avenue of the Americas, 9th Floor, New York, NY 10020-1586.

For information on how individual consumers can place orders, please write to Mail Order Department, Simon & Schuster, Inc., 100 Front Street, Riverside, NJ 08075.

THE
NARROWBACK

Michael Ledwidge

POCKET **STAR** BOOKS

New York   London   Toronto   Sydney   Singapore

The sale of this book without its cover is unauthorized. If you purchased this book without a cover, you should be aware that it was reported to the publisher as "unsold and destroyed." Neither the author nor the publisher has received payment for the sale of this "stripped book."

This book is a work of fiction. Names, characters, places and incidents are products of the author's imagination or are used fictitiously. Any resemblance to actual events or lcoales or persons, living or dead, is entirely coincidental.

 A Pocket Star Book published by
POCKET BOOKS, a division of Simon & Schuster, Inc.
1230 Avenue of the Americas, New York, NY 10020

Copyright © 1999 by Michael Ledwidge

Published by arrangement with Grove/Atlantic, Inc.

All rights reserved, including the right to reproduce this book or portions thereof in any form whatsoever. For information address Grove/Atlantic, Inc., 841 Broadway, New York, NY 10003

ISBN: 0-7434-0354-1

First Pocket Books printing April 2001

10 9 8 7 6 5 4 3 2 1

POCKET STAR BOOKS and colophon are registered trademarks of Simon & Schuster, Inc.

Front cover photo by David H. Wells/Photonica

Printed in the U.S.A.

TO MY WIFE MARY,
FOR HER MAD FAITH

FIC
LEDWIDGE
M

ACKNOWLEDGMENTS

WHEN I FIRST STARTED WRITING THE STORY THAT would turn out to be this book, it was a way of killing the long dismal hours between three and eleven P.M. in the freight elevator of the building where I was working. It took the magic of some very special people to take it on the long, strange journey from there to here. Those people are: Tom and Mollie Broussard, who were the first outside of my family to read and regard it; Dr. Malachi Martin, who so kindly came down to my job and offered me invaluable insight and encouragement; Dr. Mary Ann O'Donnell, my advisor from college and beyond, who sat me down and pointed me in the right direction; both my family and my wife's who provided typing skills and reams of paper along with their support; Joe Kelly and Danny Miller, who, when not busy inspiring much of the spirit of the book, gave me their friendship; Morgan Entrekin, my editor and publisher, for taking a shot on a kid from the Bronx; Eric Price for being a nice guy; my agent, Richard S. Pine, who has to be just about the coolest dude I've ever come across, for being my editor and advocate and friend, I thank you. Lastly, I would like to extend special thanks to Jim Patterson. If I wrote a book about all the incredible things he's done for me nobody would publish it. They would say it was too far-fetched.

PRELUDE

SUNDAY MORNING THE BOYS SIT ALONG A WOODEN bench bolted into a cement wall. The room is cold, as there is no door—only an open threshold—and shirtless and in their shorts they sit still to keep warm. There is another doorway in the dark back of the room, and from it comes the drip of water, the smell of piss. At long last, the coach comes in with his bundled bag. From a darkened corner, a black-haired youth silently gauges his teammates with wide eyes. Outside, a train atop the elevated subway yard flanking their playing field hisses in the outrush of its brakes like a cold horse, and the coach takes the shirts from his bag.

The green jerseys are thick and rough. Multicolored thread from countless rips can be seen at the seams and runs down the long sleeves like scars. They are sequentially numbered, each number signifying position upon the field. Except for the two very best players on the team—who are always the centers—the rest are constantly moved about. It is as if the numbers are the thing and the boys only pale, mutable actors. Their cleats click off the cement floor as each is called to fetch his jersey. They align themselves now in the open middle of the rough-walled room in a condensed semblance of their design. Arrayed fully, they all but burn with anticipation. The coach smiles.

Out upon the field their opponents are already practicing. They are from somewhere outside the city and wear blue shirts with socks to match. They practice drills none of the city boys have seen before. Their parents in the old stands behind them drink from thermoses and call out words of encouragement. On the side of the urchins only the coach stands in their stead, wild haired, red eyed. The truth of the matter is, these city youths don't practice often, and their record shows this. For the coach, fielding a team is trouble enough. He has to round them up from the street corners and school yards like suspects the mornings before game times. The rumor is that theirs will be the last Irish football team from their parish as the ranks of neighborhood Irish are thinned by the promise of the suburbs.

Throughout the first half, the city team is

thrashed by its suburban adversary. From the side-lines, the coach wails as if in pain. He screams with such force and feeling it is as if his very life is on the line and is being lost by the indifference of his players. At halftime, they are down considerably. The coach broods as he doles out cans of warm soda to the muddy, tired bunch. His silence carries weight after such violent exclamation.

At the start of the second half, it begins to rain heavily. At long last, the ball is kicked toward the black-haired boy. He has not seen the ball all day. Like most on that team, he is not a superior athlete; if anything distinguishes him from his peers, it is, perhaps, his awareness of the true depth of this rivalry, and it has filled him with a rancor he cannot put words to.

The ball falls out of the gray sky, and he runs up for it. His opposite, the blue fullback, follows. They jump. The heavy leather ball smacks into the city boy's chest, almost knocking out his breath, and he rips it down and turns running. The full-back rushes at him, and the city boy handpasses the ball to his teammate, who gives-and-goes it back to him as he cuts ahead. There is only the goalie now before him, and as he begins his kick, he feels the impact at his back and the ball slips from his hands and all he can do as he falls is watch, stunned, as the goalie scoops it up and boots it back downfield.

He waits, but there is no whistle. His coach is yelling at the official in an uproar that is checked now only by a new hoarseness in his voice. Covered in mud, the city boy stands and glances at his teammate, who indicates the fullback with a pointed chin. The city boy rushes up and hits the turned fullback low in the legs with his shoulder and topples him to the ground. The fullback rises and brings back his fist to throw a punch, but one of his fellow suburbanites grabs his arm to break it up and the city boy does not waste this opportunity. He is not big, but he knows how to hit, and he steps in and slaps the larger boy in the cheek with a haymaker that pops out across the field. The fullback screams out as he falls to his knees. Confusion alights on the features of the suburban youths as they glance nervously toward their sidelines. The city boys upon the field bristle and the coach on the sidelines is yelling "no, no," but it is hard to hear him now.

The ball is left discarded in the mud of the field, and the boys swarm. In the elevated subway yard, a train slowly clatters out, its blue electric sparks illuminating the fray. Adults rush off the sidelines to break it up, but they are helpless as the boys pile. The city boy is at the bottom of the pile, and he is kicking with his cleats at the fullback, kicking and smiling.

1

AT FIRST THE BLACK SPECK IN THE EVENING SKY seemed like a bag, perhaps a black garbage bag borne aloft by the strong wind. When it dropped and unfurled, Farrell realized it was a crow. High above the jagged tenement skyline the bird circled and then swooped down and alit on a television aerial. Leaning back against the cold stone wall of the roof, Farrell stared out at the black bird etched sharply on the gray horizon, dark and still among the twining metal boughs.

He turned. A long-haired man with a goatee stood beside him studying the street below with binoculars. The man's name was Mullen.

"What do you think?" Farrell asked. He had to raise his voice over the wind.

It was November and cold out on the rough tar rooftop. Mullen's long, stringy hair whipped about him.

"I think," he said, lowering the binoculars, "we better get the fuck out of this wind."

The air in the stairwell was warm and sour. Farrell held the cheap, metal-plated door behind him to close it gently. They went down two flights of worn, stained, marble steps into Farrell's fourth-floor apartment. He threw shut the three new locks on the front door before following Mullen into the living room. The sawed-off lay on the cracked coffee table where Mullen had left it, its barrels blue in the dim light of the standing lamp. Mullen sat on the couch and retrieved his cigarettes. He took one, lit it, and tossed the pack to Farrell. Mullen smoked pensively, staring into space.

"Yeah," he said finally. "We could do that motherfucker without too much fuss. He's cocky. He looks like the type never saw a white man he was too afraid of. That's our advantage."

"He's cocky, all right," said Farrell.

"How'd he get in here again?"

"Jimmied the hinge side of the door frame with a pry bar."

"A regular one-man crime spree, huh. That cocksucker. OK, I'm thinkin it this way. I clean myself up, slap a couple of Jersey tags on the Chevy, get in the whole suburban cowboy mode, right? Then I glide up for a transaction. One look at my pasty white face puts him at ease, and when he goes down for the dope, I drop both barrels on him. You situate yourself down the block and when he falls, you come up and roll him. And before you can say 'drug-related,' we're in Reilly's sippin stout with our bank."

Farrell smoked, thinking.

"You think it could go down that simple?"

"It ain't rocket science."

"What about his boys on the sidewalk?"

"You have your pistol out. You see anybody pointing anything at me, you take 'em out. I do the same for you. We won't have to worry about it, though, since once they see their boss's head come off they're not gonna be doing anything except running. Unless of course you count crappin in their pants."

"When you thinking?" asked Farrell.

Mullen picked the shotgun off the table and draped it on his shoulder. He smiled—the cigarette in the corner of his mouth making him squint.

"Ain't no time like the present," he said.

It was night when they got back with the plates. From the car up the block they watched the man doing business. Wearing an enormous puffed parka, he reclined astride a thumping Suzuki Samurai in a stiff posture of threat. As cars pulled up, he leaned in and out of them with such speed and lack of gesture it seemed only words were exchanged—as if he were some priest or wise man and those in the cars pilgrims in need of quick counsel.

Mullen took a deep breath.

"You get goin," he said.

When Farrell didn't move, he turned to him.

"What's up? You pussying out on me here?"

Farrell stared out. The Number One Broadway local trundled by on the elevated track in the distance, its windows backlit by a streetlight like the last empty frames of film through a projector.

"Fuck it," Farrell said finally.

"Fuck it? Fuck what? Everything?"

"No, this."

"Listen, if you're scared . . . "

"Oh, I'm scared. But it's not that."

"You've been inside, Tommy. If this guy did this to you inside, what would you do?"

"This ain't inside."

Mullen looked out the window, incredulously, at the gated windows, the garbage-strewn side-walks.

"Close enough, you ask me. I mean, what's the story? You gonna pull this shit again when we go do the other thing? You said we go at Christmas. How the fuck we go in a month with no stake?"

"We postpone."

"Till when? Next fuckin Christmas?"

"No, the summer."

"The summer? We gotta wait six fucking months because you got cold feet. You're not even pullin the trigger."

"Fuck it," said Farrell. He looked at Mullen for the first time since they sat there. "My way or fuck the whole thing."

"You're a pain in the ass," said Mullen after a while.

"Yeah, first you said I'm a genius. Now I'm a pain in the ass."

Mullen blew into his hands, staring out at the dealer.

"You're sure?" he asked.

He sounded disappointed.

Farrell awoke to the blaring alarm, and in half darkness he turned and set it silent with a slap. From the open, shadeless window came the sounds of the street—tires on pavement, the whine of brakes, a far-off horn. Headlights swept across the rough, pocked walls of the small room, and after a moment he rose naked and walked across the bare wood floor.

The bathroom light sent forms scurrying, and he showered quickly and shaved. He retrieved the garment bag from the otherwise empty closet and put it on the bed. He opened the bag and felt the rich fabric of the suit. How, at thirty years of age, could something so standard have eluded him so completely? He dressed in the mirror above the scarred bureau by the glow of electric light coming from the window.

He was an average-sized man but lean, which gave him an appearance of height. His face was plain and pale, the skin pulled tight on his cheeks, and there was tension to his glance. His medium-length hair was black and combed neatly, and his eyes reflected whatever he wore. In the somber business suit they seemed almost black, forgettable. He could have been any of the businessmen he passed in the street every day.

From under the bed he retrieved a used leather briefcase. He popped it open and laid it on the bed. From under the mattress he took out the gun. It was a silver Smith & Wesson 9-millimeter, and he held it, staring for a while. Then he clacked back the slide, chambered a round, flicked on the safety with his thumb, and placed it in the briefcase.

The box of Marlboros and I ♥ NY zippo he had bought at a newsstand the day before were on top of the nightstand, and he picked them up and packed the cigarettes against his palm in slow ceremony. He went to the window, took out a cigarette, and lit it with a clip-clop of the lighter. It was his first in six months, and a twinge of remorse came with the head rush.

On the street the pink neon offerings of "LIQUOR" and "TAROT CARDS" and "BUDDY BOOTHS" burned like beacons in the dark. He would have waited down on the corner, but he knew that in July at four A.M. the human residue that called the streets of Times Square home was just getting its second wind. Dressed as he was, he didn't need to risk having to show the contents of the briefcase to anyone prematurely. Already the stale air of the room was warming, promising scorching heat for the day to come. That he had lived in this mangy place for so long stone sober still surprised him. The amount of horror a man was willing to inflict upon himself obviously knew no bounds.

A beat-up blue van pulled out of traffic and stopped in the street down in front. He flicked the cigarette out into the night. He went to the bed, picked up the briefcase, and came out of the dingy room, leaving the door wide open.

It was even warmer in the dark street. The night did nothing to dispel the stench of the city that hung heavy in the doorways and wafted up from the stained sidewalks, the smell of piss and cement and car exhaust. He didn't try to look for omens as he came away; any sign of promise—if any had ever existed—had fled that place long ago.

"That's a good disguise," Mullen said from behind the wheel as Farrell entered. "You actually look halfway respectable."

Mullen was clean shaven now, and his hair was pulled back neatly in a pony tail. He bore a dark tattoo of an elaborate Celtic cross on his pale, wiry forearm like a brand.

Farrell smiled, slamming the door shut.

"Well, let's just hope it goes over," he replied.

He turned. Three men were sitting in the back of the van. Two were big and stocky and had long hair and sideburns and wore mustaches in the style known as Fu Manchu. The third was small and clean shaven, almost childlike but for the grim expression steadying his features. All wore blue work clothes and ski masks scrunched on their foreheads. All smoked. Each man sat sweating and holding a bulky, ink-black Uzi in his lap. There was a large, gray, metal gas tank with dials and hoses feeding out of it on a metal hand truck behind them, and there was a canvas tool bag beside it.

"How we doin' back here?" Farrell asked.

"For fuck's sake," the smallest of them barked, "let's get it done."

The two big brothers, Roy and Billy Burns—or the Sideburns, as they were collectively known—were acquaintances of Mullen, and like him they hailed from Hell's Kitchen on Manhattan's West Side. The smaller man's name was Durkin, and by manner of his speech, evidently was from Ireland. He was a welder by trade and had been recruited by Billy Burns in an after-hours bar in the Bainbridge section of the Bronx not two weeks before.

Five men in a confederacy based on common gain. Although it was Farrell's plan that brought them together, he avowed no leadership. Whatever might drive his accomplices, he speculated, lay solely in their own perhaps dark, but wholly wild, hearts.

"You heard the man," Farrell said. "Let's roll."

They pulled out and made a right at the corner and proceeded carefully cross town. Farrell felt an urge to go over everything one more time, but let it pass. In the silence he lit a second Marlboro and stared out at the night. The cigarette ads on the last diehard taxis cut the air above the dark streets like shark fins. A WWII surplus truck came to a screeching halt in front of the clapboard newsstand just long enough for its driver to savagely kick a bloated stack of papers out of its doorless cab before a clutch-rending departure. Garbagemen down a block wordlessly fed black bags into the beetle-backed hydraulic pits of their crunching, beeping machines. Farrell liked the down time between four and six A.M. Emptied of the crowds and traffic, the massive buildings and wide avenues seemed boundless and the bleak beauty of the city lay bared. It was the other twenty-two hours that killed it for you.

At the wide promenade of Park Avenue the van made a left and headed uptown. The hovering Metlife building behind them watched their progress. At 66th they passed the building where Farrell used to work; he looked over at the morning papers piled at the door. At 71st they made a U-turn and slowed to a stop. Mullen handed Farrell a black radio, which he put in his briefcase. Farrell retrieved a pair of round-framed glasses from the inside pocket of his jacket and put them on. He winked at Mullen, picked up his briefcase, and got out of the van.

It took a full minute to hail a taxi.

Farrell gave the driver his destination, and the cab stopped five blocks down. He paid wordlessly and got out.

The hotel stood catty-corner to his previous place of employment. Forty floors of beige lime-stone with cascading light down the corners of its multilayered tiers, with dramatic shadows down the length of its edifice. Farrell turned. The van idled half a block down. He took a deep breath.

The doorman smiled as he pushed through the revolving door.

"Bags, sir?" he asked.

Farrell held up his briefcase.

"You're looking at it. The rest will be along later, I hope."

"Airline had a mix-up?" the doorman asked with understanding.

"It's been a long one," said Farrell, putting weariness in his tone.

"Check-in is up and to your right."

"I appreciate it."

Farrell almost shook at the intensity of the lobby, a vast pristine chamber of white marble floored with checkerboard tile that shined like glass. He felt that same palpable sanctity as in a cathedral or a museum or a courthouse. The plainclothes security guard standing beside the bank of elevators on the back wall watched Farrell between sips of coffee. Farrell returned a disinterested glance as he approached the check-in desk to his right—each footfall ricocheting off the tile like a pistol shot.

Behind the desk were a young man and a woman typing at a terminal. The man smiled at Farrell's approach. He was cleancut and wore a blue blazer and a smile as plastic as the DANIEL MARTIN name tag on his lapel.

"Good morning, sir. How can I help you?" His cheerful tone rang hollow at four-twenty in the morning.

"Good morning, Daniel," Farrell said, reading the tag deliberately and offering back a weary grin. "I had reservations for yesterday evening and my flight was incredibly delayed, and frankly, I need to get some sleep before I collapse."

"I'm sorry to hear that, sir," the clerk replied

earnestly, looking down at his terminal. "I'll have you right on your way. Your name?"

"Peter Ullman," Farrell said. He checked his watch.

"OK, Mr. Ullman," said Martin, hitting buttons. "Here we are. The suite you reserved is still available. It's on the twenty-first floor, Central Park side. The views, I think, you will find most magnificent. Breakfast starts at seven in all three of our restaurants, and the dry-cleaning service starts at six . . ."

Farrell was no longer listening. He brought the briefcase up to the desk ledge and popped the clasps. He reached into the case and gripped the pistol. He turned over his shoulder and watched the guard. From down the stairs came the sound of commotion.

"Hey!" someone, probably the doorman, called out.

As the guard went to the stairs, Farrell brought out the Smith & Wesson. He had it trained when the guard reached for the small of his back a moment later.

"DON'T!" Farrell screamed.

The security guard looked at Farrell and froze with his hand behind his back. For an instant it seemed that he would draw, but the moment passed, and with a slackening around his eyes, he put his hands in the air.

"NOBODY FUCKING MOVE!" Roy Burns screamed as he came bursting up from the steps, training his Uzi at the guard's chest. Billy Burns and Durkin, a step behind, rushed the bewildered doorman before them.

Farrell turned back toward Martin, the desk clerk, whose soft, puzzled expression bespoke a mind not yet caught up with the split-second change that had just occurred.

"OUT FROM THE COUNTER, BOTH OF YOU!" screamed Farrell, putting the gun to Martin's temple.

The girl, like Martin, stared dumbstruck—a deer caught in oncoming headlights. Farrell pulled Martin's head onto the counter by his hair and trained the gun on her.

"MOVE!" he screamed.

She moved. Farrell got them out from behind the counter and onto the floor and took a pair of black leather gloves out of the briefcase and pulled them on. The doorman and security guard were herded by the Sideburns next to the clerks. Farrell reached around the guard's back and retrieved his gun, a snubnosed, hammerless revolver, and put it into his waistband. Billy Burns produced a thick roll of gray electrical tape. He quickly taped the arms and legs of the woman clerk and then the doorman. Farrell took the keys from the guard's belt. He locked all the elevators open with the smallest key and quickly came back to the guard.

"Front door," Farrell said, handing him the keys.

The guard stared at him. Roy Burns jabbed the Uzi's barrel off the man's temple, and then the guard selected a key and handed the ring back to Farrell. Farrell jogged down the entrance steps, locked the revolving door, and came back up. He emptied the guard's pockets, retrieving a radio, handcuffs, and the man's wallet. He opened the wallet.

"Jerry Franklin," Farrell said. "You're cooperating. That's good. You know what we're here for. We're going to take it and get right back out of your life." Farrell hefted the guard's radio. "Your partner calls down, you're going to tell him to take it easy and catch a little more shut-eye. I know your partner is snoozing, OK. I know fucking everything. Right now everything is fine, nobody's hurt. If you pull any shit and he comes down here or calls the cops—you see that pretty girl?—I'm going to drag her over here and make you watch as I put a bullet in her head. That's a guarantee. She's the first body gets kicked down to the hostage negotiation team, you got me? I want you to be informed because it's not up to me, it's up to you."

Farrell cuffed the guard's hands behind him. The girl was whimpering softly. Farrell helped Martin up by the scruff of his jacket and jammed the Smith & Wesson into his ear. He banged him through the swinging door behind the check-in desk. Durkin followed. On the back wall beyond some desks and filing cabinets was a steel gate.

"OK," said Farrell, letting him go. "I know what your bosses told you to say. You don't know the combination, blah, blah, blah. You're the man on this shift, I know you are, Danny Boy. Now you can save yourself a lot of pain by owning up to that right now, because I don't see your boss here, do you? All I see is you, me, and my friend here." Durkin produced a large, dropbladed hunting knife and held it out for Martin's inspection.

The clerk trembled.

"I'll do anything you want," he said.

"I want you to get the keys to the gate there, and then I want you to open up the safe and the safety deposit boxes."

Martin shakily retrieved a set of keys from one of the desks and opened the steel gate. Inside, foot-square stainless-steel lockers went floor to ceiling along both walls, and a waist-high combination safe sat in the back wall.

"The safe first," ordered Farrell, pushing Martin into the room.

Martin knelt by the safe, his face a film of sweat. He turned the tumbler slowly left-right-left-right-left. Farrell and Durkin looked at each other in disbelief. Martin paused, steadying his shaking hands. He pulled the handle. The door slowly swung open. A quarter way up the safe, bundled stacks of cash stared out at them.

"Good man!" said Farrell, ruffling Martin's hair. "No torch," he called into the radio.

"Rockin," Mullen called back.

Durkin inspected the door of the safe keenly.

"I could a done her," he lamented as he took some black nylon bags from his coveralls, "just as well."

They cleaned the safe. The stacks were mostly twenties and fifties, but there were more than a few hundreds. Farrell looked at Martin.

"The boxes," he said.

Martin held out one of the keys. Farrell took it

and opened a box at random. Inside diamond earrings sat on black felt. He scooped them out and dropped them into the bag. He made Martin lie down on the floor, then took out his radio.

"Time?" he called into it.

"Six minutes," Mullen blared back.

Roy Burns entered. Farrell opened the lockers as fast as he could. Watches and jewelry blurred into the bags. His hands had begun to cramp when Mullen's voice blared, "Time!" from the radio.

Farrell stopped. He wiped his sweaty face across the arm of his suit coat. Durkin and Roy were still emptying boxes.

"We're done," said Farrell.

"But . . . ," said Durkin.

"Time's up," Farrell barked.

Durkin chucked a last jewelry box into a bag. Farrell held out a packet of cash to Martin. The clerk looked at the money, puzzled. Farrell winked and Martin smiled, quickly stuffing the money down the front of his pants. Farrell then bound his arms and legs and left him face down on the floor. They left the vault.

Back in the lobby Farrell got the security guard to his feet.

"OK. Just the tapes and we're out of here."

"Tapes?"

"Don't fuck with me now," Farrell said angrily.

"First floor, first door on—," said the guard.

"No, you're gonna show me."

Farrell pulled the guard into the elevator. At the first floor he again locked the elevator, checked the empty hall, and then led the guard out. The guard indicated a door off the hallway and showed Farrell which key. Farrell put the guard on the floor, drew his gun, and keyed himself in slowly. Farrell dragged the guard in and closed the door. On the console in front of him were sixteen small black-and-white television screens showing various parts of the hotel. On one screen were the bound workers with the menacing ski-masked Burnses standing over them. Another showed the main entrance, where Farrell could just make out the grill of the van. A third revealed the trashed vault room (which surprised Farrell because he had seen no indication of a camera) with Martin trussed in the corner, now on his side. Farrell uncuffed the guard and helped him up.

"Get them," he said, training his gun.

The guard opened a compartment at the bottom of the console revealing sixteen numbered slots. He hit the stop button on the first tape and then rewind.

"I'm not taking them back to the fucking video store," Farrell said exasperated.

The guard put his hands up in nervous apology, ejected the tape, and placed it on top of the console. Fifteen others followed. Farrell piled them into his briefcase.

"That's it?" he asked.

"That's it."

"Turn around."

As Farrell re-cuffed the guard, he noticed movement on one of the screens. Durkin appeared in the vault. Farrell watched the screen, stunned, as Durkin went over to Martin and unzipped the bound man's pants. Martin lashed out instinctively, catching Durkin in the face with a knee. Durkin fell back and pulled off his mask. He dabbed his fingers to his mouth and, without putting his mask back on, produced a small gun with a long cylinder attached to its barrel from an ankle holster. He placed the gun to the clerk's head and retrieved the hidden money. Then he hid the money in his shirt, dabbed the blood from his mouth with his mask, and put the mask back on. He pressed his pistol to the man's throat for a long second, took it away, and left.

Farrell stared at the screen bewildered. The hidden gun hadn't bothered him so much as the silencer. The silencer fucking scared him. The silencer meant Durkin had plans of his own in mind. Solo plans. Farrell thought hard.

"What the fuck you waiting for!" blared Mullen from Farrell's radio. Farrell and the guard jumped.

"On our way," Farrell called. He took a deep breath and brought the guard out and down the hall.

Durkin was standing by the check-in desk as the elevator opened. Farrell brought the guard to where the doorman and girl lay, placed him face down, and quickly taped him like the rest. Without another word, Farrell turned and led Durkin and the Burns brothers out of the lobby.

He keyed open the revolving door and they filed out, and he locked it behind them. They jogged to the van and jumped into the open side door. The van lurched quickly up Park Avenue. They barreled left on 61st, sped over two blocks, and careened left again onto Third. Farrell climbed into the front passenger seat and turned, looking out the back window. No flashing lights. No sirens.

"Well?" yelled Mullen over the wail of the van's engine.

"We got it," said Farrell.

"How much?"

"I didn't get a chance to count it, but there's enough to go around."

Mullen brought the speeding van into a skid as a gypsy cab ate a red light half a block ahead. Mullen steered into the slide, missing the multicolored cab by inches. The van vowed to roll for a long awful second, but Mullen righted it, and they sped on.

"Slow the fuck down! You hear any sirens?" Farrell screamed when his heart began beating again.

"You're shitting me?" said Mullen oblivious. "We're talkin' substantial cash in the safe?"

"That's right."

"We're rich?" asked Mullen.

"We'll see," said Farrell, taking off his glasses and turning around.

In the back of the van, Durkin and the Burnses had taken off their masks and were laughing with relief. Durkin smiled at Farrell.

"Ya surprised me in there the way ya put the fear of God inta those bastards," he said.

"You weren't so bad yourself," said Farrell.

"The way ya were talkin, even I believed ya," continued Durkin.

Farrell said nothing.

Spanish Harlem blew past the window, all steel shutters and storefront churches. At the end of Third Avenue a skeletal black woman in a bikini stood on the corner and peered rapaciously in at the van as it went right. The road was flanked by a city bus depot and the sloping roadbed of the Harlem River Drive. They bore left under the highway, but instead of continuing up onto the entrance ramp they went over the curb onto a concrete embankment that hovered above the black surface of the Harlem River.

Across the water on the Bronx side, a dead electric billboard jutted a colossal pack of cigarettes at Manhattan as if offering the city a smoke. The van continued left to the gate of an abandoned construction materials site and stopped. A huge, rusted-out cement mixer behind the gate stood out against the night sky like some misbegotten carnival ride. They got out of the van, taking the bags. Mullen unlocked the gate. Inside sat a primer-colored Chevy. They transferred the bags, Farrell's briefcase, and the Uzis to the trunk of the car.

"Let's get out of here already," said Mullen, going over to the van. "Help me get rid of this fucking thing."

The Sideburns stayed by the car while Farrell

went over to the van with Durkin. Mullen opened the door and popped it into neutral and began pushing, pulling hard on the steering wheel to point it at the river. Durkin pushed at the passenger side and Farrell from the back. As the van approached the edge, Farrell glanced around the side of the van and spied Durkin bent, grabbing at something at his ankle. Farrell turned back and slid the revolver from his waistband, his heart slamming, his mouth cotton. When he peeked out again, Durkin was turned all the way around with the pistol in his hand. Their eyes met.

"What the fuck?" said Mullen from the other side. "Push!"

Farrell backpedaled as a small hole punched through the metal beside his head with a hollow ping. He lost his feet and sat in the gravel. He heard Durkin's boots quickly approaching, and he rolled under the van. He could see the boots now, and he aimed, animal fear like a clamp on the back of his neck, and shot. Durkin cried out and went down.

When Farrell scurried out from beneath the van, Durkin was lying on his side holding his ankle with both hands. Blood—black in the bad light—

poured out between his fingers and stained the gravel. His pistol lay on the ground beyond him. Farrell stepped over and picked it up.

"What the fuck you think you're doing?" Billy asked quietly beside Farrell. Farrell glanced around to face the black barrel hole of Billy Burns's Uzi.

"He tried to take us off," said Farrell.

"What makes you think that?"

"I don't know," Farrell said, breathing heavily, "maybe the fucking shot he just took at me?"

"What shot? I didn't hear no shot," Roy said.

Farrell handed him Durkin's gun and pointed to the silencer. Then he bent and reached into Durkin's shirt and took out the money he had given the clerk. He tossed it at Billy.

"I threw the clerk a little tip in the vault. Guess Durkin here thought I was too generous, because when I went up to get the tapes, I see him on one of the screens goin' back to get it. And when the kid resists, he pulls out this silenced piece here. Then he takes it out again a second ago and throws a shot at me. So I rolled under the van and caught him in the damn foot."

Farrell still clenched the revolver in his hand, and it shook a little as he finished his story.

Mullen took Durkin's .22 from Roy and looked at it. He handed it back to Farrell.

"A silencer? This guy's a fucking assassin," Mullen concluded.

Billy's face twisted in calculation, and then he put the Uzi down and shrugged his shoulders.

"OK," he said. "He said he dropped something in the vault. I didn't know. Sorry 'bout that."

"No problem. Only what do we do with him now?" Farrell asked earnestly.

Roy eyed Durkin dreadfully.

"Me and Billy brought him in," Roy said. There was an odd flatness to his voice, a peculiar calm. He glanced at his brother.

"Only right we take care of it."

"How?" Farrell was about to ask, until he suddenly realized it.

Without another word, the Sideburns walked over to the Irishman. For all his small stature, Durkin didn't cry out or change his implacable expression as the two brothers converged on him.

Billy lifted him clear off the ground by his throat while Roy scooped up his legs. The grim procession moved off behind the piled rubble.

Farrell had been to prison, and he thought the daily malignancy he had witnessed there had hardened his heart. The sight of Durkin being dragged off into the shadows rattled him to his soul.

"This part you don't wanna see, Tommy," Mullen said, putting an arm across Farrell's shoulders and leading him back toward the car. He offered his cigarettes. Farrell took one.

"Believe me," Mullen said, giving him a light.

When Roy came back around the rubble, he was wiping at something silver in his hand with a bandanna. Then he folded it shut and put it in his jacket. His brother, following, dragged Durkin over the cement by a bare, bloody foot. When they got beside the van, Roy turned and lifted Durkin by his hands. Durkin's head lolled back exaggeratedly.

"One," they said in unison, swinging the diminutive Irishman back.

"Two."

"Three."

They let him go. Durkin's arms spread to the sides as he sailed through the air, as if he wished them one last embrace, and then he disappeared into the darkened side door of the van with a negligible thump. Roy slid the door shut with a bang. The Burnses rolled the van off the platform. It hit the water heavily and then sunk under the black surface, front end first.

The four of them got into the dust-colored Chevy. The Burnses in the back, Farrell at shotgun, Mullen at the wheel. Mullen barreled over the curb onto the entrance ramp with an angry bark of tires and gunned the car north on the highway.

"How much, Tom? For real." Mullen smiled after a few minutes.

"I don't know," said Farrell flatly.

"Didn't even need the donkey cocksucker, huh?" Mullen said.

"Nope," said Farrell, looking off. "The kid opened the vault like it was his high school gym locker."

"With all that money there?" asked Mullen.

"I don't know. I guess somebody fucked up big time."

The silent car sped north. Farrell looked out at the water and at the expanse of the South Bronx on its opposite shore. Sunrise hinted over the concrete box horizon in a touch of light blue that led into dark blue that led into a purple sky. The lights of the Bronx reflected in the black ribbon of the Harlem River, their yellow glow spread in strips upon its oily surface. Farrell lit a cigarette.

Suddenly it occurred to him that the lights in the water didn't seem like reflections at all, but like emanations, glowing spirits sunk to some dark and lonely place.

2

THE MOTEL WAS IN THE BRONX, OFF BROADWAY, NEAR the city line. If it held any distinction whatsoever, it was that the clerk behind the scratched Plexiglas lacked an arm. The take lay piled upon the double bed before them: gold necklaces and earrings and bracelets; heavy wristwatches with second hands that did not pause but swept each moment along in a graceful, continuous revolution; a handful of loose, cut diamonds that sparkled brightly even in the room's yellowed fluorescent light. They had retrieved the diamonds from a leather satchel with a copy of the invoice. Three hundred and eighty-seven thousand dollars in class D stones. The cash, arranged neatly by denomination, covered the rest of the cheap bedspread. Among the others Farrell, still in his suit, seemed like a professional gambler set to a high-stakes game of cards with pirates. He punched the calculator in his hand.

"One hundred thirty-seven thousand," he said, looking up. "Per man."

They looked at each other dazed. Roy Burns smiled widely. Mullen nodded in approval.

"Did I tell you this was the man?" he said, pointing at Farrell. "This here's the fuckin man."

"That's not all," Farrell said, smiling. "After we fence these stones, we're lookin at another fifty apiece. Little bonus for a job well done."

"You just keep it comin, don't you?" Mullen grinned. He looked over at the Sideburns. "He seems wired tight, don't he, Roy? But it's like I was tellin you before. My boy here's a stone psycho. It's like a couple of years ago we were drivin around all fucked up, right? He's behind the wheel, and all of a sudden we stop. I look out the window and we're smack dab in the middle of Harlem—I mean spook fucking central—in front of this place, the Ebony. So I said, 'What the fuck you doin?'and he says, 'I'm thirsty. I'm getting a drink,' and then in he goes. Five minutes go by. Nothing. So I figure I have to go in and at least try to retrieve his body, right? I walk in, and this place is packed, standin room only, with brothers, like at a rap concert or something. Except there isn't any music. In fact, the whole place is deathly silent except for Tommy here, who's slapping the bar, going, 'Service! Service here!' "

The Sideburns laughed. A slight, uncontrollable smile came over Farrell's face.

"So then the crowd turns and sees me, and there's a loud sigh, 'Shit, man. Fuckin cops,' they're whining. And this huge motherfucker comes up to me, sticks his finger in my face, and says, 'Why you pigs gots to be razzin us all the time?' I got no answer for the guy. I mean at this point, I'm fucking speechless with fear, so I just shrug my shoulders and walk past to stand next to the Great White Hope here. There's a point there where I think they want to go for broke—cops or no cops—but they ease off for some reason, and then the place clears and there's only me, Farrell, and the bartender—this big, fat mama. 'You boys from the three o?' she asks. I nod my head, my voice still out to lunch, and this guy, this maniac here, takes out of his wallet a picture of some girl. His fuckin high school prom date or something, and he says to the mama real sincerely, 'Have you seen this girl?' Like some white girl ever set foot in the place. She stares at Farrell for a few seconds—she can see the picture's a hundred years old—and says, 'No, never.' And then he mumbles about how he saw some guys rollin dice when he came in, and how would she like to get her liquor license revoked. So she goes to the till and hands us twenty bucks apiece, and we leave. I swear to God, I thought they would kill us on the sidewalk, but there was nobody."

"You shook down a Harlem bar?" Roy asked Farrell, stunned.

"I was loaded," Farrell protested halfheartedly.

"Hey, no man, I think it's beautiful," said Roy.

They all laughed together.

"How did you know they'd think you were cops?" asked Billy.

"I didn't know my own name," said Farrell.

"I guess, what else could they think? That you were just a couple of crazy white boys fuckin' with them? If they knew you were just a couple of stumblebum drunks, they would have killed you," said Roy.

"Some people skydive, some bungee jump. You gotta get your thrills somewhere, right?" said Mullen. He looked at Farrell benevolently. "You might not have been from the neighborhood, but dammit you shoulda been."

Farrell nodded, smiling. He looked at the money. His father had once told him that he'd never make a dime. Take that, prick, he thought. He stood.

"Let me get the fuck out of this already," he said, loosening his tie.

He grabbed his knapsack off the floor and walked into the bathroom and closed the door and stripped. He took a pair of electric clippers from his bag and shaved his head in the paint-flecked mirror above the sink. His black hair fell in clumps to the filthy floor. When he was done, he smiled, rubbing at the stubble on the back of his head. It had been a long time since it had been so short.

Farrell showered for the second time that morning. He dressed in jeans and construction boots from the bag he had packed. He took out the gun he had stolen from the guard. It was a Ruger snubnose .357, not a .38 as he'd thought. He pulled the latch with his thumb and tipped out the chamber. Then he slipped out the one spent casing and held it to his eyes.

In the early stages of the robbery's planning, he and Mullen had almost killed a drug dealer for stake money. A man who had wronged Farrell. A man whose death might have eased some suffering in the world. He had declined, thinking that such a heinous act was beyond him.

The overhead light flickered off the brass between his fingers. Durkin. He tried to assuage his guilt with the assurance that there was no way to allow for every eventuality. But an uneasy realization kept coming back: He had no idea what he was capable of.

It had been a year in the planning. He had gotten a job as night doorman on Park Avenue straight out of prison. It came to him like deliverance his second week there. He saw it from the gated mailroom window. An armored car stopping at the curb of the hotel across the street, two guards going in and coming out five minutes later, laden with currency bags.

He had studied the hotel nightly. Noted shift changes, radio car patrols, the comings and goings of guests. Within three months, every movement could be predicted with certainty. Anything further would have to be gathered from inside.

He'd met with Mullen on an afternoon in October. It had been two years since the last time he had seen him. Farrell laid out the detailed blueprint of his intentions, and when he was done, the wild Irish American sat poker-faced and asked if he could use his phone. Dialing, he explained how he'd been loading chicken trucks on lower

Eleventh Avenue for the past six months. Then speaking into the phone, he'd said, "Lenny? Hi. Do you know who this is? Good. I just wanted to let you know that it's time for you to go get yourself some other fuckin' nigger, you fat prick, because I quit." Hanging up, he'd turned to Farrell and smiled. "What was that you were saying?"

He had sent Mullen into the hotel with a video camera hidden in a briefcase. Mullen had checked in half an hour before the weekly pickup. He asked the clerk to keep the briefcase behind the desk for a person who would be coming for it later. The next morning, they saw the taped transaction from atop a desk in the back office: the clerk leading the guards into the back office and through to the vault. The clerk was the man to go for.

Mullen had brought the Sideburns in a month before. Two brothers whose family business was concentrated solely in armed robbery, they could be counted on to both intimidate and keep their heads. Even so, Farrell had misgivings. If the vault was on a timelock, they were fucked. So, when Roy said he'd just met a welder who could open safes, Farrell had agreed to let him in for a cut.

Durkin had sliced open a plate of high carbon steel with an acetylene torch in under eight minutes. Then he had done it in under six. Durkin was young, but his easy confidence and his craftsmanship belied his years. He had seemed just like what they were looking for, a piece of luck. He had turned out to be luck all right, Farrell thought, all of it bad.

Farrell put the casing in his pocket and flicked the chamber back. He laid the revolver down. He took Durkin's .22 out of his bag. He slid out the clip and counted eight rounds into his hand and then put them back and slapped it home. It was a Colt Woodsman with a homemade silencer, balanced, oiled, well maintained. A shooter's gun, a professional's. The fact that Durkin was no longer around to use it wasn't giving him any relief. He unscrewed the silencer and dropped it in his bag.

He put on a T-shirt from his bag and stood. He took the Smith & Wesson automatic from the pocket of his suit hanging on the door and stuck it in his belt. He picked up the revolver and placed it at the small of his back and put on the suit coat to hide it. Finally, he stuffed the .22 into his boot. Armed to the teeth, he went back into the motel room.

Mullen and the Sideburns glanced up at Farrell's new appearance and then turned back to the TV.

Theirs was the second story. It showed a picture of the hotel. A reporter spoke about the heist and ended with the statement that the police seemed to have no leads but speculated that it was an inside job. Then Mullen shut off the battered set.

"Hear that?" Mullen asked merrily. "Inside job. Just like you said, Tom. Short of us fuckin turning ourselves in, we don't get caught."

Billy Burns wore a frown.

"What the fuck's your problem?" asked Mullen. "Don't tell me you're still upset about Durkin."

"Excuse me. Hang with a dude, get to know him a little, and then have to sink his ass to the bottom of a river don't exactly make me feel like doin cartwheels, score or not."

" 'Score or not,' like we just knocked over a fucking liquor store. Listen, for the last two weeks, all that sweet-bogs-of-Kilarney shit was startin to grow on me, too, OK? But you want to try and snuff me and take away the money I just risked my ass for? Fuck you."

"That's what I don't get," said Billy. "He seem like the type would snuff us out?"

"The nut popped a cap at Tommy," said Mullen. "Tommy didn't take him down, he'da done us all. He could have been here right now countin his share, but he got greedy. So fuck him. I'm not gonna let him piss on my parade."

"You're a real sensitive guy, Mulls," said Roy, cracking a smile.

"It's the Jesus in my heart, Roy," Mullen assured him.

They packed up and checked out and went for breakfast in the adjoining grill. It was empty save for the dirty-aproned cook. They ordered breakfast at the counter and sat down at a booth.

"What's this fence again, a guinea?" Roy asked Farrell.

"Albanian," said Farrell.

"Al-what?"

"Albanian," said Mullen. "They're like Russians, right, Tom? These little commie motherfuckers ain't happy unless they're bustin into a supermarket, cutting into the cash machines, and stealing everything they can get their hands on. They got crews workin all over Westchester, Jersey. Tom's got a line on some guy whose uncle's a big-time fence."

"They can move our shit?" asked Roy.

"The way I was told," said Farrell, "they can move anything."

"How you know this guy?" asked Billy.

"Tenant in the building I was workin in locked himself out one night, so I called this locksmith that the day guy told me kicks you back forty bucks. This Albanian shows up and we started talkin, and he lets me know maybe he could come in handy in case one of the tenants tossed out somethin might be valuable."

"Why him?" asked Roy. "Twenty guys from the neighborhood could move it."

"What's the first thing Johnny Griffin or Malarkey's gonna say when they get pulled over for runnin a light, huh? They're gonna say, 'I can get you those dumb assholes who robbed that fancy hotel, officer. These guys were so goddamned stupid, they fenced the shit through me.' When was the last time you heard an undercover cop could speak fuckin Albanian?" Mullen asked.

"I don't trust commies," Roy persisted.

"Listen to Ronnie Reagan," laughed Mullen. "You trusted that hee-haw, and he almost took our heads off. Fuck your trust."

"OK," Roy relented. "When?"

"Tonight or maybe tomorrow," said Farrell. "But we stick together until then. I'm not hangin with everybody out on a shopping spree."

The cook brought them their food. The

Sideburns finished first and went out into the now bright day in search of a paper. Farrell sipped his coffee. Mullen produced a silver flask and unscrewed the top and poured some of its contents into his own coffee. He gestured it toward Farrell.

"I'm all right," Farrell said.

"Fuck that wagon shit for a while, Tommy. We're done. Celebrate a little."

"Not a good idea," said Farrell.

"Pussy," said Mullen.

"You should put in for a counselor position at AA," said Farrell, taking a napkin from the dispenser and patting sweat from his face. He picked up the flask. It was burnished and heavy and there was a crest flanked by two rearing horses upon it.

"You're a pretty classy drunk," Farrell said.

"Yeah, well, I figure what's the use in bein an alky if you can't do it with a little style." Mullen smiled back. He looked out the window onto the traffic on Broadway.

"How you really feelin about our dearly departed Hibernian friend? Because I want you to know, what I told Billy is the truth. You saved all our asses."

Farrell sipped his coffee.

"You know what I keep thinkin?" Farrell said.

"What's that?"

"Remember that punk coke dealer? Maybe if we took him out like you wanted that night and we had more funds, we could have cased it out a little better, figured out for sure the clerk had the combination."

"Planned more! You could have built the fuckin place with all the planning you did. The video camera? The police scanner? It wasn't your fault. This hit was the biggest, most professional job I'll ever be in on. Same goes for those two knuckleheads. You got like a gift, you know, like a callin. I've seen tons more shit go down for a lot less. Count your blessings."

Farrell shook his head.

"What about the silenced piece? He was really nuts. Why didn't he go hell-bent for glory in the van with the Uzi? That seem a little funny to you?" asked Farrell.

"Like he might not have been workin alone?"

"Exactly," Farrell said uneasily.

"I might have been having some thoughts along those lines myself."

"So what does it mean?" said Farrell.

"Means maybe you really did haul our shit out of the fire. Can you believe Roy and Billy? Of all the goddamn welders in the city to recruit, they bring in one who's IRA."

Farrell looked at him.

"IRA?"

"I don't know. Make your own conclusions. You heard that brogue. Plus, it wasn't the fuckin welders' union gave him that gun or that silencer. I don't know too much about our rebellious brethren from the Emerald Isle, but I know they pull off heists. Remember that armored car up in Boston last year? They like to collect funds any way they can. What better way than to pull a double cross on a heist that's already planned? Plus, he was lookin to make stiffs out of all of us with that assassin piece. Gruesome fuckin work for your regular hard-workin, jig-dancin, off-the-boat bog-trotter, don't you think?"

"Shame you didn't put this together before," Farrell said.

"Hey, listen. You're the fucking genius. I'm just the chauffeur. But I will give you some advice."

"What's that?"

"Anybody with a brogue asks you if you know any welders, shoot first and ask questions later."

"What about Roy and Billy? You let them in on your little theory?"

"Nope. Less they know, the better. You know what I'm saying. They're big boys. You saw them. Feel worse for the poor souls who fuck with them."

Farrell looked out the window and then at the silver flask.

"Well, I guess you better find some new bars to drink in for a while," said Farrell.

"Fuck that," Mullen said. He smiled brightly. "I get into any trouble, I'll just drop a dime to the INS, get 'em all deported. Now what do you say you, me, and Tara hit a real place tonight? Do it right—champagne, seven courses, cigars, brandy."

"Champagne," said Farrell, leaning back. "Now that's another story entirely."

Farrell liked Mullen. He always reminded him of his older brother, Terry. Cool and laid back but tough, loyal. He was a good friend, the oldest one he still had. Mullen was the only visitor he'd had the whole time he had been away. Mullen grinned as he took Farrell's cigarettes from the table and lit one. He held up Farrell's I ♥ NY lighter.

"See, I always took you for a high roller," he said. "Now let me ask you something. What are you planning on doing with your newfound wealth?"

"I don't know," Farrell said. "I was thinking of taking a nice long drive out of this shithole. Maybe head out west."

Mullen looked at him sideways.

"Goin out to Cali? Fuck that bullshit, Tommy. Stay here and hang like old times. I'm gonna be openin up that bar, like I told you."

Farrell laughed.

"Well, if you're an expert on anything, that's it."

"No, man. This place ain't gonna be no gin mill. It's gonna be nice. All wood, a little grill on the side. A class joint."

"I take it you're gonna be the silent partner."

"Fuck you, cocksucker," Mullen said, smiling. "Go ahead and leave. Who needs ya?"

As they finished, the phone behind the counter rang loudly. The cook picked it up.

"Yo," he held the phone toward their table. They exchanged puzzled looks. Farrell's stomach turned. Mullen stood, walked over, and took the receiver. He spoke into it for a moment, hung it up, and walked back.

"It's Tweedledum and Tweedledee. They found an open bar around the corner."

They drove out, turned left, and parked a few blocks up, across the street from a bar called the

Kindling Forge. It was a narrow, dark place with a curtained glass door. They went in to the back. Besides the Sideburns there were two ancient men nursing boilermakers. Farrell ordered coffee and lit up a cigarette. He closed his eyes, breathing in the sweet, cool smell of the place.

The barman attended them closely. A smile crossed his face at this unexpected boon of early business. They carried the two old men down the bar without thanks or acknowledgment. The brothers sat talking and laughing among themselves. Farrell stubbed out his cigarette and nodded to Mullen, who nursed a whiskey highball. He went to the pay phone.

"Who is it?" came the gruff voice at Farrell's dialing.

"Yeah. Frank there?"

"Who is it?" the voice repeated louder. Farrell couldn't decide which he disliked more, the tone or the thick accent.

"Put Frank on the fucking phone," said Farrell.

"You give me a name because I never hear your voice before."

"Why don't you ask a little nicer? You tell him Tom is on the phone. You want me to spell that?"

"Tom," came a voice without a break in the line. "How are you?"

"Frank. I'm just fine. That's some receptionist you got there. Real charmer."

"What can I tell you?" said Frank. "He's not a morning person like some of us. You're calling to confirm what we talked of before?"

"That's exactly what I'm doing. Same time, same place?"

"I'll be there, Tom, and if this is what I assume, some congratulations are in order."

"I don't know what the fuck you're talkin about," Farrell said firmly.

Frank chuckled, a light, pleasant sound.

"Whatever you say," the Albanian said pleasantly. "See you tonight."

Tonight, thought Farrell, and he hung up the phone.

3

IN THE PREDAWN DARK, A FORM APPEARED IN THE
white glow of the headstones on the cemetery rise
like a shadow stirring among the pale slabs. A lean
figure walking in jeans, a plaid shirt, and dusty
boots. A middle-aged man with furrowed features
treading silently across the rough, sanctified earth.
A witness to this marcher might have mistaken
him for an insomnolent soul more willing to walk
the world than lie beneath it. The man's name was
Ryan. He was still alive, and he was on his way to
work.

He had taken the bus around the Woodlawn
Cemetery to the subway station on Jerome Avenue
for years, but on a whim one morning he had
hopped the wall and cut through. Here he had
found a certain peace, suspended time, and some
history. Trees and grass and stone and the dead.
No unfamiliar company.

By a reflecting pond halfway through, he

paused and stood looking off to the darker forms of the shade trees that swayed slightly in the already warm breeze. He listened. The light, preemptive traffic on the Bronx River Parkway far below could barely be heard, like the soft rush of waves on some placid beach. Taking a deep breath, he picked up his pace on the rolling hills and five minutes later reached a stone wall and scaled it back into the land of the living.

Jerome Avenue was different so early—almost hopeful—with no traffic and the tentative whistles of birds in the warming murk. Down along the cemetery wall, the road widened. The elevated Woodlawn subway station came into view. Massive and ornamented in wrought iron, with decades of paint enameling its eaves and balustrades, it stood housed atop its dark girders like something from another era, superannuated and preserved for the sake of posterity. There was an all-night grocery in its eternal shadow where Ryan dropped his change on the newspapers upon the rusted stand in front and slid one out. As he approached the stairs, he paused. A mural was painted there. It was a depiction of the Vietnam Memorial Statue, the one of the three grunts walking on a daunting and confusing path. This, too, was a part of his morning ritual, and he stood stiffly staring for a moment. Then he turned and went up to wait for his train.

As he came through the turnstile, a train was pulling in. He could feel the cement platform sway slightly beneath his feet. After a search he selected a car free of homeless. The doors bing-bonged closed, and the train lurched forward. He stared out at the first fingers of sun peeking above the black tenement rooftops. At each stop, tired-looking men and women in jeans and work clothes got on. People embarking on the train this early rarely wore suits. They took their places around him, squinty-eyed and shoulder to shoulder, jostling with the train's rushing wobble.

At Eighty-sixth Street he stood, dropped his paper on his seat, and disembarked. He climbed up the filthy, worn steps onto Lexington Avenue. It was hot already, and his jeans and boots felt heavy, constraining in the warming air. He passed joggers and dog walkers as he headed west. A woman in a tailored suit came down the steps of a townhouse. She was thirtyish, and her hair was still wet from her shower, her makeup fresh and shiny. Her face was beautiful, but the eyes were glossed over, blank with concerns more important than the admiring glance of some over-the-hill construction worker. Had he been a younger man, she might have looked back at him, but these days such encounters rarely yielded him anything but the joy of aesthetic contemplation.

In a coffee shop off Madison, he bought a cup of tea to go. Between Madison and Fifth Avenue there was a wood-enclosed storefront and some stairs beside it. He walked up, sat on the stairs, and sipped his tea. On the horizon was a dark office building. He watched sunlight catch its top floors and flare brilliant green down the vertical lake of its glass. On Fifth Avenue the traffic was steadily increasing, and there was a sudden influx of pedestrians. Suits began to appear on the sidewalks all around him.

He was draining the dregs of his tea when the work van pulled up. Kelly, the foreman, leaned out of the passenger window.

"You know what I think, fellas?" the white-haired Irishman said toward the back of the van. "I think Paddy lives around here somewhere, don't ya, Paddy? I mean, how is it he's always early. Yer an eccentric millionaire, aren't ya?"

"You busted me," said Ryan, getting up and walking over to the van. "I got a co-op over there on Park, but I'm thinkin of sellin." He paused for emphasis. "Kerrymen started movin in."

The driver laughed, as did the two men in the back. Kelly, a Kerryman, tried to look pissed off but couldn't and then laughed himself.

They got out of the van.

Kelly, with his wan drinker's face, was an old-looking forty. But with his long hair and tight clothes he seemed like he didn't realize it. Kelly lived in Woodside, Queens. He'd been in New York twenty years, but from his thick accent he seemed as newly arrived as the three young men in their work crew. Donnell, Cosmo, and seven-teen-year-old Kevin had been in New York less than a year, and their naked enthusiasm still showed. It was after they'd become accustomed to the steady work and the decent paycheck that they'd be eager to point out the things wrong with it. They always did. These three lads were still fresh though, still excited by the adventure of being on their own in a big country.

Kelly went to the padlock on the front of the site and opened it with the key that Ryan knew he had bribed the general contractor for. From the back of the van they removed flat wood panels and wood strips. Then came their toolboxes, nails, the router, and table saws. The air inside was thick with the smell of sawdust. When they set down their tools, they sat against the raw plaster walls and waited to start work as the other tradesmen—the electricians, the plumbers, the painters—arrived.

Ryan clipped on his leather belt. By eight-thirty the air was filled with the scream of saws and the pounding of hammers. Ryan measured out wood paneling, sawed it to length, and hammered it up on the walls. It was a shoe store they were working on, but you'd never know it from the materials they were using. From the marble and rich woods and sophisticated lighting system you'd think they were building a restaurant or a gallery. Ryan had learned a long time ago, though, to take his satisfaction from doing the work conscientiously and to just pick up his paycheck.

Sawdust was thick in his throat. The taste always reminded him of his late father, who had emigrated from Galway at the age of seventeen and worked for thirty years in the carpentry union before retiring. He remembered as a child watching him drive nails. His lined face serene in concentration, his right hand swinging the hammer with an easy strength, three, four shots sending them home. His father had had the hands—carpenter's hands—veined, muscular, large. Ryan's hands were small, ladylike—really better suited to finer work, but he didn't care. He was almost getting the hang of it.

They broke at ten. He put down his hammer. Kevin, the youngest and therefore designated gofer, was sent with tea, soda, and beer orders to the deli. The other tradesmen had followed the carpenters' lead, and gradually the cavernous enclosure's cacophony of toolwork turned to deep silence.

Ryan went out to the street, hoping for a breeze. It was blazing now, and the sidewalks were crowded. Fifth and Madison were both clogged with traffic and the blast of horns. The slight breeze felt hot and dirty against the skin, like a blast of bus exhaust. Waves of heat came off the blacktop on Eighty-sixth, and the opposite side of the street wavered and flapped as if on the verge of ignition.

Up beside Fifth Avenue there was a road crew. With shirts off, they worked in the slow, deliberate movement of a chain gang. Ryan noticed that one of their number, indistinct in size and musculature, had merely rolled the sleeves of his denim shirt to the elbows in deference to the heat and rode a jackhammer unswervingly. It wasn't so much that the man worked harder or faster than the rest of his crew, it was that he didn't stop. When he finally laid the hammer to the street it was only to walk to the work truck, grab a shovel, and come back and clear out the aperture he'd just created. Done with this, he began his drilling again, his head intently fixed on the street before him as if some artifact of great interest might lie beneath it. At times the rest of the crew stopped to catcall at passing women, but the man with the jack just kept at his unflagging excavation.

When a yellow school bus ground loudly off Madison, Ryan turned. It was old. Filth caked in its half-open windows, and its paint was sunbleached almost white. As it slowed, Ryan turned in to the work-site entrance. He knew where it would stop. It was one of those "coalitions." He'd seen them on other sites. They fronted like they were some kind of civil rights group, but they would come and hurt people and threaten the site to shake down no-show jobs. There were some lengths of galvanized pipe leaning in a corner, and Ryan quickly selected a three-foot piece.

The bus stopped curbside. It had been a long time since those filthy windows had had children

behind them. Angry black faces—fifteen or
twenty—stared out. Large, desperate-looking, and
wild-eyed, in dusty semblances of work clothes,
the men smiled widely at Ryan as he stood in the
entrance. A chant started, halfheartedly at first but
then grew louder, accompanied by the slap of
hands and tools against the metal body of the bus.

"WE DON'T WORK, NO ONE WORKS! WE
DON'T WORK, NO ONE WORKS!"

When Ryan saw Kevin coming up with the bags,
he tried to warn him off with his eyes. The young
Irishman paused for a moment at the commotion
and then came up alongside the bus as its door
folded open with a rusty scream. The first man off
the bus wore a sleeveless plaid shirt. His muscular
arms were scarred and bore green ink tattoos. The
man who followed him was tall and thin and wore
a yellow hard hat cocked back on his head. He
wore a toolbelt with four hammers dangling from
it around his waist. The muscular black darted forward at Kevin, and the Irishman froze, the bags in
his hands falling to the sidewalk.

Perhaps the man didn't see the pipe at Ryan's
leg, or maybe he'd simply dismissed the middle-
aged man that held it. But as he reached out for

Kevin, Ryan stepped forward and swung. Ryan caught him solidly in the ribs, and the man toppled to the cement, screaming. When Ryan turned, the one with the hard hat was fumbling at his belt for a hammer. Ryan was at him in three steps. He feinted with the pipe, and the man backpedaled. He then whipped the pipe around and grazed him in the side. The man turned and fled into the open doorway of the bus. Ryan went over to the fallen man, who moaned loudly.

"Up," said Ryan.

The man stared at him in pain.

"You motherfucker," he whined highly, the voice of a child no longer wanting to play.

"Up," Ryan repeated. He placed the pipe on his shoulder and bent over the man.

The man cradled his side and stood slowly. Ryan followed him to the door of the bus. It was silent now, the threatening expressions in the windows gone. The man gained the steps, and the bus roared to life. The hard-hatted leader stuck his head out a window. He looked up at the site.

"Don't worry," he yelled. "We'll be back."

Ryan resisted an urge to smash out a window. The bus roared up to Fifth, turned, and was gone.

Ryan dropped the pipe. It rolled off the cement loudly. He turned to the entrance that was crowded with the workers brought out by the bus's departure. Kelly stood at the rear, watching him uneasily. Next to Ryan, Kevin stared after the bus, pained.

"Listen to me," said Ryan before the younger man could speak. "You had the balls to walk past them. Look at the rest of those bastards." Ryan swept a hand toward the doorway. "Where were they? There was only one other man I saw standing out here."

Kevin looked at him hopefully.

"Ya think?"

"I know," said Ryan, placing his hand on Kevin's shoulder. "A couple more busloads like that and we'll make a Yank out of you yet."

The workers dispersed as they came over. Ryan's face wore a look of naked disgust.

"Ah, Paddy," Kelly said, frowning. "That wasn't the way to handle that. They'll only be back, and next time someone will really get hurt. What'll the G.C. say?"

"I don't know about the contractor," said Ryan, "but if you say one more word, I'm going to knock all your teeth out."

Kelly opened his mouth and then closed it again.

"Listen, me and the boy here are taking the rest of the day off," Ryan continued. "With pay, you understand. Make up for all the help you boys so kindly gave us."

Kevin stared at Ryan and then at the foreman.

"Uh, Paddy?" the young Irishman said weakly. "Still a day's work to do . . ."

Ryan shook his head slowly, feeling for the first time the soak of sweat on his skin from his exertion. He looked at the young man.

"A lot more than a day's for you," he said.

As he walked away, they stared after him as if he were a stranger. He walked down the dusty ramp and out into the hot sun. As he crossed the street he heard the jackhammer stop, and he turned. Up the street, the roadman he'd been watching seemed to smile at him, and then he turned back to his hammer, attacking the street as if to rend the very plates of the earth.

The first bar he found was on Lexington, an English pub attempt called King Henry's. It was overpriced but cold and empty. He was on his third draft when he felt the vibration of the beeper on his belt. Not recognizing the number, he thought at first it might be the contractor calling to fire him. He went to the pay phone and called.

"What the fuck do you want?" he yelled when it was picked up.

"Is this Patrick Ryan?"

Ryan recognized the harsh Belfast accent immediately. Fuck, he thought.

"Yes," he said.

"This is a friend of Clancy's. Can you talk?"

Ryan looked at the Union Jack behind the bar.

"Go."

"The Sportsmen in Bainbridge. Ten tonight."

The phone clicked dead.

Ryan went back to his beer. He looked at his crinkle-faced image in the smoked mirror behind the liquor bottles. After all this fucking time, he thought. He drained his beer, left a tip, and went out of the dark coolness into the hot, noisy world.

4

FRANCIS MCCARRY GOT THE SEDAN UP TO A HUN-
dred at the crest of the Tappan Zee Bridge. He
glanced at the glowing 4:38 A.M. on the dash and
tapped the gas again slightly, sending the whine of
the engine to a slightly higher pitch and the rear
end up another fraction of an inch. Over the blur of
the guardrail, the glow of dawn was rumored
behind the dark hills of Westchester. He cut across
three empty lanes, taking the inside curve of the
roadway, and slowed reluctantly for the tollbooths
that loomed ahead.

He looked to spot any state trooper cars behind
the toll station. Seeing none, he aligned the car to
an exact-change lane in the empty plaza and sped
up. There was no stick across the lane, only a red
light, and as he roared past the booth, the alarm of
his unpaid passage clanged behind him like the
win bell at a casino. Fifteen minutes later, he

pulled off the thruway at the Van Cortlandt Park South exit with a smile on his face.

He would make it after all.

He ate the red light at the top of the ramp and bore right. At Broadway, he went left beneath the rusting iron framework of an elevated subway track. At 238th Street, he made another right and parked the car. He came out into the silent darkness and walked quickly along a dogshit-mined sidewalk to the back of a rundown brick building and keyed himself in. He walked up three flights of darkened stairs and down a hall to the office at the end.

"If it isn't Minute Man McCarry," said a gruff middle-aged man as he came in. "How's it goin there, Minute Man?"

The speaker stood in the gray light of two small black-and-white video monitors that sat in a large metal console. Audio equipment and headphones were on the desk in front of the monitor, and a bound log sat beside it. The stench of cigar smoke was strong. The man was an old forty-five: short, fat, balding, generally unhealthy. No wonder they had him pulling nights, McCarry thought. Who wants to look at this guy? The man wrote down a last entry and, after he stretched and yawned, began gathering up Tupperware that was scattered all over the office.

"Where's my coffee, Minute Mouse?" asked the man.

"Running real late today," said McCarry indifferently. "You wouldn't do me a real big favor and swing by Mickey Dee's and pick me up a cup?"

"Why don't you call up the deli around the corner. I hear they have free delivery," said the older agent with a grin.

The agent's name was Brown, and from what McCarry had gathered on him, he was a loser. Why else would he—fifteen years in—be pulling a shittier detail than McCarry, who had less than four.

McCarry had heard stories of Brown and a fistfight with a present deputy director ten years earlier over a confidential informant who had gotten killed. Blow a career over some shitbag CI? Brown was a dunce.

"Hey, fuck you, Mr. Brown," said McCarry jovially.

"No. Fuck you, McCarry," said Brown, staring coldly into the younger agent's eyes before he slammed the door on his way out. The man had sounded serious, thought McCarry. Angry. Perhaps he was finally cracking. He'd have to mention it to someone.

As McCarry sat and skimmed the night log, he gave himself mental high fives for being on time. This was his closest call yet. You wouldn't think being a few minutes late would make a difference in the high adventure that was being an FBI Special Agent, but you would be wrong. Tardiness was seen as a symptom of some larger weakness, and in the four years McCarry had been an agent, he had never been late. He'd never taken a sick day either. One had to remember that in the Bureau, such personal records were seismographic readings of a person's soul, and he wanted to be up for sainthood.

He finished the log without surprise. Nothing had happened the night before. It was the third week of the stakeout, and nothing ever happened.

He went to the window and opened it to let out Brown's tobacco stench and gazed across the street at the object of the federal government's covert scrutiny, Gaelic Park.

From the distance it looked oddly military, a cluster of single-story, green and white cement buildings next to a fenced-in grass playing area

roughly the same size as a soccer field. The buildings consisted of locker rooms, a banquet hall, and
what no stadium was complete without, a tremendous, fully stocked bar. McCarry had gone on
reconnaissance the Sunday before during the
games and had had a beer. The burnished brass-
railed bar went twenty feet straight from the front
entrance, turned left, and went another twenty or
so out toward the field. A second bar outside
under a wooden awning served draft beer. It could
not be said that the park was remiss in providing a
complement—or alternative—to the athletic con-
tests waged.

The place would have seemed quaintly antique
if it weren't still in use. The stands along the field
made McCarry shudder every time he looked at
them. They looked like the antediluvian remnants
of cheap seats quickly erected for a turn-of-the-
century prizefight. The better seats had steel and
concrete supports—perhaps added on after some
tragic collapse. But the ones in the more remote
parts of the park were made out of wood. Not a
water-sealed, treated type of wood either, but a
hewn, weather-rotted timber that had taken on the
dry, graywhite color of bleached bone. Weeds tan-
gled under and through these seats in an act of

nature repossessing its own. The park's perimeter was secured by an ancient, corrugated-steel fence whose age might be determined by the thick, hieroglyphic layers of graffiti upon it. The old fence did its job, though. Its sharp, rusting top invited tetanus, and as if that weren't deterrence enough, there were the hounds.

How many dogs and what breeds were indeterminate. He would see them on the screen sometimes, a black mass of closely moving, raggedy mutts that roamed the grounds at night, keeping out teenagers and potential thieves. Sometimes the junkyard dogs in the auto body shop across the street would start barking, and the ones from the park would answer, and the air would be filled with their mournful baying.

All of it lay in the shadow of the constantly rattling and hissing elevated Broadway local train yard.

The FBI was looking for terrorists, Provisional Irish Republican Army. The end of the Cold War had turned much of the huge counterintelligence section of the FBI toward antiterrorism. The IRA, being one of the biggest and most dangerous terrorist organizations in the world, needed its movements monitored.

The bureau had cameras on the entrance and parking lot and taps on the bar and pay phones, but so far the only crime they had observed was drunk driving. The bar wasn't open every night, and the thought was that any illicit activity would be done when the place was supposed to be closed. But there was no activity when it was closed and even less when it was open. They seemed to be barking up the wrong tree here. After tomorrow, thought McCarry, they would have to reevaluate.

Tomorrow night at the park, there would be a benefit for a widow of an IRA provisional killed by a British soldier, and every man, woman, and child coming in or out of the place would be photographed and identified. They would have to work from there because either the park was clean or someone had been tipped off.

It was disappointing because he'd initiated the surveillance. The assistant agent in charge had authorized it, but McCarry was the one who had given him the idea. It came to him after being in an after-hours place in Woodside with a law school buddy after a bachelor's party. Some Irishman had come around with a donation can and some pro-IRA pamphlets. He'd figured that such organized fund-raising meant strong IRA presence in New York. He remembered Gaelic Park from his childhood. It was where his father had gone to congregate with his fellow Irishmen, and when he found out it was still open, he figured it would be a good place to start looking. But it was turning out that he was wrong.

McCarry sipped water and stared out the window. Up the block from the park sat a police radio car. McCarry knew how the officers felt—fast food and too much coffee burning their bellies with indigestion, impossible to get comfortable in the cramped interior of the car. The difference between him and them was that he actually did his work; he wasn't copping shuteye. He wondered if they had been notified of the federal surveillance and decided they couldn't have, because if they had, they wouldn't allow the possibility of being seen not doing their jobs. Those cops were catching a good three, four hours of straight, uninterrupted sleep every night.

McCarry took out his personal log, the one he kept to back up and document everything that happened every day, and wrote "5:07 A.M. Radio car 1435 sitting in same spot as yesterday." He didn't know exactly how this information would help him at a future date, but if it could, he would have it.

He took a quick survey of the park out the window and on the screen. Finding nothing, he got some water from the cooler in the corner and then sat down and reread Brown's discarded newspaper from the day before.

At precisely eight o'clock, the cubicle lock clicked, and McCarry's partner, Neil Wallace, came through the door bearing brown paper bags.

"I knew you wouldn't let me down, Wally," said McCarry, kicking the other sliding office chair over to the man. Wallace sat down and took coffee cups out of the sacks.

Wallace was thirty-five and had about five years in. He'd come from the NYPD, and in the unwritten parameters of the FBI's career path trajectory, McCarry knew he would never make it far beyond his current rating. He was a short, stocky man with a mustache (another personal detail that didn't fly so well with the powers that were) and was a good agent. Reliable, intelligent, street smart. The only thing about him that was a little offputting was his tendency to listen more than he spoke, something that McCarry himself had found useful in the full-contact sport of federal employment politics.

Theirs was a mostly silent partnership. It got awkward at times, each waiting for the other to speak, like two boxers endlessly circling each other, but otherwise it was fine. McCarry liked working with him because he was a good agent and because he really wasn't any competition.

And he always brought coffee.

"Anything?" asked Wallace, draping his suit coat over the back of the chair.

"Nope," said McCarry. "Does dog barking count?"

"Those fucking dogs," said Wallace by the window now, looking through binoculars.

McCarry put sugar in his coffee. He checked his watch.

"Any sign of him yet?"

"Nope," said Wallace. Then, "Wait a second. Here he is."

McCarry got up, taking the other set of binoculars from the sill.

A late-model blue Mercury pulled up in front of the bar, and a large, middle-aged, white-haired man hoisted his bulk from the car. He was dressed in the barman's uniform of cheap dress shirt, sleeves rolled manfully to the elbows, bargain slacks, and soft-soled shoes. This barkeep was the day caretaker of the place, and he held the ever so unlikely moniker of Timothy Finnegan. His British TIGER file (Terrorist Intelligence Gathering Evaluation and Review) showed a Belfast upbringing steeped in fringe IRA activity—petrol bombings, rock throwing. Nothing solid that the English could pin on him, but some suspicion there. Of course, now he was a law-abiding American citizen—had been for the last twenty years. Had a daughter going to Fordham University, if the current file was right. The files were exhaustive. It sometimes seemed like every Catholic out of Belfast or Inniskillen or Newry had a suspected terrorist jacket on him. They couldn't all be IRA, could they? It seemed kind of paranoid to him, not that he could blame the British government. The British had been the recipients of the longest reign of terrorism in the history of the modern world and had plenty of reason to jump at shadows. But was there really enough evidence for the U.S. government to be tailing law-abiding American citizens? In light of the inactivity of the last three weeks, McCarry didn't think so. It looked like he would have to admit failure on this one, before more time and resources were wasted.

This opinion would be included on the report he

had been requested to write and present at the antiterrorism task force meeting tomorrow morning. His boss would be there and his boss's boss, as well as agents from Immigration and ATF. He was taking a risk here, he knew, at making a recommendation. What if something happened after he pulled the plug? They'd blame him, wouldn't they?

McCarry contemplated for the hundredth time. Was there something he was overlooking? Finnegan? He thought. Why was he feeling sympathetic for him? It was uncharacteristic for him to feel empathy for those he was watching. Something came to him. So simple he had overlooked it. Finnegan reminded him of his father.

It was the bartender part. His old man had side-jobbed behind the stick in the local gin mill in their Queens neighborhood when McCarry was a kid. During the week, he drove a city bus out of Flushing, but on the weekends he worked all Saturday and Sunday in the bar. One might have said that it was good of him to work so hard for his family, if the fact wasn't that he worked only from eight in the morning to five in the evening and didn't get home until two A.M. No, bartending weekends, you could say, was a labor of love for Mr. McCarry.

Across the street Finnegan came out of the front
door with a broom and a dustpan and began
sweeping the sidewalk in front of the establish-
ment. A memory came to McCarry then of himself
at ten or eleven, coming home from church on a
Sunday morning and stopping in to see the old
man. There was his dad, leaning back behind the
tall, dirty brass-railed bar, keeping court with the
light crowd of morning drunks. Young Francis
waves and walks down to the empty end of the
bar, hops on a stool, and waits. Young Francis gets
the feeling something is wrong. He has come in
before to have a quick ginger ale with his father
and talk sports, but today everyone is silent, staring over at him. His father stares also, as if he
doesn't recognize his own son. Thinking along
with them, Who is this kid? Francis almost has the
urge to call out, "Hey, it's me, Francis, your son,"
but at that particular moment—his old man standing stiffly with the others, chewed bar straw dangling from the hard grimace accentuating his per-
petually morose features—it seems to Francis that
perhaps he is wrong. That maybe he did come into
the wrong place. His old man saunters down and
gives him the curt brushoff "Not today." Not even
"Not today, Francis" but just "Not today" like he is

some sot off the street begging a drink. Young Francis hops off the stool and walks out of the place without a glance at anyone, and as he steps into the light and the tears start coming, he vows he will never be like his father.

McCarry put the binoculars down.

Was that what this was about? Did he lack objectivity toward the surveillance because of some kind of veiled guilt? Was his decision making being clouded by some Freudian bullshit? Maybe it was. Maybe he had been selected for the surveillance for precisely that reason: They wanted to see where his allegiance lay. He had thought his suggestion had been complied with because of his familiarity with the culture, his ability to move in it if the need dictated. But he was having his doubts. His father had been off the boat—born and raised in County Mayo—had raised Francis and his family not too far away from this place. For all McCarry knew, his father had been a member of the fucking IRA. Maybe the bureau knew that. Maybe it had come up on that extensive background check they had done on him when he applied. Maybe the Bureau wanted to see what an Irish Catholic agent would do against one of his own.

The decision before him was becoming clearer. Even though there was no evidence of activity, he couldn't rush to denounce the surveillance. He would ask for an extension—a couple of weeks. He would show his superiors that he held no allegiance but to the Constitution of the United States of America, just as he had sworn when he took the job. If they wanted to plumb the depths of his dedication, they wouldn't be disappointed.

"What's up?" Wallace said, giving him a smile. "Looks like a lightbulb just went on over your head."

"Nothing," said McCarry, startled. He quickly raised the binoculars to his eyes. "Just remembered where I left something."

Poker face, McCarry chastised himself, watching the bartender across the street reenter the bar. Poker face at all times.

5

IT WAS ALMOST EVENING WHEN THEY CROSSED THE George Washington Bridge in the dust-colored Chevy. A red sun hung low in the western sky. On the Hudson far below, a rusted tanker trudged slowly up the wide, gray expanse. Farrell glanced back over his shoulder as they approached the bridge's end. In the distant fading light, Manhattan lay like a dream city, its stone towers flushed golden, its countless windows set shimmering like mercury. Then the cloven basalt face of the Palisades rose up and sliced it from view.

The modern office buildings just beyond the bridge looked deserted, their yellowed glass greasy to the touch. The ramshackle motels beside them advertised "$19.99 A DAY" and "CLEAN SHEETS."

Mullen drove the car one handed, the grin that had appeared at the end of the robbery still pasting his features. The Sideburns in the backseat stared out at the road like curious schoolchildren on a class trip. Farrell wondered if this was the farthest west they had ever been.

They had left the Kindling Forge that morning when a light crowd had come in. They'd spent some hours at a pool hall close by, where Farrell had bested each man in turn at nine ball and then again at straight pool. They had returned to the city that afternoon and placed the cash in a safety deposit box in a Midtown bank. The key to the box was in Farrell's wallet by unanimous agreement. They had just finished a leisurely meal at a diner on lower Sixth Avenue, where Farrell had winked at the waitress when she paused in shock at her fifty dollar tip. The swag, packed now in Farrell's briefcase, was in the trunk of the car.

Farrell had selected one watch from the cache. It was an antique Phillipe Patik, and he wore it on his wrist for safekeeping. They had put the three Uzis, now inside the car, on the floor beneath their seats.

Farrell cupped his lighter from the warm breeze of the open window and lit a cigarette. He looked out at the thin stand of trees flicking past on the side of the road. Within them, pointed boards of backyard walls appeared at intervals like the battlements of forts.

His shock at the recent events had dissipated. What he felt was a relaxed numbness that had grown familiar in the past year since his release from prison. A strange, almost lulling, sense that anything at all could occur.

While he was in prison so many things had changed. His old neighborhood had disappeared. The only things recognizable upon his homecoming were the buildings. It was as if measures had been taken to erase his past. The German deli where he had gotten his first job delivering groceries had turned into a bodega with bulletproof glass. The bar where his brother had taught him to shoot pool was a Cuban restaurant. The nights that at one time had been filled with the cries of him and his friends playing now thumped with loud rap from car stereos and occasional gunfire.

The night doorman job had been part of his parole. At first, he had thought it might not be that bad. It was simple, and after so much complication in his life, there was something to that. Less than a month had cured him of that notion. He realized he'd only stepped out of one prison into another.

Throughout, the only thing he held on to was his drawing. It was corny maybe, and he kept it to himself, but he had come to find that it was the only thing he had. He'd been a good artist when he was a kid. It had come easily to him, the only thing in which he could lose himself. He'd fill notebooks, mostly with comic book heroes and cartoons, but occasionally he would do thumb sketches with textures and shading. Even now a ninety-nine-cent empty notebook brought him joy. He had gone to a high school for art, but when he was kicked out for missing class he dropped drawing altogether. He picked it up again when he was in prison. At first it was just to kill time, but after a while he had discovered a passion for it that amazed him. It was shocking to find, at that low point, something that made him feel alive again. So when he was released, he had planned to continue, try to take some classes. He hadn't counted on the state of his old neighborhood, though. The impossibility of getting anything going in the cramped, cold-water, one-bedroom he had rented not far from the building where he'd grown up. What he needed, he realized, and what he was willing to risk a return to prison for, was a chance to get away from everything and pursue what he should have done when he was a kid but didn't. Go out west somewhere to draw, paint. Attend a school. Do it right. Fuck that starving shit. He'd been starving all his life. It wasn't like he even wanted to show his paintings to anyone or sell them. He just wanted to do them. It would cost money, he knew. One smart score's worth. That he had completed it successfully still seemed odd. Coming out on top was a brand-new experience for him.

"We need gas," Mullen said, interrupting his thoughts.

Farrell checked his watch.

"We got time," he said.

They pulled into a two-pump island station that was overseen by an Arab in a bulletproof hut. Mullen turned off the car, got out, and pumped gas.

"You know what would be a great way to rob this place?" Billy observed from the backseat.

"You forget, you don't have to go around knocking over gas stations for a while," said Farrell, smiling without turning around.

"Yeah, I know," said Billy impatiently. "But I still can't help comin up with these great angles. This is what I'd do. Wouldn't even need a roscoe. As I'm fillin up my car, I'd get a container—a Prestone can or somethin—and fill that up, too. Then I'd stroll on back to the booth, pour the gas through the slot, light a match, and tell the sand nigger to hand over the cash or experience the flammability of his product firsthand," he finished proudly.

Farrell shook his head.

"Yeah, he'd probably laugh and tell you to go ahead," said Roy. "The way they water the shit down, it probably wouldn't light."

Farrell laughed uneasily. He'd seen the brothers with Durkin. They were probably serious. He eyed Mullen outside.

"What the fuck is this?" Farrell heard Mullen say as he paid for the gas. "I gave you a fifty."

The Arab in the booth looked out blankly. "No, you give me twenty." He held up a bill as if it were inarguable proof.

"You think wavin a fuckin twenty around is gonna send me packin? You're in for an awakening," Mullen heatedly informed him.

"Fuck him," Farrell called over impatiently. "Let's go."

"This wily piece of shit is robbin us," Mullen complained.

"Today's his lucky day," said Farrell. "Come on."

"Stay in your box, motherfucker," Mullen said, putting his face up against the booth's glass. "Stay in that fucking box because it's a dangerous world out here."

"What's your problem?" Mullen asked when they were back in traffic.

"You want to get the state troopers up our ass?" asked Farrell.

Mullen rolled his eyes.

"I know a way you coulda got it back," offered Billy from the backseat.

Traffic got tighter down the turnpike. After twenty minutes, Mullen squeezed the Chevy onto an exit ramp. The strip malls off the crossroads seemed upscale, camouflaged with colonial-style facades. A left off the main thoroughfare ten minutes later had them in a tree-flanked neighborhood of palatial, landscaped homes. Cruising slowly down the empty, gently sloping roads, Farrell thought they must be in the wrong place.

He wouldn't have seen the driveway if he hadn't been counting the addresses. No house was visible, just some stray gravel dividing a row of hedges. Two stone piers overgrown with ivy gated the approach. He motioned to Mullen.

"There," he pointed.

Mullen nodded and sped the Chevy around the

block. Billy took the machine guns from the floor of the car. Roy taped clips upside down to one another. The metallic clacks of the guns being readied were loud in the interior of the car.

"You know this is all unnecessary, of course," said Farrell warily. "This man does business."

"Sure," said Roy, squinting down the barrel of his Uzi. "We know."

When they came back around, Mullen slowed as they entered the driveway. The house appeared over a short rise, an elegant, white, two-story colonial. A wrought-iron light fixture hung within its pillared portico like a frozen pendulum. Mullen stopped in front of the two-car garage on the side of the house. The chatter of crickets was loud in the darkening trees. They left the machine guns on the seats as they got out of the car. The double doors of the garage opened with an electric hum.

Five men stood in the door of the garage. They were pale and had black hair and mustaches. They wore suits and silk shirts open at the throat and gold jewelry. Standing together they seemed interrupted from a celebration, some wedding, a christening perhaps. The Irish Americans, with their long hair, beards, tattoos, and ratty clothes, looked like the last remnants of some routed rebel force. All the two groups shared was mutual scrutiny, which was unblinking in the failing light.

"Shit," Billy said with genuine wonder. "Fuckin gypsies."

Farrell grabbed the briefcase from the trunk and headed toward the men. One of the Albanians came out to meet him.

"Frank," Farrell said evenly.

"Thomas," the young Albanian said, holding out his hand. "It's nice to see you again."

They shook.

"Come on. We're set up in the garage."

Farrell turned, nodded to Mullen, and followed Frank inside. One of the men by the door followed. He was middle-aged, short, and stocky. His eyes were such a light shade of blue they would have been striking were they not so flat, so dead. The man was smoking a cigarette, and as he walked he lit a new one off its end and then flicked the butt away.

"So, you are the master thief," the man said. It was hard to determine his tone. His voice was deep and thickly accented, Russian sounding.

Farrell looked at Frank, puzzled.

"Sorry, Thomas. This is my uncle, George. This is his house here."

Neither offered a hand.

They sat at a table, the two Albanians with their backs to the wall, Farrell before them. Farrell placed the briefcase on the table, popped the clasps, and opened it. When he turned it around, he couldn't detect a reaction in either man's face as their eyes darted over the contents. Farrell lifted out the jeweler's case and unzipped it, revealing the diamonds. George deftly plucked one up and held it to the light. He produced a jeweler's glass from his pocket and squinted at the stone. He said nothing. He put the gem down, reached for another, smoking all the while. Frank went through the rest of the contraband, hefting and turning watches and jewelry and making quick notes on a pad. After a few minutes, Frank stopped and pushed the pad next to George, who put down the diamond he was looking at and spread the rest across the felt. George looked at the pad and then at Farrell.

"One hundred," he said firmly.

"Without the diamonds maybe," countered Farrell calmly. "A hundred ain't worth the ride out here."

The Albanian shook his head. "I have seen better. Really, this is not so good. Really," he said.

"Really, huh? Like you wouldn't lie to me or anything. Listen, Frank tells me you're discreet. That's valuable to me. But if a hundred's the best you can do, I guess I'll just have to take my chances."

"One-fifty," George offered.

Farrell stood. The three at the mouth of the garage turned quickly.

When Farrell went to close the briefcase, George held its lid.

"One-eighty," George said, nodding at Frank. Immediately, Frank took out a small nylon satchel and started counting out hundred dollar bills.

"That is final."

Farrell stared dumbstruck at George.

"That is not final. You're smokin dope," he said. "Those rocks are D's, motherfucker. Flawless."

Frank stopped his count and stared at Farrell, amazed. Then he quickly put his head down and continued.

"What do you say?" George said angrily.

Farrell looked at Frank.

"What the hell is this, Frank? I thought you said you were a businessman. What kind of bullshit is this?"

Frank looked up at Farrell briefly. He shrugged

his shoulders slightly. It was out of his hands.

"I am the fucker of my mother?" George asked, his barren, laser-beam eyes widening. "Yes? The fucker of my mother? You say this?"

"Fuck this," Farrell said.

Farrell pushed down the lid of the briefcase. George reached out and held it open easily with his thick hand. Then George took out the diamonds and put them inside his jacket, holding Farrell insolently in his eerily placid gaze.

"I will ignore that you have said this. I will ignore that you have wasted my time." George sat back and took out his cigarettes and lit one. He crossed his legs.

"Take the money. Or take nothing. Go."

Farrell stood there struck silent. Rage pulsed through him like an electric current. Suddenly he was in prison again. Another one taking him for a chump, sizing him up for a punk.

Holding his fury at bay, Farrell glanced toward the Albanians at the mouth of the garage. They were still locked in vigilance with Mullen and the Sideburns outside. Without looking at George, he sat and counted the money quickly and then dropped it in the open briefcase. He closed the lid. An unexpected confidence surged through him as he stood, a flowing sureness of purpose that he hadn't felt in sometime. He pulled the revolver from his back. George was in the midst of rising when Farrell leaned across the table and struck him squarely in the temple. The man sat back down slowly as if suddenly fatigued. Then when he raised his face in wide-eyed wonder, Farrell pistol-whipped him again.

Frank's mouth fell open as George crumpled silently to the floor.

Farrell stepped around the table and took the diamonds from inside George's jacket.

Leaving the garage, he raised the pistol as the first Albanian turned.

"Get out of my way," he warned.

When Mullen and the Sideburns saw him coming, they instantly produced the automatic weapons from the car. The Albanians looked dazed. Two had their hands inside their jackets. One had his hand behind his back. Their glances skipped from Farrell and his partners to their fallen leader on the floor.

"Let's do 'em," Roy Burns cried out in the silence.

The Albanians parted as Farrell passed through them. He drew the Smith & Wesson out now also as he backed to the car. Mullen got into the front seat and gunned the engine. Farrell came around, opened the passenger door, and held both pistols across the roof.

"Go," he called to the Sideburns. The brothers got in the backseat, and then Farrell jumped in as Mullen floored it in reverse. They backed out screeching into the quiet street. A hubcap came off with a whine and clanged against the opposite curb as Mullen slapped it into drive. The engine groaned as Mullen laid distance between them and the Albanians.

Roy spoke up as they raced onto the turnpike.

"You kill him?" he asked.

"No," said Farrell, his heart hammering and his voice sounding strangely calm in his own ears. "I clocked him." He held up the revolver still clenched tightly in his hand. There was blood in the grooves of the cylinder.

"What happened?" Roy asked.

"He took the diamonds," Farrell answered.

"What do you mean he took the diamonds?" Mullen asked.

"We can't agree on a price, so he fucking takes them and puts them in his pocket and tells me they're the cost of me wasting his time."

"Get the fuck out of here!" Mullen cried, slamming the steering wheel. "He took the fucking diamonds? He's got them?"

"Oh no," Farrell said. "That's why I clocked him. To get them back."

Mullen punched him in the arm approvingly.

"Jesus Christ, I didn't know you had it in ya. Don't worry, we'll find another fence."

"We could hold off on that," Farrell said. "I got the money, too."

"What money?" Billy asked.

"Their offer for the diamonds. For everything."

"How much you get?"

"A hundred and eighty."

"Grand?" Billy asked excitedly.

Farrell nodded silently, eyes fixed on the bloody gun.

"You're right, Mulls," Roy rasped, chuckling. He squinted ahead at Farrell. "This boy is certifiable."

There was pride in his voice.

Night was complete as they headed back across the bridge. Manhattan glittered, sharp and awesome against the darkness as if the stars had been rent from the night above by some cataclysm to fall in sparkling heaps.

The place they chose for celebration was deep in the Bronx. A lone Irish name in a block full of Spanish: farmacias, carnicerías, bodegas. As they parked, Farrell counted out twenty thousand from the money he had taken off the Albanians. He handed each man five thousand and pocketed his share.

"Little pocket change, motherfuckers," he said jovially.

He stuffed the rest of the cash in the briefcase along with their booty and carried it out with him.

The bar was dark as a cave, but for the shamrock-green neon light behind the bar. A spare crowd of aging drunkards was lit unbecomingly in its emerald pall. Farrell sat at leisure with the Sideburns at a table in the back while Mullen spoke with a bearded man at the bar. Mullen went outside with the man, and when he returned to the table a few minutes later, Roy Burns smiled knowingly.

Mullen brought a closed fist up to the tabletop and stared at Farrell.

"Who's it gonna be, gentlemen?"

Farrell stared at the fist.

"I'll pass," he said after a pause.

Mullen moaned as if in pain.

They left Farrell sitting and headed off somewhere to a dark corner of the place. Mullen came back alone and went to the bar and returned with drinks—two beers, two whiskeys. He handed Farrell a whiskey and put an arm around his shoulder.

"To you, my brother. I gotta admit I had my doubts, but you proved me wrong. Now if you say you're not gonna drink with me, I swear to God I'm gonna pistol-whip *you*."

Farrell raised his glass. He took a deep breath.

"Bottoms up, you miserable fuck," he said.

They downed their shots. How it burned. Mullen drank his whiskey and held his head back and chased it with beer from a foot above his mouth. It splashed on his face, but he continued anyway, emptying the bottle while soaking his face and hair. He slicked back his hair, smiling, his face wet as if he'd been crying.

A couple came in, and the jukebox was turned on. Farrell could feel its vibration through the floor. The light behind the bar began to seem festive.

"A couple more, and we lose our compatriots, OK? I told Tara we'd meet her at Reilly's in an hour," said Mullen.

Farrell nodded, placing the empty shot glass upside down on the table. He pulled on his cold beer, closing his eyes.

The Sideburns came back. There was an old, made-up bar hag at the end of the bar. Mullen stood and walked over to her and took her hand delicately, standing her up to dance. She accepted with a lurid, painted smile across her ruined face. Mullen box-stepped with her gallantly to the loud music. Farrell laughed along heartily with the Sideburns. When Mullen grabbed the old lady's ass, even the dour-faced barman—who'd been shaking his head at the low display—cracked a smile. The hag, lapping up even this attention, kissed Mullen on the lips—and he let her for a moment—and then cheek to cheek he turned with her to his friends wearing such an exaggerated grimace of horror, they stamped their feet in their mirth.

Farrell was downstairs in the bathroom later pissing when he heard the first blast. He thought at first someone had dropped a tray of glasses upstairs. A scream told him otherwise. He had left his two guns in the pockets of his suit coat on the back of his chair, but he still had Durkin's small pistol, and he took it from his boot as he left the bathroom. At the bottom of the stairs he listened to the loud detonations. Shotguns, two, perhaps three, by the sound. People screaming and glass breaking between the shots. The gunfire ceased, and he just stood there dumbly with the pistol in his hand, staring up at the darkness, paralyzed. Only when there was a crunch of a careful footstep over broken glass and a hushed call in a language he did not understand but recognized from an hour ago did he back away. Then he felt the push bar of the rear fire exit door, and he turned and fled.

There were boxes of empty bottles in the blackened courtyard and an alleyway to the left. He ran up the sloping corridor and banged through the metal gate at the top, and he was out on the street and running. He felt gloried at his ability to move, arms pumping, booted feet slapping pavement with a heartening rapidity. He passed people, children in the darkened street, men glaring at him from the stoops of buildings. He caught a gypsy cab out in front of a bodega. When the driver asked him in Spanish where he wanted to go, at first he didn't know.

"Times Square," he answered after a moment, and then he scrunched down in the backseat as they pulled away from the curb.

6

THE FIRST BAR FARRELL FOUND WAS EMPTY. IT WAS A few blocks south of Times Square, where the gypsy cab had let him off. Passing warily through the crowded streets, he'd stopped short when he spied the line of vacant leather stools through the door glass. The heavy wooden door opened without a sound.

It was dark and cool inside. Red light from a neon beer sign lay in a soft puddle on the varnished surface of the bar. The bartender regarded him through slitted eyes. When Farrell took out a fifty and ordered a whiskey with a beer back, the man's expression took on an instant friendliness that would have seemed genuine had it not been for the eye-blink speed at which the transformation took place.

The bartender poured whiskey into a heavy shot glass and placed a bottle of beer next to it and took his money. Farrell waited for his change before he drank. The whiskey tasted of wood and smoke. He held its slow burn in his mouth, staring at the eddies of vapor emanating from the dark lip of the beer bottle. Then he slowly lifted the bottle to his lips and chased the shot back. Even with the events just unfolded, his lips curled into a smile at the calming rush.

He motioned to the bartender. More whiskey was poured. He had to steady his hands to light a cigarette. He put his cigarettes on the bar next to his change and placed the Zippo on top of them. He sipped at the second shot.

The realization struck him as he placed the shot glass down.

He was cursed.

It occurred to him not as the chilling pang of a man who has just been told he has a short time to live, but in an almost warming embrace of sudden illumination—like when the name one's been searching for suddenly pops into the head.

He was tainted.

There was no other explanation.

He had paid his dues this time. He had not drank. He had not used drugs. He had not been stupid.

Every move had been approached with precision and forethought without precedence. He had controlled every factor as much as humanly possible. Had forged all the pain of thirty years of grim failures into one daring act of discipline and intelligence, and still it fell apart right before his eyes.

It had been his belief that the origin of his ongoing misfortune had come as the result of getting booted from school when he was thirteen. His acceptance and the scholarship to the private school were a surprise, to say the least. He remembered his mother's deep frown lines disappearing at the news. And yet his response to this unlikely accomplishment had been to cut class and to drink and to fail every subject. He had been kicked out at the end of that year, and all the years since he had blamed himself for this colossal failure, this choking at the only shot he had ever been offered.

Lifting up the whiskey glass—the weight of it so familiar, so right in his fingers—he realized that it didn't matter. If he'd graduated from that place and gone to Harvard, the result would have been the same. He'd have been sitting here or somewhere similar contemplating the carnage of his life. How oddly comforting to understand his misery was not wholly self-inflicted. How strangely liberating to find out at last that his woe was merely the intent of a universe turned resolutely and inexplicably against his every move.

He drained the glass and motioned to the bartender for a third. He looked around the empty room and then out through the dark diamond of glass on the door to the street. He wondered what the night had in store for him.

After the third whiskey, he finished the beer and stood. His legs were only slightly wobbly. He went to the pay phone, picked up the receiver and held it dumbly in his hand for a moment, and then hung it back up. He leaned against the wall, staring down at the faded tiles, and took out the loose wad of cash from his pocket. It was his share from the fence. The sheaf of hundred dollar bills seemed fake. He knew the smart thing to do would be to get a room, hang until morning, then clear the money from the bank and leave. But he also knew that there was no way he was going to do it. He wadded the bills again and stuffed them in his jeans and checked his watch. It was 9:35. He remembered Mullen's mention of his girlfriend, Tara. A lone friendly face in a world gone suddenly cold. He left a twenty on the bar and went out.

At the corner, he followed a flock of white-shirted businessmen into an all-nude bar. He paid the cover and entered. Inside, loud music pounded in the dark as men sat still and silent in rows of hard-backed chairs. Upon the long stage, two figures swayed before a smudged mirror, at intervals setting themselves toward the audience in configurations that seemed at once athletic and awkward. He stood at the bar. When the greasy-looking bartender asked him if he wanted to see the VIP room, Farrell just glared at him until he retreated. These fuckin places. Sometimes he felt like burning them to the ground. He went to the stage, turned, and glanced out upon the audience, but he couldn't see what he was looking for, so he left the place and went back out onto the street.

It was in the second all-nude bar that he found the man he was looking for. In the bathroom, Farrell stood in a doorless stall with a short, swarthy man. He wet his pinky and dipped it into the small envelope the man had just handed him and rubbed it against his gums. Farrell smiled at the numbing freeze, handed the man some money, tucked the envelope into his pocket, and went out.

He bought a quart bottle of Heineken from a grocery store and got the proprietor to open it up and bag it. He went over to Fifth Avenue and made a left.

He walked uptown with headlights in his eyes, the passing people all backlit and faceless. He stopped once and sat on the steps at St. Patrick's Cathedral. He lit a cigarette and turned to stare at the stone saints carved so intricately in their niches. Then he looked across to the black metal Atlas bent to his task in front of Rockefeller Center across the street. Behind him, the cathedral doors were huge, and he imagined that perhaps they had been built in anticipation of the day Atlas would despair of his shitty job and have need to put down the world and cross Fifth Avenue for consolation.

He walked up to Fifty-ninth Street, crossed over, and walked west on the cobbled sidewalk beneath the dark overhanging trees of Central Park. Across the street in the high copper-rimmed windows of the Plaza, dinner-jacketed waiters passed in the dark of the crowded Oak Room like elegant ghosts. He walked, drinking and staring at the well-dressed people in the yellow light of the hotel awnings. At Sixth, he passed a group of top-hatted horse-and-buggy drivers counting money at the black marble base of a statue of some mounted patriot, their cutoff-gloved hands flicking bills with bankerly precision. Their raggedy nags stood at the curb, heads bowed as if shamed by the obsidian stallions that reared on the pedestals above them. He walked and stared down the avenue at the lines of buildings receding to the south—at their dark, broken shapes that tapered the lighter sky behind them into funneled wedges like tornadoes summoned to cleanse the metropolis of its unredeemable sins. Farther up, as he passed by the Merchant Gate entrance to Central Park, a rat scuttled about beneath the stone prow of the *Maine* memorial as if looking for a place to board.

When he turned the corner west on Fifty-eighth past the Coliseum, he could already feel the change. Here, the first tentative mar of graffiti appeared on a building front. The sidewalks became darker stained, the streets less lit. Even at this late hour, a line of diesel trucks ticked loudly beside a construction site. Along the sidewalks, lines of garbage bags were propped up haphazardly as if in poor preparation for an imminent flood. A man entered a basement bar as Farrell passed, and its raucous din momentarily spilled out into the street. Farrell walked on.

The first time he'd walked here was the Christmas he'd been dishonorably discharged from the Marines. He remembered coming out of the Port Authority that morning to a full Hell's Kitchen holiday greeting of filthy snow and gray buildings and an even grayer sky and wanting anything but to take the twenty-minute subway ride home. Every place he tried was still closed until he stumbled onto a place on Eleventh. It was a windowless cement box flanked by two empty lots, and there was a handwritten poster outside that said, "Welcome Sailors." The place was packed, the jukebox blaring, and people were actually still dancing at ten in the morning. He had sat and had a beer, and he remembered someone putting on the famine relief song that was popular at the time. Everyone had joined in heartily, laughing their asses off, and by the time a "Hands across the Bar" ceremony was underway, he had thought that maybe he didn't have to go home after all, thought perhaps he might already be there.

Walking now, staring off at the murky sky above the low, dark buildings to the west—smelling again the cement and grease and faint salt from the Hudson—he contemplated just how complete a fool a man could be.

He thought of his brother Terry as he walked. Terry had lived around Times Square, and that was another reason he had settled here. He wanted to find his long lost brother. He had finally found him, hadn't he? Found out he'd died of AIDS. After that, he was pretty indifferent to the concept that anything mattered. It took a trip to prison to make him believe that maybe his drawing did. But he was beginning to have doubts about even that. Serious doubts.

When he got to Reilly's, it was a little after ten. He finished the quart in the shadows across the street, watching the front door, but nobody entered and nobody left. He stared up and down the block and then put down the empty bottle and took the .22 from his boot. He put the gun in his pocket and lit a cigarette. Then he crossed the narrow street.

She was in the far corner and was already smiling at him behind her long black hair. Besides her and the bartender he counted seven people. All seemed middle-aged regulars but for a younger man of about thirty. He had a short, blond crewcut, and his hard, sharp-nosed face and arms were sunburned red. He seemed to be in construction by his still dusty clothes and boots and well into his paycheck by his glazed eyes. Farrell relaxed and returned Tara's smile as he came over.

She was wearing a dark suit with just a slim necklace of gold, and she was smoking a cigarette with red stains from her lipstick on the filter. She crossed her legs beneath the slitted skirt, her skin pale beneath the dark fabric of the stockings.

"GI Joe! What's up?" she said. "Can I?"

He bowed toward her. She scratched her long fingernails through his short hair.

Farrell sat. He turned to the hovering bartender.

"Heineken," he told him. "And another for the lady."

When he turned to her, she looked genuinely surprised. He had never seen it before.

"Has it been that long since I bought you a drink?" he said.

"And you're off the wagon?" she said.

"Not really," Farrell said, taking his beer and paying the bartender. "Just celebratin. That don't count."

"Oh, really?" She leaned in, staring at his eyes, and he caught the scent of her perfume. "The party's already started, huh?" she said, looking over his shoulder. "Mulls outside?"

Farrell tilted the bottle back, chugging. He wiped his mouth with the back of his hand.

"He and Roy and Billy went to drop Durkin out

in Queens. He asked me to babysit you until they get back."

"Durkin's the Irish guy, right? That snooty bastard who came out with us that time. The one who was actin like everything was beneath him or something."

"They can be like that," Farrell said, staring at his bottle. "Like bad guests. They come over and like the opportunity and the money, then start criticizing."

"Right. Like if this is such a bad deal, then why don't they just go back. Anyway . . . " She lowered her voice. "Everything went OK, right?"

Farrell nodded slowly, looking at the bottles behind the bar.

"Good," she said. She nodded to herself as if convinced of something. "Good," she repeated. She sipped at her drink.

Farrell sipped his beer and looked down the bar. Three of the older men were engaged in a heated conversation, trying to raise their voices over the piped-in stereo. The other three were sitting separately but shared the same vaguely retarded blank stare as they craned up at the TV above the bar. The young laborer sat staring curiously at the glass he held daintily in his hand, as if expecting it to do something. A long, burnished mirror dangled in the space between the top of the wall and the stamped-tin ceiling. When Farrell looked up into it, he saw the laborer turn a quick glance over to them and then back to his drink.

Farrell sipped at his beer again for a moment and then put it down.

"I'll be right back," he said.

He stood and passed behind the construction worker on his way to the bathroom. He locked the door and turned on the tap. He splashed water on his face, breathing deeply. He bent at the sink, putting his cool hands on the back of his neck. When he looked up at his reflection in the stainless-steel towel dispenser, he could hardly recognize himself. He waited for a minute on his watch and then came back out.

The laborer was at the pay phone as he headed back to his stool.

"Some babysitter you are," Tara started.

"Do me a big favor," said Farrell, smiling as he took her purse off the back of her stool and handed it to her. "I'll explain why in a second, but I need you to go outside and get us a taxi. I'll meet you in a second, OK?"

She looked at him.

"You're serious?"

He nodded.

She passed out the door. Farrell waited for the laborer to sit back down before he called out.

"Hey!" he yelled down to the bartender.

Conversation stopped. Sets of eyes unglued from the television screen.

"What was that?" the bartender said tautly, a hand going to his ear in an exaggerated gesture.

"Com'ere!" Farrell yelled.

"You lower that fuckin volume," the bartender commanded, coming over.

"I want to buy a drink for that man there," Farrell said, pointing at the construction worker. He watched the man's face as it squinted in puzzlement. With an angry deliberation, the bartender took a coaster from the pile in front of him, walked to the carpenter, and slapped it down.

"Four-fifty," he told Farrell, not hiding the agitation in his voice.

"Hold on," Farrell said, patting at his pockets. He took out his cigarettes and placed them on the bar. Next his wallet. When he took out the .22 and clacked the black automatic loudly upon the bartop, the background music seemed to suddenly increase in volume.

Farrell retrieved a twenty and placed it in some puddled liquor above the gun.

"There we go," he said.

The bartender looked at him seriously now, with a newfound concern. "We're not lookin for trouble here," he said diplomatically.

"Oh, no trouble," Farrell said, putting away his cigarettes and wallet. He winked at the sunburned laborer as he picked up the gun. He held it in his hand.

"No trouble at all," Farrell assured him as he passed down the bar and walked out the door.

Tara waited in the cab. Farrell slipped the pistol in his pocket as he got in.

"Times Square," he told the driver.

"What is it?" Tara asked.

"Guy at the bar was wrong."

"Which one?"

"The construction guy."

"Wrong how? Like he was a cop or something?"

"Maybe," said Farrell.

"Well, maybe you should slow down a little on the booze," Tara recommended. "Maybe you're a little out of practice."

He looked over at her. Her smile flickered white and black in the passing streetlights. He laughed.

"Maybe you're right," he said.

"Now, how are we going to meet up with every-body?"

"I'm thinkin I rent out a room at the Milford or somewhere, call Reilly's and leave a number. Why don't I drop you off somewhere?"

"I'll stay with you," she said.

"You're sure?" Farrell asked.

"Yeah," she said. "I know a place we can go." She gave the driver an address on East End Avenue. The cab made a left and headed east.

They pulled up at a corner. Farrell paid, and they got out. They walked down the block and came to a door, and she unlocked it. The apartment was on the third floor. It had a long hallway with a kitchen and bedroom off it and at the end, a large living room with new-looking white couches and a glass coffee table. She went into the kitchen. Farrell sat on the couch and looked out the window at a dark sliver of the East River that rolled at the base of the wall of a huge high-rise, the countless windows intermittently bright and dark like some cryptic binary message. He felt exhausted.

When she came back out, she was without her shoes and she carried two beer bottles. She handed him one and sat on the couch across from him.

"Nice," Farrell said, looking around. "Yours?"

"My sister's."

The white shelves held art books, small metal statues.

"She work on Wall Street or something?"

"No, she's a waitress," Tara said. "She has a rich boyfriend. He bought it for her."

"No way," said Farrell surprised.

"Lucky bitch," Tara said enviously. "She's in Tahoe with him right now."

"Where's his wife?" Farrell asked, smiling.

"In Europe or someplace," Tara said. She looked over at him. She smiled back slowly. She had looked suggestively at him before when they were all out and Mullen was talking to somebody else or gone to get cigarettes. But before tonight whether it was teasing or she got off on betrayal or she liked him, he'd never cared to know.

With one movement he took out the packet of coke and slid it across the table. She glanced down at the package and looked back at him with an intense expression that at first was outrage and then something else. She had a cocaine problem, and that's why she'd been with Mullen in the first place. She was a secretary in a Manhattan real estate office (where she had gotten Farrell the doorman job), and she was only twenty-three years old. She lived with her parents in Brooklyn during the week and spent her weekends with Mullen because she loved him and because he gave her cocaine. Mullen had told Farrell often enough that he suspected the coke might be the main reason she stayed with him. Farrell could empathize. He was not unfamiliar with the drug's effects nor dissatisfied by them. They stared at the coke, then at each other, then at the coke again.

She sat on the floor and opened the bag a little and tapped some onto the table. She went into her purse, took out a credit card, and cut a couple of lines. She took out a short metal straw and snorted one nostril, then the other. She lit a cigarette, blinking as her eyes teared.

Farrell cut his own line and snorted it and waited as the drip started at the back of his throat. What the cocaine did, and what he had always liked about it, was keep him up and drinking when he should have been passed out. With enough cocaine, you could sometimes keep the party going for days. In those first months out of the service, when he was flush with his back pay, he had gone as long as three days in the same bar, in the same clothes—ordering in food and going through the shifts of bartenders. He would have gone longer had they not become so sick of him and his incessant chatter that they refused to serve him anymore. He knew the disastrous effect it had, though, when the high came down—that grip of suicidal depression, the destructive result of a mind and body put through paces they naturally refused. But that something could keep him up and happy at times when he should have felt terrible was amazing to him.

Already his mind began to clear, his fatigue to dissipate. What mattered now? With Mullen and them all dead—Durkin practically by his own hand—what did it matter having a little coke, some lies, a betrayal? He had only a little time, another few hours perhaps, and he intended to use them well. He'd make up for his wasted labors, the painstaking preparations, the foolish regard. All that was left was his need to empty out the bitterness of his heart into a night that seemed all too eager to receive it.

He snorted again and without a word reached over and unbuttoned the top of Tara's jacket. His hand brushed beneath the thin string of gold, meeting no resistance.

In the bedroom after, he lay staring out the window. On the East River the huge black mass of a ship passed slowly by, blotting out the bottom of the high-rise. He sat up and put on his jeans. He looked over at her. He thought for a moment what it would be like to be married. It was crazy because he knew she was just some coke whore, but he thought about it anyway. He imagined a little house somewhere quiet. He could draw while she worked in the garden. Some kids, a son perhaps, raise him right. A normal life.

"Worth the wait?" she asked sarcastically.

Farrell turned.

"Every minute," he said, dashing his thoughts.

"What are you gonna do now, with the money, I mean?" she asked.

"I'm gonna get out of here."

"Where to?"

"I don't know," he answered her. "Away. What about you and Mulls?"

"Yeah, right. That son of a bitch won't even take me out to eat."

"Hey, Mulls was a great guy. He was the best friend I ever . . . "

"What did you say?" she asked, interrupting him.

"He was the best . . ."

"Was? What do you mean 'was'?" She sat up in the bed.

"Is. Was. Whatever," he said hastily.

She looked at him, horrified.

"That explains it. That's why you didn't call Reilly's. Bobby is dead, isn't he?"

"Slow down. You're talking crazy, Tara."

"You son of a bitch," she said, pulling the sheet off the bed and wrapping it around her as she stood. "You killed him, didn't you? You killed him and came over here and . . ."

Farrell walked over to her.

"You're sick in the head, Tara. Mullen went to drop . . ."

"Get the fuck out. YOU GET THE FUCK OUT OF HERE! RIGHT NOW!" she screamed.

When Farrell took another step toward her, she grabbed at something on the nightstand and let it fly. He felt it whip past his head. It smashed against the wall. He gathered his clothes. She ran out and then rushed back in the room as he was putting on his boots. She held something in her hand and was running at him. It was a butcher knife, and he rose quickly, grabbed her arm, and pitched her hard across the bed. She took out the lamp on the far nightstand, and it bounced loudly off the wall.

"You're fuckin nuts!" he screamed as he fled the room.

When he came out on the street, an object smashed at his feet. She was hurling something else when he looked up. He stepped aside. Something metal clanged off the sidewalk and banged off the side of a parked car. Farrell jogged away. At the corner a man with a dog stopped and shook his head at Farrell sympathetically as he passed.

"Murderer!" she screamed after him. Farrell turned the corner quickly and crossed the street, sticking to the shadows.

7

IT WAS A LITTLE AFTER NINE WHEN RYAN ENTERED the Sportsmen. It was a large, open place; men and women were packed around the curved horseshoe bar, and dusty-skirted men were shooting pool, shooting darts—a good crowd for so early. That neighborhood of Bainbridge was a haven for new immigrant Irish. Though they had until four A.M., the loud pay-day crowd before him seemed to be intent on getting their drinking in before eleven, Ireland's last call.

Ryan looked different. Slacks, sport coat, shoes. Not formal, but serious. A man about to attend to some business. He'd spent the rest of his unexpected afternoon off watching television in his small basement apartment, and he'd come here early, not to get any preemptive lay of the land, but just so he could have his meeting as early as possible and get the hell out of here.

He spotted an empty stool, and he walked across the beer-stained wood floor and slid onto it. He saw that they had Guinness on tap, and when he finally flagged down one of the bartenders, he ordered one. He watched the barman tilt the glass beneath the spigot and lower the lever. The thick, black liquid slowly swirled in the glass and then was stopped for a pause and then started again. After a while the barkeep topped it off expertly, presented it to Ryan, and took his money. Ryan appreciated its perfection for a moment, then lifted it up and took a gulp.

He looked around the bar at the ruddy faces smiling, laughing. But for the piles of money on the bartop, it could have been Dublin or Belfast. He'd lived in Ireland years ago, and, drinking being perhaps a more serious business in that country, he'd found that sacred wood reserved for spirits alone.

He sat listening to the jukebox. Some sad song backed by ancient flutes and drums. He had always loved Irish music, those quiet, old-fashioned, mordant tunes of homesickness and heartache and tragedy.

His three sisters had done Irish dancing, and the

jig record would be played over and over again in the living room, where they practiced. Sometimes his father would come in from work and yell and do a reeling jig stomp along with them, making the record skip and them all die laughing. His father had been a good man. He'd put in sixty-hour weeks of back-breaking work to provide for his family, and he loved them all—his mother, three sisters, him—even told them so, which perhaps wasn't in keeping with the times. He'd immigrated at seventeen, right after WWII, doing nonunion day laboring and glad to get it.

Not like some, Ryan thought.

He thought of the kid Kevin from the work site. A person like that would never learn. The boy had seen how his "friends" had left him hanging, and yet he'd gone back to them. Ryan had given him the opportunity to step up and be a man, but the kid had declined. Chalk up another one for the bastards, Ryan thought.

He sipped his stout and looked around the room. Out of that crowd of faces, he found one looking back from the far opposite end of the bar. A brown-haired woman, near his age, smiling. He assessed her. She still had some looks on her, but there was something in her gaze, some glaze of desperation that was a little frightening, and he looked away. Not that road yet, he thought.

After a while the door spilled open, and a party came in. A group of men carrying small duffels with hurling sticks jutting out of them, strips of black electrical tape wrapped around the curved wooden hafts. The volume on the jukebox was increased, and the room became even smokier. There was a sign for a beer garden pointing toward the back of the place, and Ryan lifted his pint from the wood carefully and walked through the bodies for the door.

Some rusting metal tables with matching rusting chairs sat in a small, unlit, cement courtyard surrounded by a chain-link fence. Cases of empties were stacked up against the fence and the wall of the bar. Beyond the fence were the crumbling backs of several buildings and between them the slow stream of cars on the Mosholu Parkway. Besides weeds from cracks in the cement, no fauna or flora was in sight. Ryan let the door and the dull roar of revelry close behind him.

When his eyes adjusted, he saw a man sitting at one of the tables with his back to him.

"Is that you, Mr. Ryan?" The form spoke quietly without turning around.

Ryan walked over to the table and stood where he could see the other man's face. He was a large man, in his late thirties, with thinning brown hair and glasses. Ryan did not know him. The man had a bottle and a glass in front of him, and he leaned back in his chair, leisurely studying Ryan. Ryan set down his pint, pulled over a chair with a screech, and sat down.

"You are?" asked Ryan.

"Seamus." The man extended a big callused hand across the table. Ryan took it. "Seamus Gallagher."

Ryan could tell from his accent that he was not from the North. It was not surprising. Many of those he had known had been from the Republic. Gallagher leaned back in his chair again silently. A dog barked somewhere. Ryan sipped his drink, put it back down.

"Well, here I am," he said.

"We have a mutual friend," Gallagher said. "A Mr. Clancy from Inniskillen. He told me if I ever was in dire need of help, I could contact you. He also told me something he said you would understand."

"What's that?" Ryan asked disinterestedly.

"Ask not what your country can do for you."

Ryan winced inwardly at the words as he looked off into the sky above the buildings.

"Horseman, pass by," Ryan said, giving that long-ago prescribed reply.

"Ah, brilliant. I have heard a lot about you, Mr. Ryan. Can I get you something to eat?"

Ryan shook his head.

"How is old Clancy?" he asked.

"Hurting, I'm sad to say, Mr. Ryan, as are we all with the cessation. No activity allowed, you see, and the boys are gettin antsy. Fine for the politicos to make gestures, but it's hard to keep things together without activity, you know. When a union strikes, at least you can get the men to go out and picket. Not practical in our business though, is it? You heard the Brits wanted us to hand over our weapons?"

"I'm sure they did," said Ryan.

"The balls," said Gallagher. "Imagine. Hand up the only thing that got us sitting at the table in the first place. Ahh, don't get me started." Gallagher paused. He moved forward and laced his fingers together carefully on the table. When he started again, he lowered his tone.

"I am sorry to bother you. I know this was the last phone call you expected to get. A few of ours got pinched in Boston, and we are dying for man-power. A situation has arisen. A man in our unit is missing."

"Missing?"

"Do you know what the Westies are?" Gallagher asked.

Ryan nodded his head.

"A man of mine, Liam Durkin, was in on a little business with some of them last night."

"What kind of business?"

Gallagher looked up, squinting in search of the most appropriate word.

"Fund-raising."

Ryan looked heavenward. Why the fuck did he wake up this morning? He thought for a second.

"What are we talking about here? That hotel robbery? He was involved in that?"

Gallagher nodded solemnly.

"What kind of man is your boy, this Durkin?" continued Ryan.

"He was a Belfast boy," Gallagher said. "Young. But dedicated, you know. He didn't leave with the money, if that's what you're thinking."

"He's probably dead then," Ryan said shortly.

Gallagher glared at him.

"How do we know that?"

"I haven't heard too much about those boys from Hell's Kitchen, but what I have heard is they're not too squeamish about shooting a man."

"Neither am I," said Gallagher coldly. "Neither are you, from what I hear."

"Do both of us a favor," Ryan said, lifting his glass. "Don't presume anything about me. You want my help finding your boy or finding out what happened to him, I got a long weekend coming up. No problem. Anything past that, you're on your own."

Gallagher stared from across the table, his eyes slits behind the spectacles.

"I guess we'll just have to find him then," he said. He picked up the bottle, poured a drink, leaned back. He drank. "We'll just have to find him."

The bar door swung open, throwing a rectangle of yellow light onto that tiny, decrepit plaza. The bartender stood in the threshold.

"Seamus," he called over.

Gallagher placed his drink on the table and stood.

"Hold on. Right back," he said.

When the door closed, Ryan took his drink and walked over to the fence, looking out over the dusty, darkened yards. What kind of bullshit was he getting himself involved in? Wouldn't he ever learn? He should leave this instant, he knew, but he felt obligated. The promise he had made was decades old, but there it was. He could do a little legwork and pay back that long-ago favor. Then all ledgers would be even. Anything rough came along, he'd do just what he said—walk. He looked out, drinking, convincing himself.

When the door opened again, it was Gallagher.

"Come on," he called urgently.

Ryan put his half-finished pint on the table and went for the light. As he followed Gallagher into the bar, there was some commotion in the crowd. One of the bartenders and a tall bouncer were trying to reason with an even taller inebriated patron.

"I'm not your buddy!" the drunk screamed as he shrugged off the hand the bouncer had laid on his arm. Gallagher rolled his eyes and walked deliberately behind the bar.

"I'm not your buddy!" the sot wailed again as the bouncer grabbed him around the waist. The drunk wrapped his huge hands around the brass rail and held himself there fast. Even when the bartender joined in, they couldn't budge this drunken passive resister. Gallagher shoved through the crowd quickly, holding something in his hand. It was a small mallet, and he brought it down twice on his uncooperative customer's hands.

"Ohhhhhhh," the drunken giant moaned, putting his hands beneath his armpits and doing a comic dance as he backpedaled to keep his footing. He was still moaning as he was bum-rushed out the door. Gallagher put the hammer on the bar and came over to Ryan, the crowd parting before him.

"I just got a call. One of the Westies Durkin was with last night just stepped into a bar downtown," Gallagher said, leading Ryan out. "I called in the rest of the boys to meet us there. I have my car up the block here. We can be there in twenty-five minutes if there's no traffic."

They stopped at a dilapidated station wagon. Gallagher unlocked it and opened the passenger door from the inside. He threw tools and papers and coffee cups off the seat into the back, and Ryan sat. The car smelled immediately of gasoline when Gallagher started it. Ryan rolled down the window.

Just as they pulled onto the Mosholu Parkway, Gallagher's beeper went off.

"Shite," he said.

Gallagher stopped at a corner pay phone and got out.

Ryan turned and looked behind him. The backseat was folded down, and there were tools—dusty sledgehammers and crowbars, a sawzall, a worn, red metal toolbox. There were also holes in the floor of the wagon where rust had eaten through, a big one near the tailgate showing the street beneath. When he turned and looked out the windshield, Gallagher was attacking the pay phone with the receiver. He threw it one last violent time, let it hang, and rushed back.

"My man lost him," Gallagher said, sitting. He slammed the door viciously. "He says the coy bastard pulled a gun and left. There are a couple of more places he can look. He's going to call me back in an hour or so."

"Well, I'll tell you what," Ryan said. "I'm gonna swing on home. You have my beeper number. You know Woodlawn?"

Gallagher nodded.

Ryan got out and closed the door.

"You get a line on your friend, you beep me and I'll be at the gas station on the corner of Katonah and 233rd."

"I'll drop you there," Gallagher said.

"That's OK," Ryan said. "I like the walk."

Ryan walked up Bainbridge Avenue. Full bars bookended nearly every block. When he was fifteen or sixteen, he and his friends used to come here. It had always been an immigrant Irish neighborhood, with bartenders notoriously lax in their age-proofing policies, so they would travel south from Woodlawn Friday nights to take advantage. He remembered the tensions that unfolded at times between the young Bronx-born and the brogue-voiced immigrant clientele. He had broken a bottle over an Irishman's head on one of these corners on an occasion when a pack of them were chasing him down during a brawl. Funny how things worked out, he thought, how unpredictably alliances transformed things.

He walked up the hill past the Oval Park and past Montefiore Hospital. He crossed Gun Hill Road and walked down to Jerome Avenue and past the Woodlawn station again. He walked along the cemetery wall but did not go in. He was in no rush tonight. Across the street the dark trees of Van Cortlandt Park undulated slightly, soundless in the scant warm breeze. He stared into the thick shadow of those trees and then with effort looked away. That park was vast, and its deep forest contained within it many unsettling things, Ryan knew.

He had been to Vietnam and had seen and done things there that had affected his mind. He had been a sniper and the long bouts of fear-drenched solitude in that far-off wilderness presented difficulty for his readjustment to normal life. One manifestation of this difficulty was a newfound proclivity after his homecoming to slip out of his parents' home under cover of night and travel up to the park and walk its trails until dawn. Something in the immensity of Van Cortlandt spoke to his disturbed mind. He had heard people say it was haunted by the souls of Revolutionary War dead or by Indians. Whatever it was, he had felt it pull at him as the jungle had, some unnamable affinity.

He would skirt silently, stealthily, along both the Mosholu and Saw Mill parkways, the Mosholu and Van Cortlandt golf courses, the Van Cortlandt lake. He'd follow along the old Putnam line tracks and sit for hours atop the wall of the Revolutionary War Cemetery up in the rocks above the flats. Waiting, listening, searching, going through the motions of some deranged campaign.

There were the skeletons of burned-out cars, some in clearings rimmed so tight with old trees it seemed that the only way a car could have come there was if it had been air-dropped. He had seen wild turkeys and pheasant, and one time he thought he'd seen a wolf, but then it had started howling and he realized it was a coyote. Along some trails, he had seen marks in rocks that had triangles painted on them and small indentations. On one night he had seen lights in the forest and, when he got closer, the sheeted procession. Figures in white cowls chanting, incense in the trees. Perhaps he had made it up, hallucinated it. God knows, it was possible at the time, with all the drinking he'd been doing. But the next morning, there was dried wax on the stones and a cleared-out place where there had been a larger fire. A fucked-up time it had been, to be sure.

He had gone on in this manner until his father discovered his nightly missions and took Ryan on a plane to Ireland to see if he could save his life. It was agreed that he would stay on his uncle's farm in Wicklow, but then one day a month later, he found himself in Belfast signing up for the work he had started in Vietnam but did not seem to have finished.

Perhaps not even now, he thought.

He picked up his pace. It was all too much, too soon. His past had lain dormant for so long, he had thought the bad things in it had lost their strength to affect him. Wrong again. When he turned right at East 233rd, he could see a dark group drinking by the backstop of the ballfield there. He could hear the low, tinny sound of their radio. If any of those teenagers happened to glance across the street at that moment, perhaps they kept it to themselves—struck silent by the vision of a man standing with an unnatural stillness beneath the stone cemetery wall, the streetlight above cutting dark shadows in the hollows of his eyes and sharp cheeks. Ryan stood there and wished for a moment that he had the last of the Guinness he'd left on the table in the back of the bar, and then he turned slowly and walked down the street heading home.

8

MCCARRY FIRED AND FIRED AND FIRED, BUT THE crouching figure in his sights didn't even flinch. After the last round, McCarry pulled the trigger again, ejecting the empty clip from the Glock, and then fluidly slapped in a full one with his other hand. He let burst with the gun again, the quick-spaced reports clacking out like the sound of an industrial machine punching holes in metal. It was difficult to aim with the recoil and the moving slide, but he was used to it. With two hands, he held the jumping gun down as shell casings chased themselves out the port, the brass tinkling almost musically off the cement.

McCarry laid the gun down on the wood shelf, took off his goggles, and pressed the button to move the target in. He took down the paper and assessed the damage he had inflicted on his assailant. There were concentrated groupings in the head and chest of the paper figure, the same "bad guy" he gunned down every week—a white, middle-aged male with black hair and a .38 special directed right at him. He always seemed to McCarry an outdated, comical figure—a disgruntled plumber turned by the Great Depression, perhaps, to a life of crime. If they wanted to update it, McCarry thought—make it a little more realistic— they could draw a fourteen year old with dreadlocks and an AK47. McCarry gathered his brass up off the floor and put it in the stall's receptacle. Then he picked up the empty clips and loaded them again from the box of nine-millimeter rounds on the shelf. He put the box with the remaining bullets in his bag along with his goggles. He reloaded the gun with one of the clips, clicked on the safety, and slid it back into the leather holster on his right hip. He rolled his sleeves down and straightened his tie before putting his jacket back on. He didn't look at the other shooters as he passed them. He left the earmuffs on until he came out the door of the range. Without a word, he handed them to the clerk at the desk and left.

Last light had been falling when he entered the range forty-five minutes earlier, and now it was completely dark. He walked across the parking lot through the inky warmth. When he got in the car,

was bigger than the rental the six of them had been a family in, and he'd paid for it himself. He was the youngest of four kids, and he was the first real estate owner his family had produced thus far. The mail was all junk and bills, and he left them there on the counter as he took his beer inside.

He went over to the window, turned on the air conditioner, and lay back on the couch before it. He was a lot of firsts for his family, he thought. First to graduate from college, not to mention law school. As far as he could surmise, he came from a long line of people who just accepted their lot in life with nary a thought or a protest, and he seemed to be the first of his ilk to try and reverse that. He had gotten into Regis High School, which was free to those who passed its arduous entrance exam, and he'd gone to St. John's on full scholarship and taken out loans for four years of nights at Brooklyn Law. Paid his own way throughout, too, without a request for or an offer of anything from anyone.

He equated his going for the FBI with the penchant that had almost made him go for the priesthood. There was something about it that was vaguely similar, the relaxed control in dealing with matters of vast importance. Being educated by

Jesuits had shown him that there were realms other than money—namely, the importance of being part of a tradition larger than oneself, and the power granted to initiates of such traditions. And though the government paycheck could be seen as a vow of poverty, even at this bottom rung the badge's cachet demanded certain perks—instant respect from men, occasional intense interest of women.

He drained the beer. He was willing to wait and to make the connections necessary to put him somewhere real in the next fifteen years or so. He stood and went into the kitchen and put the empty bottle in the sink. He thought about having another one but then remembered the report. He went into his office and turned on his computer.

When he was done, he printed out several copies, some to hand out at the meeting and one for his records. It was a good report. Like any shrewd legal document, ambiguous enough to hold many interpretations equally. The fervor with which he'd planned to dismiss the surveillance of the park shook him up a bit. He'd almost made a huge mistake.

He took off his tie and his shirt and headed to the shower.

When he came back into the darkened bedroom, the phone was ringing. He let the machine pick it up.

"Yeah. Hi," came a vaguely familiar voice. "This is Vince Spano."

McCarry picked up the phone without turning on the light.

"Hey, Vince. What's up?"

"Francis. How the hell are ya?"

"Hangin in there, man. What have you got for me?"

"Remember you asked me to let you know if we saw any new faces with Gallagher? Well, we got one."

"Oh, yeah? Who?" asked McCarry.

"That's just it. We don't know. He's just a middle-aged dude in a sport coat at this point. He doesn't match anybody we've got in our files. He came with Gallagher out of his bar about an hour ago, and then Gallagher came back alone."

"A boyo?" asked McCarry.

"Maybe. Got a serious look on his face from the look we got."

"Interesting," said McCarry, taking out his notebook. He started writing. "Could you do me a real big favor, Vince? Run everything you got by my office tomorrow morning. I got to be in bright and early for the big meeting."

"That's right. You're one of the keynote speakers, I hear. Kid's moving up in the world, huh?"

"We'll see, Vince. Thanks for the call."

"Don't worry about it. There's nothing else to do in this godforsaken van except watch your brethren destroy themselves with alcohol."

"You should be thankful, Vince. You know what they say."

"What's that?"

"God invented whiskey so the Irish wouldn't rule the world."

"Is that right?" said Spano. "Well, from where I'm sitting, it looks like God invented the Irish to soak up the world's supply of whiskey. Take care now."

McCarry hung up laughing. Spano was an agent of the INS and also a part of the multi-agency, antiterrorist initiative. The man Spano had mentioned, Seamus Gallagher, was a suspected IRA unit leader. His name had come up in the investigation of an armored car holdup in Boston the year before. There was no evidence to convict him, but three of his Irish-American associates had been convicted and sent to prison. He had moved down to New York and set himself up as a general contractor, specializing, not so ironically, in demolition. He also owned a bar called the Sportsmen in the Bainbridge section of the Bronx. Gallagher was the strongest evidence of terrorist activity they had in the area, so they kept him and his bar under sporadic surveillance. But even he was on his best behavior these days.

The man who'd left the bar with him probably only wanted his bathroom redone, but you could never be too sure. Though he was almost positive the initiative would not produce anything this time out, McCarry was compiling lists of names and connections in his own database. If something happened farther down the road, it might come in handy. Investigations could stop and start up again, and if he were the one to put two and two together at a crucial point, it would bode well for him. Such attention to detail, he knew, was the grist from which promotions were made.

Smiling, McCarry turned and hit the switch for the computer. In the darkness he peered intently at the screen, listening to its shrill chirpings, waiting for the damn thing to come on.

As he waited, he remembered the message on his answering machine, and he played it. It was his mother reminding him about dinner on Sunday. He had swung by his mother's apartment that afternoon. When she went into the kitchen to make tea, he sat staring at the framed picture of his father on her lace tablecloth. For some reason, he'd remembered his father's old suitcase in the closet, so he went and got it out. His father having been a frugal man in life, there wasn't much. A wedding ring, a penknife, an old cheap watch, a tin whistle.

The tin whistle had brought back memories, though. He remembered the times, three in the morning they'd be awakened by shrill reels of his father blowing it in the kitchen. He remembered when his mother had hidden it to prevent those nocturnal recitals and how a few times the household was awakened by the crash of his father dropping boxes from the closet shelves in search of it. Thereafter it had been left on the kitchen table next to his knife and fork for his cold dinner waiting in the fridge.

"I should have been a song-and-dance man," he would say, consoling himself wearily in the darkened kitchen between songs. My dad, McCarry thought, Ward Cleaver.

There were some photographs on the bottom of the case, and he searched through them. A grainy brown-and-white baby portrait, and another of two strong-looking, middle-aged women in shawls and sack dresses standing in front of a thatched cottage, patchwork fields behind dotted with hedges. A third photograph made his mouth drop open. It showed his father as a young man. He was standing in a rutted, tire-track, dirt road in the country somewhere with a shotgun draped on his shoulder. He called his mother in and asked her about the picture, and she said it was his father hunting on the farm he had grown up on.

"What's he hunting? English soldiers?" he'd asked.

His mother had asked him if he was feeling all right, and he'd dropped it. It bothered him though. He took the photograph out as he sat waiting, wondering who the man really was.

9

ALL THREE BARS FARRELL HAD BEEN IN AS HE MADE
his way crosstown were crowded with rich college
kids—milling ranks of blond hair and baseball
hats and button-down shirts. He had had a
whiskey in each place. Some rowdy adolescents
entered as he was exiting the last. One stopped,
blocking the doorway, as he howled out to his
friends. Farrell didn't say a word, nor did he hesi-
tate. He just hard-shouldered the youth in his
path, the door banging out like gunshot against its
frame as he stepped over him onto the sidewalk.
Not even a curse followed him to the corner.

He walked westward through the Upper East
Side along rows of black, iron-gated townhouses,
past curtained restaurants, bleak-faced drivers
leaning on the hoods of limousines drinking their
coffee. At Park he waited on the light. Thick, silver
steam escaped from a manhole and stood in low

cover across the street, pulsing and darkening in the passing headlights. At the middle grassy mall, he sat and lit a cigarette. Down the avenue, the tower of the hotel that he had plundered was still lit brightly against the dark sky, and in the vertical strata of the receding buildings beyond, he could just make out the sliver of gray that was his old workplace. He wondered about the people he had worked with—and thought about how shitty it had been to work there. No matter what happened, at least he'd never have to go back there. He heard the metal hum of the Metro North train approaching. Its roar burst from the wire grate beneath with a breath of hot air, the steel clatter screaming and reverberating and passing upward like a buried storm that sought release.

When he got to Madison, he turned left and headed downtown. It was a fashionable shopping district here, but all the stores were closed and just a few people were waiting for buses, a few strolling. He passed by the darkened windows of boutiques, small art galleries, and silver shops. Beyond cardboard barriers in a few of these doorways, forms lay sleeping. Strangely innocuous in their slumber—even in the heat some wrapped in blankets—filthy figures curled upon the cement like overgrown babies dropped on ill-chosen doorsteps.

A few blocks farther south he came across the café. The doors were opened wide to the street, and its tables spilled onto the sidewalk. Tanned and richly attired men and women crowded round linen-covered tables and were three deep at the bar along the righthand wall. On the opposite wall, some silver art deco lamps emitted a bluish light, and everything white in the dim of the restaurant glowed incandescent—tablecloths, waiters' aprons, flashes of teeth.

Conversation and laughter and the clinking of glasses, along with the scents of cigar smoke, perfume, and rich cooking, drifted across the street. Farrell stopped, surveying the high-class revelry. Mullen would have liked it here, he thought. Mullen—a man who had lived in the same rent-controlled rattrap his whole life—would have walked into this place in his rags and celebrated by getting drunk on Dom Perignon and two-hundred-dollar bottles of brandy. An expensive task with less extravagant liquor.

Farrell was drunk himself, and suddenly he felt a great need to do something his departed compatriot would appreciate. He crossed the street.

The woman entering before him was over six feet tall and had short blond hair. The dress she wore was backless and all but see-through, and if she wore underclothing beneath, there was no sign of it anywhere. The maitre d' shook his head vigorously at Farrell's approach. He looked disgustedly at his jeans, his boots. Farrell slid a hundred dollar bill into the man's hand. The maitre d' glanced at the money and then back at Farrell— visibly torn. A thin man with slicked-back hair came through the crowd, took the money from the maitre d's fingers, and flicked it back at Farrell without a word, letting it fall to the floor. Farrell's face darkened. As he stepped after the man into the place, he was grabbed roughly from behind and pulled out. His arm was twisted behind him, and he was bent over the hood of a parked car. Someone stuffed his money back into his shirt pocket.

"Get the fuck out of here," said a serious voice in his ear.

When his arm was released, he resisted an intense urge to take out the pistol. Turning, it wasn't so much the bouncer's height but his width that was striking. The man was barely six feet tall but must have weighed three hundred pounds. He wore a short-sleeved black shirt, and his huge fore-arms and hands held a map of thick, raised veins. Farrell turned away.

"Don't come back," the giant warned him.

Farrell spotted the sailors up on Fifth Avenue. Every year the Independence Day celebration in the harbor brought ships, and when Farrell came to the corner, he saw three white-suited young men across the street enjoying some shore leave. They were sitting on a shadowed bench beneath the eaves of the Central Park trees, passing around a bottle.

"How would you boys like to help a fella out?" Farrell asked as he came up.

Farrell explained what he wanted, and when he was done, they stared at him dumbly. They were just some country boys who had perhaps banded together in their mutual ignorance to explore this city they had only seen and heard about on TV. The largest of them spoke up in a thick southern drawl.

"What the hell's in it for us?" he asked.

Farrell smiled. He'd been stationed in Virginia when he was in the Marines, and the sound of the man's voice brought back good memories.

Farrell took out three hundred-dollar bills and

tore them in half and handed a half to each man.

"It's not that I don't trust you," Farrell said, placing an arm on the shoulder of the sailor who had asked the question. "It's just, I need to know you're gonna be there."

"Get paid for stompin ass?" the man asked enthusiastically. He pocketed his half. "You just point the fucker out."

One of his friends laughed at this as he was drinking, and liquor sprayed out of his nose and mouth as he snorted.

Farrell came at the café for the second time. The bouncer, on spotting him, left his post and walked out to the sidewalk rolling his huge shoulders. Farrell held up empty palms as he approached. He watched as the sailors arrived one, two, three between parked cars down from the bouncer, and then holding the bouncer's gaze, he took an empty chair from the sidewalk table beside him and hurled it high into the interior of the restaurant.

Glass crashed loudly. A woman screamed. The crowd suddenly went silent. The bouncer rushed at Farrell. He moved fast for such a big man. Not fast enough. The sailors caught him in three steps, hitting him en masse. Two took a leg apiece while the third hit him up top, choking him as they all came toppling down at Farrell's feet.

The sailors earned their money. Blows rained down with quick, workmanlike rapidity. One of the sailors bashed a chair across the wide back of the bouncer, but it did not break like in the movies. It remained incredibly solid. When he did it again, the bouncer screamed. But even under this onslaught, the bouncer raised himself onto his hands. When the man gained his knees, Farrell hauled back and kicked him in the ear. He was wearing steel-toed boots, and the bouncer seemed to think better of this eleventh-hour resistance. A soft, sorrowful moan emanated from his lips, and then he curled into a tight fetal position, covering up his head with his hands.

Farrell looked to the crowd. They were penned up against the walls of the interior of the restaurant away from the melee like cattle in a slaughter-yard. He searched but couldn't pick out the man who had thrown the money back in his face. He turned to the sailors, who were still feverishly attacking the now motionless bouncer. They'd torn his shirt off and were about to slap his skull in with the WAIT TO BE SEATED sign when Farrell grabbed one of them.

"That's it!" he called out.

He jogged away with them down the block and handed over the other halves of the bills as they turned the corner.

"Thanks," Farrell said to the Southerner.

"Pleasure," the sailor said sincerely. He tipped his white cap graciously as Farrell cut ahead.

A siren started somewhere in the distance as Farrell flagged a cab on Fifth. He saw the last of the sailors in a blur of white through the rear wind-shield as they hopped the bench they'd been drinking on and disappeared like clumsy deer into the trees of Central Park.

He went to a club off Forty-second Street and then to one in a far West Side warehouse. The one that he found himself in now was housed in a desacral-ized church. In the surreal violet light of what might have been the nave, he bought some cocaine off a shirtless Hispanic who had a tattooed teardrop in the corner of his left eye. It was a cheap prison-house tattoo that Farrell knew was sup-posed to mean the man had killed someone.

"Where can I get one of those?" Farrell slurred loudly, pointing to the corner of his own eye. The man didn't even look up. He just handed over his product, added Farrell's money to his thick roll, and stepped off into the loud and frenzied darkness.

Farrell teetered on the edge of the dance floor, smiling out at the churning forms. He was very drunk now, but he had the cocaine that would sustain him as it had always done—prop him up now that all else had failed him. He looked around and then put one foot carefully in front of the other seeking a bathroom.

He was in the bathroom for some time. You couldn't tell who it was for by its occupants—men, women, odd approximations of each. When he came back out, the music and the flash and movement of the lights seemed clearer, more precise, newly understandable. Each gesture of sound and light that had seemed like so much confusion just a short time ago revealed itself to him now as perfect accompaniment to his troubled soul. Discordant and tortured, but still loud and alive.

He cut through the dance floor, where pews had once been. The flickering strobe light burned a rapid-fire montage of frozen portraits from the dark: dramatic, alluring, and dreadful. In the middle of the floor a group was dancing in a circle, at times one dancer breaking out into the middle.

Farrell watched carefully. The more he watched, the more their purpose became revealed to him, the more evident the likeness of their minds to his own. He waited patiently, and at the moment prescribed by their signal, he moved. He came through the circle to the center, and he twirled. He could see them smiling and laughing as he spun, and now he unzipped while still spinning. The high arc of his piss glittered in the flashing light. They danced on for a moment as he splashed them. Then they realized what was happening, and they fled in a violent rush. He spun alone with his back arched and his head back, his face a rictus of abandon and pleasure set high up into the blackened rafters.

The bouncers came quickly. He saw them coming and barely managed to adjust himself before he was knocked back. He went down, sliding across the floor. He studied the features of the men who roughly grabbed him and dragged him through the crowd into the alleyway. It seemed important that he do so.

That they did not beat him was to their advantage. The pistol from his ankle was in his hand as he got up, but the door had already banged shut. He heard a sound, some scuffle on the stone behind him, and he turned, swinging the pistol in the darkness. But it was nothing, so he turned and ran for the mouth of the alley.

He gave the next cab driver the address of a club he had known farther downtown. There was nothing at the address, but down the block there was a crowd of people and a velvet rope before a steel, graffiti-scrawled door. He paid the driver and got out. He went roughly through to the front of the crowd and slapped a hundred dollar bill into the hulking bouncer's hand. The door opened, and he went through.

It was dark here but quieter, with wood walls, furniture, carpet. From somewhere back in the smoky room came the sound of horns, the light crash of cymbals. He sought the bar. He was standing at it with a whiskey before him on its slick, black surface when a hand rubbed at the stubbled back of his skull.

When he turned around, the eyes that he looked into were wide, black-rimmed, and of a deep, dark gray that seemed at once filled with portent and splendor. The color of an angry sea or a troubled sky. Farrell just stared at her speechless, and then he realized that she was talking to him.

"What?" he said.

"I said, you're the guy who kicked the shit out of Ronny with those sailors," she said assuredly.

"I don't know what you're talkin about," Farrell said, looking away with effort. He realized she was the woman who had entered the sidewalk café before him.

"You're full of shit. I saw you. Don't worry. I'm glad you kicked his ass. What was up with those sailors? Were they friends of yours or something?"

Farrell lifted an eyebrow. Finally, he smiled.

"No," he said. "I just couldn't find any Marines."

She laughed, staring back at him.

"Is that what you are?" she asked, interested.

"Not anymore," he said.

"Don't worry," she said. "I think you still got it."

He looked at her. She was beautiful, but she seemed bored with it, as if it had lost its ability to make her happy. She couldn't have been more than twenty. She glanced over her shoulder. She smiled at him.

"You want to buy me a drink," she told him in his ear.

He ordered her a vodka, and she took his cigarettes off the bar and lit one with the lighter, smiling. When her drink came, he clinked his whiskey to her glass and glanced to where she had been looking. The owner of the café where he had fought sat at a curved booth, staring at them. Farrell smiled. Around her back he pointed to the girl and then to himself. Then he set his face in a mask of placid malevolence and placed a finger toward the slight, tanned entrepreneur and drew it slowly across his throat. The owner's mouth dropped open. When Farrell stood, the slight man bolted, disappearing into the crowd. Farrell took the girl's hand.

"Come on," he said. "I have to show you something."

He took her to a dark corner. He tapped some coke onto the web of his thumb. She snorted greedily. In this manner he fed her and then fed himself. He didn't even want to kiss her, he just wanted to look. Those wide eyes, the full lips. He wished he had a camera.

It had happened before. Unhinged on alcohol, he'd get lucky. Not with bad-looking women either. They could sense something off him perhaps, a recklessness they found thrilling. What they couldn't tell was that he really didn't care if he lived or died. They thought it was just a game.

He looked at her. For a moment a voice told him

to get up and just leave her there. A small voice. He ignored it. Yeah, he could show her some things. It was the least he could do.

They had more drinks and more cocaine, but then they were out. She looked at him, disappointed.

"Don't worry," he said, taking her hand again. "I know where we can get some more."

The subway station was a block over on Broadway. Between the glow of the lit green newel lamps, they passed down the flight of dark steps, the edges rimmed white and smooth as river stones from where a million feet had polished the iron. They pushed the heated air before them. Farrell bought their tokens at the plastic box from a clerk who didn't lift an eye. They passed through the turnstile. Its electronic beep, metal scrape, and click of its arm as it fell and caught sounded out loud and distinct in the silence of the empty station.

They walked to the end of a cement platform so stained that it looked like earth beneath their feet, a turned field. Farrell lit cigarettes and passed her one. He wouldn't look at her, only down the distant curve of track, at the compacted garbage between the ties, across the dead space of express tracks where, but for a quicksilver sliver where light caught rail, the ground and ties and gravel and steel girders were all the color of ash. The empty platform opposite was lit beyond this murk like a stage upon which a drama was about to unfold.

She moved in front of him. So striking on that grim backdrop, under that fluorescent light. She knelt before him. There with the distant sound of trains, far-off detonations in the tunnels, and the clink of pipe on pipe somewhere up in the low, vaulted ceiling she was at him. Down in the darkness of express track a headlight appeared and then another like the eyes of an awakening creature, and then it was there. A blur of silver, thundering and rattling between the girders before him, and he turned his head, following it until it was just the windows, cruciform panes against the light sliding off into the darkness. Slowly he looked down.

By the time their train arrived they were done. They stepped onto the empty car and sat on the colored plastic seats. Neither spoke. After a while she held his hand. Farrell stared out the scratched Plexiglas into the rushing darkness. Emergency tunnel lights streamed by at intervals, flashing in pinball reflections off the silver walls, the metal poles, the plastic. There was a fracture in the window across from them, and its jagged edges crackled in the passing light like distant strikes of lightning. They rode uptown, the doors rattling open at the empty stations, the fouled white-and-mosaic-tiled walls like sacked Roman baths. Not one person got on. As the train emerged from the tunnel at Dyckman Street station, he stood. When it stopped, he stepped out of the air-conditioned cool into the warm black, the girl a step behind him. They descended the stairs to the street.

The doors of the station swung out under the el. They stood for a moment, looking out from beneath that tonnage of dark metal. There were potholes in the street and within them the rough brickface of cobblestones from another era. Flat, brown slabs of projects towered to their right. Beyond these, across the black incision of the Harlem River, lights of buildings in the low hills of the Bronx burned from their slotted windows like caged fires. Far off, a kitted-out car stereo thumped, the throb of its resonant bass like the approaching footfalls of something huge.

Farrell took out his cigarettes. There was one left, and he shook it out, lit it with the lighter, and dropped the empty pack to the filthy cement.

"Home sweet home," he said.

He led her across the street, past shadowed blocks of stores that were just walls of corrugated steel from one end to the other. Stringed flags from some ancient grand opening were strung from rooftop to broken street lamp, limp and faded in the warm, dead air.

It had been such a night almost a year ago when they had come to rob him. He had seen them right away from the station—two gold-toothed youths with lightning eyes—as he came across the street. They hadn't counted on the Smith & Wesson he drew on them. He could tell from the expressions of appeasement that chased the cocksure viciousness from their faces. They couldn't have known that the pistol was his first acquisition upon release from jail, or of the promise he'd made to himself as he waited for the train outside the gates that parole or no parole, victimization was a possibility he would no longer entertain.

His apartment had been burglarized the next week. He had cause to suspect the main dealer on the block, a young Dominican named Enrique, who had sat laughing on the stoop of his building as he'd come in. What wasn't stolen lay in pieces on the floor, the furniture slashed, the walls soiled. Perhaps his efforts at self-defense hadn't been appreciated.

When he and Mullen had thought to make a quick score to bankroll the heist, Enrique seemed like the perfect candidate, but then when it came down to business, he'd balked.

"Hold on," Farrell said now. He stepped into the recess of a garbage way and took the .22 out of his pocket. The girl watched, enraptured.

There was some satisfaction in the idea that not all of his mistakes were unrectifiable.

A gypsy cab slowed on the cracked asphalt. Farrell stared through the smoked glass until it passed. When the girl touched his face with her delicate fingertips, he laughed. So out of place in her evening gown. She smiled at him and turned eagerly, taking in the raw surroundings. Even that far in, she was too ignorant to be afraid, too arrogant in her beauty to believe it might run out of power to protect her.

He turned away from her and started walking again. They turned a corner and walked up a narrow street. In the distance, firecrackers went off in a rapid-fire burst. It would be the Fourth of July in less than a week.

He remembered the Bicentennial when he was a kid. How they'd painted all the fire hydrants red, white, and blue. How everyone from his building had walked in a huge, slow procession over to the park for the fireworks. The smell of gunpowder and him and Terry lighting off the gross of bottle rockets one by one, kneeling in the dust beneath the trees. The father fortunately absent. His mother at a bench with all the neighbors talking and laughing, still young and pretty in the floating, colored light. So long ago.

He turned left at the next corner, and you could see them lined at intervals in the distance like carnival barkers right out in the street. As if it were legal. As if stalls had only been precluded by the narrowness of the avenue.

They passed the corner bodega where he had shopped, but it was closed, the colored lights dead atop the plastic yellow eaves. Passed by the laundromat where they had video rentals and the small store in the basement of a building that sold T-shirts but was really just another type of laundry, the kind for money. They walked past the corroding buildings. Some had wood-beamed tudor facades and some art deco stonework, many with intricate cornices or faded spaces where cornices had been taken away or perhaps fallen. Buildings fronted with pebbled cement balusters worked into vases, alabaster pillars, and arched stone doorways with sunken spandrels, stone fleur-de-lis pendants in the walls, iron on fire escapes hammered in delicate flowered designs. All frayed, all fading. High architecture saddened, withered away by time and perhaps by the sum of ignobility it had witnessed in the streets before it, among the walls within. His own included.

A block up, and there he sat. They saw each other at the same time. Enrique was bigger, more muscular since the winter. He was only about seventeen, so either he'd just matured or he was on steroids. He was sitting on the jut of a shielding wall of a basement apartment in shorts and a tank top, overseeing a younger Hispanic who stood out on the street making furtive gestures at the occasional passing car. Farrell turned to the girl.

"You just follow my lead," he told her seriously.

For the first time, a look of something other than excitement entered her eyes.

Farrell had come off the high of the cocaine, and he felt the load of alcohol he had drank shifting on him, bearing down. Though its dulling ease siphoned off the fear that threatened to overtake him and circumvent this deed six months past due, he wasn't sure if he would be able to make it, wasn't sure if he could get through it at all. Smiling, he stepped from the curb.

Enrique stood as they made the block. Farrell could see the fanny pack pulled in front for easy access. As they came up, Enrique seemed to talk to himself, then a figure stepped out from beneath the shadowed doorway. This man was tall and thin and wore a black shirt and jeans with pointy cowboy boots and a black leather cowboy hat. The eyes within his sharp, lined, Indian's face matched his clothes. Within the metal horseshoe of the man's belt buckle, a painted enamel Virgin Mary stared out sympathetically.

"Enrique," Farrell said softly, still smiling.

Enrique's eyes were on the girl.

"I know you?" he asked.

"You remember me," Farrell said. "I used to live in the building over there." He gestured back with his chin.

Enrique turned to him for the first time, squinting.

"Oh, yeah," he laughed. "You that herb got vicked in there."

The young street salesman had wandered over, and he laughed at this, a grating, incendiary braying in Farrell's face. The vaquero said nothing, just held Farrell in his vacant glare.

Farrell nodded his head, still smiling.

"That's right," he said. "You got a good memory. I'm downtown now. Nice night tonight. Thought I'd come by the old neighborhood, check things out, maybe make a little purchase for my friend, Barbie, here. She's plannin a party."

"That right?" Enrique said, turning to the girl. "You plannin a party, bitch?" he asked.

The girl looked over at Farrell.

"Fine. You don't want our business, there's only about a couple of hundred other people around here might. C'mon honey," Farrell said to her.

"How much?" Enrique asked.

"I don't know," Farrell said, rubbing his chin. "Four ounces should do it, I think."

Slowly Enrique checked the girl out head to toe. When he was finished, he bowed his head a little and proffered a guiding hand toward the building.

"Le's go," he said.

Enrique led the way. Farrell and the girl stepped behind him. When Farrell turned, he saw the youth from the street smiling and staring at the back of the girl as he bounced a few steps behind. Farrell was not worried about them finding the gun because he knew they wouldn't frisk him. It wasn't that they dismissed him as harmless, it was that the basic tenet of commerce within that industry—fucking around invited quick and savage death—seemed to preclude such formalities.

They followed the Dominican over a rough-cement, litter-strewn courtyard; the ground-floor apartment windows flanking it were dark, shaded, and barred. There was just a hole where the inside foyer door lock should have been. They entered a lobby cooled by walls of gray-streaked marble. There was more mosaic tile inlaid in designs on the floor. Then they went beneath a hand-cut arch into a rancid corridor. At its end, they went by a bank of metal mailboxes with some missing doors like a set of broken teeth on their way to the worn marble steps.

Farrell remembered getting caught beneath such stairs in the lobby of his building when he was a kid. Coming out from the grocery with milk for his father's tea, he'd seen some Spanish girls, all of thirteen but fully developed, dark-eyed and stunning. Maybe he'd looked too long, and a bunch of their boyfriends or brothers had come after him. They caught him in his hallway and got him down on the cool marble, one of them flicking out a butterfly knife. It was just to scare him, but he thought he was dead. Then the front door opened, and he'd heard familiar steps, careful, heavy footfalls beneath a load. He remembered looking up pleadingly at his father coming around the corner, but the old man paused only for a moment, his sodden senses taking in the situation, before passing up the steps without a word.

The staircase and landings stank of fried food and piss. On the third floor, they stopped before a door with a small square opening cut into it. Enrique rapped on it loudly. When the aperture slid open, the black maw of a shotgun appeared and then a set of eyes. Locks clicked loudly for a moment, and then the door opened.

Enrique led the way. The door warden was a fat, older man with a mustache who held an automatic shotgun casually upon his shoulder. He glanced at Farrell but concentrated mostly on the girl—his eyes roving and lingering slowly, shamelessly. The hardwood floors of the apartment were dirty and splattered with ancient paint. Gouged plaster walls showed slatted wood. There was an eat-in kitchen by the door with a refrigerator and stove but no table or chairs, and it had a strong chemical smell, hairspray or a burnt tire perhaps. There were some rooms off the corridor, but the doors were closed.

They walked out at the end of the hall into the living room. The metal table beneath the strung bulb held three items: an electronic scale, cocaine in a plastic bag, and a silver .357. Next to the table a young man with stocky features similar to those of Enrique sat on a wooden chair, the room's only other piece of furniture. When this man stood, Farrell heard a chain, and then a pitbull came out from under the table. It was a full-grown albino male, and it growled as it locked its dark eyes into Farrell's own.

"I don't think he likes you," Enrique said, walking toward the dog.

"Don't worry," said Farrell to the dog. "I won't bite."

Enrique sat in the chair. He took a sheet of foil from the floor and laid it on the scale. Using a baker's spatula, he scooped an amount of cocaine onto the foil deftly, a practiced motion. He raised an eye at Farrell to read the number on the scale, and Farrell nodded in satisfaction. The Dominican folded the big package tightly and laid it on the far side of the table. Farrell came forward.

"Six G's," Enrique said.

"Sounds good," said Farrell. "I just got to run down to the car to get it."

"Get it?" Enrique hollered. "Why the fuck you come up here you got no money?"

"I didn't want to get jumped," Farrell explained. "I'll be a minute. Come on, honey," he said to the girl.

Enrique cursed in Spanish, shaking his head.

"You jus be a minute. Then why don't she wait till you get back, make sure your drunk ass don't play no fuckin game with me. I don't like no games."

Farrell looked at the girl. She'd been holding it together, but as this was said, he watched terror flash in her face.

"I'll just be a minute," he told her. Looking at Enrique again, he turned and headed for the corridor.

The youth from the street followed him until the doorman opened the front door to the hallway. Behind, Farrell heard laughing and then rabidly festive Spanish music. He didn't look at the doorman as he passed, but he could smell his vile breath. With the door closing behind him, he lifted his ankle to his hand in a quick motion and took out the .22. The door barked off his foot, still in the threshold.

"Shit. My keys. She's got my keys," Farrell called out. The doorman cursed, pulling the door back open, and then Farrell placed the barrel to his head.

"*Mierda*," the fat man whispered.

Farrell pushed the door wide open, waiting for the man to shout or struggle so he could shoot him, but the man did neither. He just leaned stiffly against the wall with his eyes clenched shut. Farrell ripped the shotgun out of his hands and turned him around. He slipped the .22 into his own waistband, placed the shotgun to the back of the man's skull, grabbed the back of his belt, and led him forward. A few feet before the living room he let go of his belt and booted the fat man viciously ahead, jacking and raising the shotgun up as he followed.

He shot the dog outright. It swung its pale misshapen head in his direction, the black doll's eyes widening, and then he tore it through with the buckshot, sending it sliding across the floor trailing gore, its dropped leash behind it. He readied the gun again and had it trained before the dog stopped against the wall.

Farrell stood there. The radio blared on. He was sweating freely, but felt clear, pure with an anger that strengthened him, that reverberated within. The blast of the shotgun seemed to have dislodged something that had been stuck. This bastard here who'd invaded his home. The equal to any of the scores he'd come across in the service, in prison, in the street. The liars and killers and scum. The ones who snuffed out the possibility for grace every chance provided, no questions asked, no opportunity too small.

Enrique stood next to the table. He turned to the destroyed dog and then to Farrell and was lifting the heavy pistol off the table when Farrell fired. The shot went high and the light bulb disintegrated, and Farrell jumped down to the side in the darkness. Shots came at him—licks of orange flame in the black—near solid thumps of exploding plaster, and then he was scrambling up, the girl forgotten. He shot again blind and turned and ran down the corridor with shots following him. He made the door and flung it open. He came into the bright hallway, and booming footsteps were coming up the stairs, and he went up as well. There were anonymous screams in the stairwell, and then he punched out onto the rooftop. He dropped the shotgun in the darkness and ran. There was another building across an alleyway to the south side of the building, he knew, because he'd jumped it before when he was twelve, and now he jumped it again—the same adrenaline clench of fear and exhilaration over that cement distance— and then he landed, rolling on tar, and went into the building through another stairwell and down.

When he made it out the back of that adjoining building, he saw a red light sweep down in the rough-hewn corridor. He tossed the .22, went around to the far side of the building, and came out in the street, running.

10

THE HEAT WOKE HIM. FOR SOME TIME SUNLIGHT
had been coming in through the small, rippled
glass window high in the wall, cooking the unven-
tilated air of the cramped basement room. It was
like an oven when it finally dragged Farrell into
consciousness. He opened his eyes, bewildered in
the sweltering dust and murk, the metallic taste of
fear rising from his belly into his burned throat. He
started up, and then something within the bumpy
mound he lay sprawled upon shifted, and he went
down in a rain of falling debris.

The cement floor beneath his cheek was almost
cool. He looked around without turning his head.
He was in a storeroom of some kind—old chests
and luggage, an aluminum walker, a broken hob-
byhorse. He was wedged between some old head-
boards, one from a dusty crib, its white-painted
slats peeling. He'd been sweating in his slumber,
and he could feel the dust deep in the pores of his

skin. He rose, tormented and scratching, sending more junk crashing to the floor. Standing was more difficult than he imagined, so he sat against a wall.

He looked around and realized that he was in the storage room of the building he'd grown up in. He'd hidden here playing ring-a-levio with the other street urchins in the neighborhood when he was a kid. Some were dead, he knew, to drugs, others to AIDS, like his brother. Some were in jail, as he had been. The lucky ones had become cops, firemen, gotten into Con Ed or the phone company. They were all long gone though, had been for years. Except for him. He thought of the times he'd had with Terry. The nights they'd string two garbage can lids together with fishing line across the street and run heaving from laughing so hard as passing cars dragged them clattering up the block. The chases they'd get, during the winter, from throwing snowballs at cars. And the time they'd shoveled out the walkway of a house and when they had gone back to get the agreed-upon ten dollars, the man had indicated the driveway also and they had buried the cleared pathway again and rang his bell and asked him if that was better. So many times.

Sometimes he wished they'd never happened at

all, with the way things had turned out. Maybe if nothing were all he had ever known, he wouldn't know the difference.

He closed his eyes and wiped his filth-streaked face with his hands. Last night his alcohol-emersed consciousness must have selected this childhood sanctuary as a good destination. It was not the first time he had awakened in an odd place and didn't remember how he'd gotten there.

It all came back to him then, in shuddering waves. The succor of blackout was gone. The expression on the desk clerk's face when he stuck the gun in his ear, the one on Durkin's when the Sideburns dragged him off, the way the Albanian had fallen when he hit him, the gunblasts in the bar, Tara, the bouncer, Enrique and the dog and the girl. Jesus God—the girl—he'd abandoned her in that place. He sat there paralyzed, trying to carry—to contain—the full extent of what he had done. The sum of it was like the weight of the world bearing down on his chest. He held his head in his hands, not weeping but feeling an intense cold despite the heat, a frigid branding burning in his chest.

Eventually, he rose, clawing at the naked brick for support. He patted himself down. The gun was gone, but he still had his wallet with the bank key and his money. The cheap wooden door was draped slightly sideways in its frame where he had broken it. He pushed it out and stepped through. At the end of the dark corridor to the right he could see the burning white line of daylight at the bottom of an outside door, and he went the other way. He came into the empty laundry room and went over to the slop sink, turned on the cold water, and drank deeply. After a while he stripped off his shirt and bent over the sink, closing his eyes under the glorious water, and he stayed that way for some time. He would have taken off all his clothes and bathed in it were he not afraid someone would come in. He washed his shirt under the tap and put it on while it was still dripping wet. Then he went back down the corridor.

He left the building through the garbage way and squinted in the bright daylight. He crossed the street and walked down a block to Broadway. The digital clock outside a small bank said the time was 9:27 and the temperature 91 degrees. Lots of people were out—young mothers with carriages, packs of kids, people crowded at bus stops—traffic was snarled in the cramped streets.

He walked toward the Harlem River. Proprietors of discount clothing stores had rolled their racked wares onto the sidewalks. Old air conditioners above the doorways of rundown shops dripped water to the stained cement. He walked through the carpet of litter that lay high in the gutters, on the sidewalks, and over the dark, pebbled-steel basement shutters.

He could see the rusting iron of the el as he came down the hill. There was a bodega on the corner in the shadow beneath it. He opened its door and walked in. Three long, chest-high shelves went to the back of the store, but there wasn't much on them. Some yellowed greeting cards, a lone box of detergent, and four soup cans lined a dusty shelf like deserted stragglers of a sorry regiment. There were some beers in the cooler though; he could see the red lettering on the white cans through the glass door on the back wall. He walked down the aisle, opened the door, and freed two from their plastic ring.

The middle-aged Hispanic behind the counter smiled widely as Farrell placed his purchase on the counter. He had a mustache and a Yankee cap and seemed quite pleased by Farrell's appearance.

"How's it goin?" Farrell asked, smiling back.

"How about a box of Marlboros to go with it."

The man nodded his head but didn't move. He kept his hands beneath the worn, plastic stand. There wasn't any cash register that Farrell could see, nor were there even any of the little plastic pens of candies they usually kept behind the counter. Farrell took out a hundred dollar bill.

He slid the money across. "As much as I can get with that, taking out for the beers and smokes, of course."

The man called out something in Spanish.

"How the Bombers doin?" Farrell asked, referring to the man's hat.

"No so good," said the man, with his hands still under the counter. "No pitching."

Farrell nodded. After a while, a tall, brown-haired man appeared in the doorway behind the counter and slipped a small package into Farrell's hand. Farrell didn't even look at it. He just put it in his pocket. Only then did the counterman bag the beers.

"How about those smokes?" asked Farrell, picking up the brown paper bag.

"No Mar-bro. Newports."

"Hand 'em over," he said.

Farrell left the bodega and climbed the stairs to

the train station. He drank his beer sitting on the end of the downtown platform. He looked behind him at the sweltering wilderness of tenements, the dusty windows, the faded brick, the rusting fire escapes like jagged cracks through the edifices. He looked at the tracks toward the Broadway Bridge, but nothing was coming. The water of the Harlem River before him shined like tar. There was a cable company on the shore right before the river, and the fence surrounding its big parking lot was rimmed with double strands of razor wire glimmering like lethal garland in the hot light. It reminded him of Marion. It was as hot as this when they had driven them up. He had seen it miles away from the bus window, a lone field afire with shimmering steel. It was morning yard when they brought them along the path by the fences— the population freezing their activities absurdly, like in some investment commercial, and then swarming up against the gates to get a look. The huge blacks pumped bigger than any football players or body builders he'd ever seen. What had his lawyer said at the sentencing? Two years is nothing? Farrell took another sip. He knew what two years could be.

Farrell took out the cigarettes and packed them

hard against the heel of his hand. He peeled off the wrapper, took one out, and lit it.

Guns had been what got him sent to prison. He'd sold a converted mini Ruger M-14 to an undercover ATF agent, and they'd given him two years. He'd learned all about guns in the Corps, and when he got out and found himself living in the Kitchen, he realized that he possessed knowledge of a lucrative trade. He'd met an old crook in a gun shop in Jersey where he'd gone to buy some parts to fix a pistol for Mullen. The man was on line before him and had looked at his purchase. When Farrell left the store, the stranger was outside waiting for him. His name was Marvin and he had something set up, and he needed someone to help fix and sell. He offered Farrell a partnership, and he'd agreed. It had been good money while it lasted.

He flicked the last of the cigarette down between the ties as the train approached. Then he stood, drained the first beer, and put it down on the platform. When the doors opened, he took the empty seat in the corner to the left and opened the other tallboy. An old woman across the car looked at him in disgust as he took a long pull from the can.

"Ahhhhh," he said loud enough for her to hear.

When he glanced back at her, the woman was still staring. She was an old white lady in a sleeveless sundress. Cellulite dripped like cottage cheese off her ancient bones. Farrell smiled at her widely, offered the can, and winked. He watched her get up, shuffle to the opposite end of the car, and go through the door to the next one.

He got off at Columbus Circle, took his empty with him, and chucked it in a garbage can. In the dark wall by the stairs to the street was a friezed tile of a caravel, the *Santa Maria* perhaps. He passed his hand over the Maltese cross on its billowed sail. On the street to the south, Columbus himself stood on his epicentered pedestal forever staring toward Times Square. The Hitachi billboard far above him gave the time as 10:17. Farrell had taken this way to work, and he noted that this was the first time he'd arisen in the eyes of the hovering buildings' windows and swirl of traffic without the threat of job loss harrying him, the need to rush. He scratched at the stubble on his chin, and as he stepped off the curb, a bus roared past an inch in front of his face. He carefully crossed Central Park West and went into the park.

He walked along a softly curving path beneath thick old trees, came up on Central Park Drive, and

crossed over. A minute later he approached the
Sheep Meadow. People were already set up on the
far end with beach towels. He hopped the short
fence, walked across the field, and sat in the thick
grass in the shade beneath some trees. He took out
his cigarettes, lit one, and was still smoking it
when a man approached him. He was a grizzled-
looking, older man without a shirt. He had a long,
gray ponytail and was wearing cutoff jeans and
sandals. Farrell assumed the man would try to
bum some change.

"Sest?"

Pleasantly surprised, Farrell smiled up at him.

"You don't have any papers, do you?" he asked.
The old hippie nodded his head.

"I'll take a dime then," Farrell decided.

Farrell rolled a tight, fat joint and smoked it,
cupping it in his palm, holding the putrid smoke
in his lungs until it burned. When he was done, he
lit a cigarette and lay back, feeling a numbing ease
course through him. Fucking sest, he thought. The
last time he'd smoked weed was when he was
what? Eighteen? He'd smoked enough of it then,
though, hadn't he? Sest, buddha, skunk, home-
grown, Jamaican, or Hawaiian if he could get it.
Him and friends from the neighborhood, they'd

drop acid or mesc, eat some shrooms—dumb kids fuckin around. This was before he joined the Marines to supposedly cut all that shit out.

He remembered the first time he'd gotten high. It was the summer before he was gonna start his fancy school, and he was home drawing and watching TV. Terry had a summer job at the gas station down the block, and he'd come home during his lunch. Farrell had walked in to talk to him and saw him blowing rancid smoke out the window. Terry had told him to get the fuck out, but Farrell was curious, and he threatened to tell if Terry didn't let him try it. Terry reluctantly agreed, telling him to bolt the front door. Why hadn't he done it? He must have asked himself that question a million times. They had the radio up pretty high, so they hadn't heard their father come in early from work. When Farrell looked up with the joint to his lips, his father was standing there wide-eyed.

Their father had grabbed Terry, pushed him out of the apartment, and told him never to come back. "That drug addict stays under this roof over my dead body," he said to their mother's plea of leniency. As if he weren't an addict himself. The father seemed joyful as he sat in front of the TV drinking beer after beer that night. As if he'd won something, pleased with himself for getting at least one of them out of his house.

When Farrell got to school that September, his father still hadn't relented. Terry had to spend his seventeenth birthday on the street, alone. Farrell started messing up soon after that. Started to fuck up his life as if it were some inalienable right. He wanted to be with his brother again more than anything in the world.

If his memory served him right, he'd gotten high in this actual meadow before. He was thirteen years old, and it was the third day of his freshman year in high school. He remembered he'd blown off the day with some seniors. They'd ended up here and bought some weed. High as a kite, stretched out on this nice soft grass. His whole life before him, big city buildings peeking out over the trees. The whole world still to conquer. Farrell sat up on his elbows and looked out on those same buildings. No giggling now. He flicked his cigarette away. Calm before the fucking storm, he thought.

He lay back, took out his wallet, and shook the bank key into his palm. Half a million dollars. He'd counted it with his own hands, but it still hardly seemed real. He wouldn't even have to share it. No one left to split it with.

He thought of Roy and Billy and of Mullen and how they'd taken the hotel. How everyone had done his job and watched each other's back and they'd come out clean. He remembered their faces as he walked out of the Albanians' garage. The death in their eyes to protect him. Their laughter in the bar after. What had Tara called him in the street after he'd fucked her? Murderer? Maybe so. They never put in for him pistol-whipping the Albanian, but they'd been made to pay for it. He squeezed the key in his palm. It couldn't be easy. After everything, it couldn't just be cut and dried, take the money and run, like the song. His life had never been a song, had it? A fucking dirge maybe. No, he couldn't get away from it. To leave now would be to leave his friends on the floor of the bar where their killers had left them, in pools of their own blood, bar muck, and liquor. It would mean they had died for nothing, the eradication of their lives for shit.

He sat up and closed his eyes, thinking. He took out his keys. He had a key chain with Frank's locksmith business address on it, somewhere in the Pelham section of the Bronx. It had to be where the

Albanians hung out because there was always some thug answering the phone. Maybe, he thought. God knew they wouldn't be expecting it. No, an attempt had to be made to set things straight.

He stood up and walked out from the shade into the sunlight. He exited the park through an opening on Fifth not far from the bench the sailors had been drinking on last night. He walked to Madison, hailed a cab, and went uptown.

At 83rd he paid and got out. He headed for a men's clothing store he had seen the night before. He stood a moment before the plate window, looking at an expensive Italian suit—dark, austere, gracefully cut. Inside, more suits were lit up with track lighting in niches along the white walls like paintings in a gallery. A little man with a white shirt buttoned to the chin approached, doubt pinching his features. Farrell brought out his immense roll of cash.

"I need a suit," Farrell told him.

The man stopped and looked Farrell up and down.

"I believe you," he said in a high, vaguely Southern voice.

The suit he agreed upon was a lightweight, dark

gray, two-button that was a little under two thousand dollars. With the bone-colored silk shirt, T-shirt, underwear, socks, and black leather oxfords, the total came to a little under twenty-five hundred. He left his old clothes and boots in the corner of the dressing room.

He'd go see Marvin now. If there was one person left who might help him, it was Marvin. The federal DA had wanted Farrell to roll over on his partner when he was busted, but Farrell had told him to fuck off. Sending Marvin to jail would have been like putting a bullet in his head. Farrell hadn't stopped by to see him since his release because Marvin was a man who didn't let a good deed go unpaid, and he didn't want to appear to be looking for a handout. He checked himself out in the full-length mirror. Less chance of that now.

While he was waiting for the pants to be hemmed, he sat in the dressing room and took out the glassine envelope he'd purchased in the bodega. He tapped some powder onto the web of his thumb. He took a few snorts. He smiled bitterly at himself as false strength began to surge through him.

If the clothier heard his nasal activity in the dressing room, he kept it to himself when he brought in his pants. Farrell counted off the crisp bills, paid, and left the store.

Outside, he headed over to Fifth to get a taxi going downtown. A well-dressed matron with a poodle arched an eyebrow at him on the corner. She could have been one of the ladies he had gotten taxis for those twelve long months. He grinned rakishly at her as he passed.

The address he gave the driver was in SoHo. Canal Street was teeming with people when they finally got there. No stores here. Just long, open stalls piled with clothes and toys, small radios, CDs. Card tables in front spilling over with children's books, sunglasses, counterfeit handbags. Angry horns tore out from the bottlenecked traffic in the street. Oriental men with rolled-up shirt sleeves stood smoking, watching their establishments, still and silent in the flowing torrent of humanity.

He passed by it twice before he spotted the small, chipped, plastic sign at the bottom of a crowded stairwell.

STEINHILBER
WATCHES

The stairs were so steep it was like climbing a ladder. There was a black steel door at the top with a small peephole in it. He rang the bell, waited, and rang again. On the fourth ring, the door was opened, and a small, bald man stood in the threshold. A smile lit up his old face.

"I'm seeing a fucking ghost," the man said.

"Not yet, old man," Farrell said, smiling back.

"Get in here," Marvin said.

They went into the shop. Marvin clicked the heavy steel door shut. Along a wall in the front room were some glass cases filled with rows of wristwatches. A huge, old cash register was set behind them. There was a curtain over a doorway in back of the cases. Marvin led him through it to a room. Along the wall were shelves holding small cardboard boxes and a workbench piled with watch parts—tiny toothed gears, some small calipers, a magnifying glass. Marvin cleared some papers off a desk in the corner, and they sat. Then he opened a drawer and brought out a bottle of Cutty Sark and a couple of paper cups.

"A little early in the morning," Marvin said, handing Farrell his drink. His voice was even rougher than Farrell remembered it, as if he'd swallowed sandpaper. "But as I remember, that never bothered a good Irish kid like you."

Farrell drank. He grinned widely.

"You better be nice, or I'm not coming to your funeral."

Marvin laughed, leaning back in his chair. His drink was propped up on his skinny chest.

"I didn't think I'd be seeing you again," he said. He indicated Farrel's suit with a hand. "Doin pretty good, looks like."

"Well, it's like you said one time," Farrell said, staring out at the traffic on Canal. " 'Don't bother goin back unless it's in a limousine.' Which reminds me, I got you something."

Farrell took the Phillipe Patik off his wrist, leaned over the desk, and placed it before the old man. Marvin took out a pair of bifocals and looked at the watch with studied intensity.

"Somethin I came across. I heard you were in the business, thought I'd save it for you."

Marvin turned, wiping at his eyes, perhaps with fatigue, perhaps something else. He put the watch down.

"I been a crook for fifty fuckin years, and I never had a partner like you, Tommy, you know that?"

Farrell waved a hand dismissively. He took
another gulp, the whiskey burning merrily in his gut.

"How's this business, Marvin? Any good?"

"Ah, OK, I guess. Nothing like we had."

"We did make some money, didn't we?"

"That's right. But you don't remember most of
it, do you? With all that shit you were on," Marvin
said bemused. He looked into Farrell's glossy eyes.
"I see you haven't lost a taste for it."

Farrell smiled.

"I can't hide nothin from you, gramps, can I?"

"You're a big boy, Tommy. Just a shame is all."

"Nice as it is to see you again, too, I can't lie. This
visit isn't purely social."

"No?" Marvin said, raising a gray eyebrow.

"There is one thing," Farrell hesitated.

Marvin looked over at him.

"Name it."

"How retired are you?"

"You need something?" Marvin asked.

Farrell nodded.

"A bigger something or a smaller something?"

Farrell paused.

"A bigger something," he said.

Marvin looked at him for a long time.

"You goddamned Irish kids," he finally said, smiling and shaking his head.

The old man got up from his desk and went into a closet past the workbench. Farrell poured himself another drink. He listened to his former partner move things around, cursing to himself. When he reappeared, he was bowed beneath the weight of a green gym bag.

"Don't get up," he said sarcastically.

Farrell stood, took the bag, clunked it on the desk, and unzipped it. In the dusty sunlight from the window, he stared at what was inside as he inhaled its reek of oil. It was a Heckler & Koch MP5 SD submachine gun, black, sleek, and lethal. Farrell shook his head, his mouth open.

"How did I know you'd show me something like this?"

"I got it off a *svatza* who stole an ESU truck. Can you believe it? I got a ceramic vest back there that'll stop a fucking bomb. You want the 'jaws-of-life'? He threw that in for free."

Farrell hefted the gun.

"You are one crazy old fucker," Farrell said, carefully placing the gun back down.

Marvin smiled at the compliment and sipped his drink.

"Just one more minor thing. I need a car for a couple of hours. One that might get damaged, but I'm willin to pay."

Without hesitating, Marvin pulled keys out of his pocket and took two off the ring. He handed them to Farrell.

"It's a Lincoln parked over in the lot on Sixth. I'll call and tell them you're comin."

"No," said Farrell. "I need something disposable."

"What the fuck? It's fully insured. How about you don't get it back to me by six this evening, I report it stolen."

Farrell took out his money.

"Don't insult me, Tommy," the old man said sternly.

Farrell put his money back in his pocket and smiled at his old partner. He stood, put the gun in the bag, and zipped it up.

"Well, shit. Thanks a lot, Marvin." They shook hands. The old man's grip was surprisingly hard. "It was nice seeing you again."

"Thank you, Tommy. I guess I never told you that, but thank you. Thanks for coming back, too. You ever got the time, we'll swing over to Peter Luger's, get us a couple of steaks."

"A couple of broads, too?" Farrell said, picking up the bag.

"Both for you maybe. I'll just watch," Marvin grated. "So long now."

Farrell turned and brushed through the curtain into the front room. He went out through the door and pulled it shut. When he got to the bottom of the steps, he realized why he loved the old man so much. He hadn't even asked him once what he was doing.

11

THE LINCOLN WAS SHINY BLACK AND HAD POWER everything and leather seats. The air-conditioning was like the blower from a freezer. After Farrell took it out, he made two stops. The first was a hardware store on West Broadway, where he bought some tools: gloves, a crowbar, a box cutter, a drop cloth, some rope, and a tool bag to carry it all. He filled the bag and dropped it in the trunk next to the gun. The second stop was a liquor store down the block, where he bought a pint of whiskey.

Getting out of lower Manhattan took the most time. He went up Third Avenue to the Willis Avenue Bridge. The cigarette billboard he'd seen two nights ago was lit up. "I LOVE NEWPORT," it scrolled off. "ALIVE WITH PLEASURE." "I don't," he said, lighting one up. He looked over to the cement pier where they'd dumped the van and Durkin's body. No police. No nothing. He held the whiskey between his legs and cracked the seal with one hand as he drove.

He got off the Deegan at the Fordham Road exit and squeezed his way down the off ramp. Throngs of people were out on the sidewalks shopping, and off to the sides were little cement parks with kids playing basketball and girls jumping rope despite the heat. He sipped whiskey behind the refrigerated glass. After a while, he got on the Pelham Parkway, its thin strip of trees and littered grass trying to keep the Bronx at bay, a valorous—if impossible—attempt.

As he drove closer to the address, he noticed planes in the close distance off to the right. They seemed to be leveling off, then descending, one right after another. This part of the Bronx must have been beneath a flight path for planes landing across the water in Queens at La Guardia. He watched one coming down, its silver fuselage winking in the sunlight. He could see its landing gear. He had worked on airfields in the military, and it never ceased to amaze him how things so big and heavy could fly.

He'd been on an airfield the night he'd been dishonorably discharged. He had been in the infantry, but it was right after Panama and before Desert Storm. For over a year he'd lived in the field, training, carrying sixty-pound rucks twenty miles to then shoot out targets the size of half-dollars at fifty yards. All that training, and he'd never been called to serve. He'd transferred out and gotten detail on an airfield. He was pulling guard duty, and he'd had a few beers and thought he'd take a shortcut back to base. With the blackouts over the humvee headlights, it was impossible to see the two Hueys. Though the aircraft and the jeep were destroyed, he'd come out without a scratch. It had been on the eve of a presidential inspection, however, and they did a blood alcohol on him, and that was that.

He took a swig of the whiskey and got off at the exit. The neighborhood was surprisingly clean and quiet. The avenue, with its small shops and trees down the sidewalks, was like the main street of a small town. The address was on a quiet street around the corner from the avenue at the end of a block of connected stores. He drove past it twice to double-check. It was an old store with a recessed entryway and double plate-glass windows. A former pizza parlor or barber shop. He drove on without slowing. When he drove around the other side of the block, he spotted a professional building that abutted the connected stores, and he slowed, looking around for a place to park.

He found a spot at a meter at the corner and put the whiskey in his suit coat. He pocketed the cellular phone Marvin had left in the car, popped the trunk, and got out. He put some quarters in the meter, took out the two bags, and slammed the trunk. He crossed the street and made for the professional building without looking around.

He went into the cool lobby. A woman with a baby was waiting for the elevator, so he turned and opened the door to the stairs. High in the wall at a landing between the first and second floors was a closed window. Farrell stopped and put the bags down. He listened, but no one was coming, so he climbed up on the banister and leaned over to the wall and opened the window. He stuck his head out and could see the oily black of the rooftop beneath him. Then he came down and grabbed the bag of tools. He brought them back up and dropped them out the window. He'd wrapped the crowbar in the dropcloth, so there wasn't any sound when they landed. He went back down the steps and draped the bag with the gun on his back.

Then he got up on the banister, pulled himself up on the dusty sill, and jumped up on the dusty sash, and then flipped himself out and down.

The drop was negligible, but he lay flat, listening. The tar was hot and soft beneath his back. The window he had come through was one of only three on that wall, and the nearest building was a block away, across the front of the avenue. Large, metal-boxed air-conditioning units hummed busily behind him. A silver exhaust fan rotated slowly in the hot light. He sat up slowly and picked up his bag. He crouched down and made his way along the low roof wall to the opposite end, above the Albanians' social club.

He put his bags down in the meager shade of the club's large air-conditioning unit. He took the bag of tools, came over to the side wall, and chanced a quick glance over. There was a small window, of a bathroom, he hoped, a few feet down, and he stepped carefully until he was certain he was directly above it. He took out the drop cloth and put on his gloves.

The tar paper split like a meatskin when he put the box cutter to it. He cut a four-by-four-foot square, slid the crowbar beneath it, and peeled it off. There was some old plywood beneath, and he cut at the paper some more until he found the seam. He dug the sharp end of the crowbar deep into the crack and levered it down until the wood split. He had accompanied Mullen on a torch job one time, and the Hell's Kitchen thief had shown him how to do it, a craftsman passing on trade secrets.

"You don't have to worry about the noise because of the insulation beneath the wood," Mullen had explained, leaning on the crowbar he was using on that long-ago darkened rooftop. "Then out with the insulation and a kick through the plaster or sheetrock ceiling, and you're in."

He ripped up a good piece of the wood and then bent and extracted the wadded yellow insulation. Sweat was pouring off him, and he was pissed he hadn't thought to bring some water. When he saw the plaster ceiling in the hole, he took the rope out of the bag. He tied one end to the foot of the AC unit and dropped the other one in the hole. Grasping the rope tightly in one hand, he used the box cutter to tap out a small hole in the plaster, and then he leaned in to put his eye to it. It was black for a while, and he waited, letting his eye adjust to the darkness. Then he recognized something white in an enclosed space. It was a slop-sink closet not the bathroom.

He pulled himself up, gathered all his things, and sat on the drop cloth with his back against the low brick wall next to the hole. He took out the snub-nosed submachine gun and laid it on his lap. Its blackness, like the tar all around, sucked up the strong light like a vacuum. He loaded it with one of the two clips and racked back the slide. He laid the gun beside him, took out the cellular phone, and dialed the Albanian's number. He tried to hear it ringing in the club beneath, but he couldn't. A voice grunted in answer on the fourth ring.

"Hi," Farrell said calmly. "This is Tom Farrell. I got a message for Frank. You tell him I'm sorry we missed each other last night, and I'll be swinging by the clubhouse in an hour to collect the diamonds. You got all that?"

"Who is this?" the voice demanded.

Farrell hung up. He called back, and the line was busy.

He put the phone into one of the bags, took out the whiskey, and unscrewed the cap. He wanted a cigarette badly, but he couldn't risk the smoke. He drank beneath the burning sun, sweat beading up on his forehead with each burning swallow. Beside the hole, with the bottle and the somber suit and the gun, he struck an odd figure upon that soft sea of black. Like a man at his own wake. A circumspect, imminent suicide pre-mourning his own demise.

He'd spent half his life on rooftops, it seemed. He was on the roof of his building the night his father died. He'd been awakened by his mother's screams and he'd come out of his room, but his father was already out the door. He had gone up to the roof to keep watch if he tried to come back. He was only fourteen at the time, but he'd suffered in silence his whole life and he'd finally scrounged up the courage to face him. For what he had done to the family, what he had done to Terry. He'd waited and waited, but he'd finally fallen asleep, and at dawn a cop woke him. They went back inside, and his mother was crying on the plastic-covered couch. There were more cops there and the parish priest. Grim-faced men in formal dark. At first he thought that she had finally come to her senses and reached out for help, but then he realized it a moment before she said it.

"He's dead. Your da is dead."

"He fell in front of the subway," the priest said. Farrell had cried, but not in sorrow. He would never get to tell him how he felt, never be able to look him in his bloodshot eyes and dismiss him, show him that they were no part of each other.

Farrell sipped the liquor.

None at all, he thought.

After a while, he heard cars braking sharply in the street and the club's front door opening beneath him. Men gathering, calling urgently to one another. The minutes passed like hours. He finished the bottle and put it down. Ten minutes before the prescribed time, he took out the last of the cocaine and sniffed at it quietly until it was gone. He crouched and adjusted the gun tightly across the front of his chest with the strap. He grabbed the rope again and leaned back into the hole, opening it wider with his hand, pulling out the bigger pieces. Soon the hole was big enough for him to fit in, so he tossed the rope into the murk and then dropped down into the lair of his enemies like a spider through a trap.

When his feet touched the top of the sink, he let go of the rope and carefully eased himself down. Sweat was in his eyes, on his face, and had soaked through all his clothes. Holding his breath, he released the gun's safety, and put his ear to the closed door. No sound. He placed a hand on the knob.

The door swung silently on its hinges when he pushed it, and he quickly entered the dusty hallway. He had come through the farthest door at the back wall, and he could see the plate window in the front. There were more Albanians in the club than had been at the house in Jersey. They stood with their backs to him, a dozen or more stocky men still draped in their Sunday finery. He couldn't see Frank or George. He heard coughing beyond his line of sight up near the front, so he raised the gun and moved forward slowly, his heart slamming in his chest.

He was at the end of the hallway when he felt a disturbance in the air, and he turned and swung the gun toward the door. A boy stood there staring at him. Ten, maybe eleven, wide-eyed with a mop of black hair, mouth turned in a comic O of surprise. Farrell had already begun to pull the trigger when he stopped himself. That the gun did not go off was an act of God. An older voice—George's perhaps—called out a question to the boy. Farrell turned and ran. He got the slop-sink door closed behind him, and a moment later he heard the boy call out. He bashed a shin on the lip of the sink, grabbed the rope, and hauled himself up the wall, his shoes scrabbling. He had already pulled himself onto the roof when the gunfire started beneath. He ran to the far end of the rooftop and flung himself over, hung a split second from its warm terracotta rim, and then dropped. He rolled when he hit the sidewalk, the gun bashing him in the chin, bringing blood. He ran for the car, limping. He unlocked the door, started the car, put the gas to the floor, and dropped it into reverse. The car slammed into the one parked behind it. A loud, almost inhuman scream started not far behind and was approaching fast. He cut the wheel, slapped it into drive, and the car rocketed forward, leaving rubber. He tore down the avenue, eating red light after red light. Only when he looked into the rearview mirror ten minutes later did he realize that he was crying.

12

MCCARRY PULLED THE GOVERNMENT CAR OFF THE
FDR drive into the clogged traffic of lower
Manhattan. It was hot, so he had the air-conditioning cranked on high. He was wearing his best suit,
the Brooks Brothers—blue, sharp, conservative.
With the suit set off by his snow-white shirt, sub-
dued burgundy tie, and mirror-black wingtips, he
looked every bit the federal judge he knew he
would be someday. His report was in the briefcase
on the passenger seat next to him, and he was running half an hour early. No, fucking around wasn't
on the to-do list this morning.

Even the scum here on Canal Street selling their
shit out of dirty cardboard boxes—all of it either
counterfeit or stolen or both—seemed to be per-
forming some vital role. He glanced right as he
passed Foley Square. If he'd had more time, he
would have liked to drive past it again. It was an

awesome place. The two huge, powder-white, alabaster courthouses seemed to mute out the surrounding city, their spare classical lines pronouncing justice, order. People complained about the expense of that type of majesty, but when it came to courthouses, McCarry didn't agree. Therein lay the highest workings of the greatest nation the modern world had ever seen. You're gonna skimp on that?

As McCarry turned back from looking at the courthouses, a car pulled right in front of him. He slammed on the brakes. He was going only about twenty miles an hour, but it wasn't slow enough. He braced himself as the sedan tires squealed and he slapped into the side of a small Toyota. He looked up and saw that he had run the red light. Traffic all around began honking. A scared-looking young woman was in the other car. There was an NYU sticker on her rear window. He thought quickly. Then he grabbed the police light from the glove compartment, put it on the dash, and plugged it into the cigarette lighter. He put on the Oakley aviator sunglasses he kept in the glove compartment and unbuttoned his jacket to show the butt of his pistol as he got out of the car.

His grill was cracked, and the Toyota's door held a solid dent. The girl's eyes were red as she opened her door to get out. McCarry stood in the door, preventing her from standing, and he flashed the badge.

"Driver's license and registration."

"What?" said the girl. She was about to cry.

"I'm not asking you," McCarry said, putting every ounce of cultivated authority he had into his voice. "Driver's license and registration."

The girl's hand shook as she took the papers out of her wallet and handed them over. A crowd had formed on the sidewalk, and they looked on as the flickering red light in McCarry's car spun on its axis.

"Don't move," he told the girl. He went back to the car, sat behind the wheel, and spoke into the handset without keying it. He took the white handkerchief from his breast pocket and patted the sweat on his forehead before getting out. He went back over to the girl, leaning above her.

"I'm gonna say this to you once as your information is being processed. That car you cut me off from was under federal surveillance. If we lose that tail, you can be held responsible under the Aiding and Abetting Act of 1984. You . . . "

"You . . . you crashed into me," she stuttered.

"You're interrupting me? Fine. We'll just wait for the arrest squad."

"What did I do?" said the girl, close to tears again. "This is my dad's car. He's gonna kill me."

McCarry cocked his head slightly. "Hold on. My radio."

He went back to the sedan and spoke frantically into the dead radio. He backed his car away from the crushed door and drove around to the side of the Toyota.

"The back-up team picked him up two blocks away from here," he said to the girl. He reached across to the passenger window and held out the girl's license and registration. "I have your information. You'll be contacted. You're free to go."

She took back her documents, and McCarry pulled off, glancing into the rearview mirror.

He wondered whether she'd taken his license plate number but decided that she was too shaken up. Maybe someone from the crowd had done so and was handing it to her right now, but he doubted it. Nobody liked to get involved, right?

Jesus. What the hell was getting into him—day-dreaming and running red lights. He took a deep breath. It was the report. Pressure started kicking in once you started making recommendations. What if you were wrong? What if somebody else had information that proved you were wrong, and they were just waiting for you to screw up? Control, he thought, control was the key. He'd shown it back with the girl, and it had overwhelmed her. He would just have to show it again at the meeting. He could do that. Yeah, he decided, he could accomplish that.

He put the car in a parking garage rather than the motor pool because the banged-up grill might be noticed. He'd have to get it fixed with his own money, too. It wasn't just the damage reports that had to be filled out (which were black marks on your record, for sure), it was the general ribbing from the agents about your faulty driving. They just wouldn't let you live it down.

He entered the squat monolith of 26 Federal Plaza, passing by the ceaselessly long line of immigrants seeking citizenship in front of the building. He flashed his badge to the sullen-faced federal policeman at the entrance and took the elevator up to the third floor.

Special Agent Jerry Banks from the Organized Crime Task Force, who had been in McCarry's academy class, was finishing a story. His audience of three veteran agents sat around the coffee machine laughing heartily. When the assistant agent in charge walked past in the hallway, they all tried to look busy. As McCarry came up, they dispersed, except for Banks.

"Well, if it isn't Francis McCarry. Top o' the mornin to ya, Francis," said Banks with a bad shanty-Irish brogue. "What gets you here so early on a Friday morning?"

"Task force meeting." McCarry put a finger to his nose and winked exaggeratedly.

Banks smiled and slowly looked to his left and then to his right.

"How about you?" asked McCarry. "The trial continues, huh?"

"I'm getting hemorrhoids sitting in that chair eight hours a day. I can see the don and his cronies cracking up every time I move around tryin to get comfortable. They know what's goin on, those scumbags. I just hope they get to share that feeling, sitting on a stone cot for the rest of their miserable lives. Hey, you're teamed up with Wallace now, aren't you?"

"That's right. He's a good guy," McCarry said.

"Yeah. I know. I heard a story about him. Did you know he has a combat cross?"

"A what?"

"A combat cross, from the NYPD. You get it if you're in a major gun battle in which you either wound or kill the other party."

"Oh, yeah?" said McCarry casually, masking his surprise.

"Yeah. The son of a bitch never mentioned it to you either, did he? I heard it off a cop in the OCTF used to work with him out of the five-two precinct in the Bronx when Wallace was a rookie."

"It happened when he was a rookie?"

"Third week on the job, the way I heard it. This is the story. Wallace is on three-to-eleven-shift foot patrol in one of the more southern reaches of the precinct. You familiar with the five-two?"

"Grand Concourse?"

"Right. Grand Concourse, Fordham Road. Not the nicest of areas, right? So he's pullin his foot post around ten-thirty, and he figures he won't bother callin a radio car to pick him up. He'll hoof back to the station."

"Bad move."

"Bet your ass it's a bad move. A veteran would be afraid to go lollygaggin through that area. But he's a kid, nineteen, twenty, and he figures what the fuck? He's a cop. He's armed, right? Anyway, he's not all too familiar with the area, so he gets a little lost and sees a shortcut through an abandoned lot. So as he's comin around the side of a burnt-out building, he walks smack-dab into the middle of a drug transaction. Literally almost bumps into this dealer who's holdin out a bag of heroin to his customer—who it turns out happens to be an escaped fugitive from Georgia by the name of Carl 'Black Snake' Greene. Mr. Greene, in fear for his freedom and probably his imminent fix, retrieves a small-caliber automatic from his belt, fires at Wallace, and misses. Wallace then takes out his service revolver, fires and does not miss, and Black Snake falls to the ground with a bullet in his head."

"You're puttin me on."

"I shit you not. The cop who told me's named Tommy Milton."

"Shoots the man dead?"

"Point blank. There's more. Here he is, a kid really, probably in shock, gun drawn in some godforsaken lot, man he just killed bleedin on his shoes, and staring into the eyes of some heroin dealer who's still holding the late Black Snake's shit in his hand. Wally reaches for the radio to call it in, but he's at a loss as to his particular location.

So what solution does his besieged psyche come up with? He scoops up Black Snake's gun and puts the still warm barrel of his own into the ear of the dealer, does a quick pat down, and cuffs the dealer to his ill-fated customer's wrist."

"Get out. Handcuffs him to the body?"

"I know. I couldn't believe it either, but he chains him to the dearly departed homey and runs out to the street to find out where the fuck he is. He gets to the corner, but there's no sign, and he runs down to the next block. Finally, he finds his locale and calls in a 10-13. Then he runs back to where he left the dealer and the dead man because his head's a little clearer and he's thinkin maybe that doesn't look so good. Maybe he hasn't gone directly by the book on that one, right? So he gets back to where he left them, but there's nothing. Nobody. Now, he knows the dealer couldn't have gotten too far because Black Snake is this big dude, over six, two hundred something, so he's lookin around with his maglight and he sees drag marks through the rubble. By this time, he can hear the radio car sirens, but he figures he better find the two or he'll have a lot of explaining to do. So he follows the trail to a basement window of the abandoned building. It's pitch black, and he figures, fuck it, he'd rather get fired than jump into that hellhole. But he flashes his light down into it, and what does he see? Black Snake splayed out on the floor of the place and no sign of the dealer. Only he looks and sees that Black Snake's hand is gone."

"Get out. The dealer took off the dead guy's hand to get away?"

"Like a wolf in a trap."

"What happened to Wallace?"

"He looks around to see how the dealer did it. There's a rusty shovel there, and he picks it up and holds it up to his light and sees the blood, and that's when the cavalry comes bursting around the corner. At first the cops think he's shot. Then they look into the hole and see the body there and him holdin the shovel, and the patrol supervisor, some old salt veteran, squints at him and asks, 'What the fuck are you doing?' "

McCarry laughed. "They thought he had done it?"

"I guess they didn't know what to think. Wallace tells the supervisor the whole story, and the supervisor tells the men to spread out and find the guy's hand, which they do, not far from the shovel. Then three of the officers jump down, and they bear Black Snake's body out of the hole and back to where Wallace shot him, and they tidy things up a bit and call in the detectives and the coroner. The coroner arrives first, and the supervisor takes him aside, gives him the guy's hand, explains the situation, and gets him to sew it back on at the morgue, and the whole thing gets blown over. At the station house, everybody's ribbin Wallace about it—saying how it was bad enough that he had to kill the guy, did he have to take a trophy as well? And, 'Give that guy a hand.' And Wallace looks at them deadpan in the locker room and says his only regret was that they got there so quickly; otherwise, he could have taken the scalp as well."

"That's crazy."

"Isn't it? They gave him a cross for it though. You have to remember, this is goin back almost fifteen years. They did things a little differently back then. That happened today, no supervisor would stick his neck out for a rookie like that, and the whole thing would be on the cover of the *Post* the next morning—'Cop Shoots and Mutilates Fugitive'—and they'd riot over the cop-killing piece of garbage."

"Incredible story," said McCarry.

"Well, if you bring it up with your partner, don't let on you heard it from me. Maybe he wants to put it behind him. I know I would. He's a tough individual though, you have to give him that."

"Yeah," said McCarry. He felt a little dizzy. "Thanks a lot. I appreciate it," he said.

When McCarry got to his cubicle, he found a manila envelope on his desk with a note. "Here you go, Francis," the note said, "Vince." He opened it and took out a black-and-white video still of the man who'd been seen with Gallagher, an older, sharp-featured man. Nobody he recognized. There was something about him, though. A distance in the eyes that gave him an air of severity. McCarry put the photograph down on the desk and sat. The hidden history of his partner was still swirling in his head. Killed a man in a close-quarter gunfight before he was twenty. It unsettled him. Try as he might, he couldn't reconcile anything in his own life or career to compare to that. Maybe he was in the wrong line of work. Maybe he should quit and get some nice little corporate position somewhere. There was time.

He was still lost in his thoughts when the assistant agent in charge came by his desk.

"What's the holdup?" he demanded. He was thin and had glasses and receding red hair. They called him the Woodpecker behind his back.

"Right there, sir," McCarry said, standing up and nearly tripping over his briefcase. He took it with him and stepped in line behind his boss. As they approached the conference room, butterflies swarmed in his belly.

13

FARRELL PULLED THE CAR IN AT A GAS STATION AT the bottom of Fordham Road and put the Heckler & Koch under the seat. He looked at himself in the rearview mirror. The cut on his chin had stopped bleeding and had scabbed up like a small goatee. There was blood on the suit coat, and he took it off. He locked the car and got out. Five bucks got him the key to the rancid bathroom. He washed his cut in the grease-streaked sink and held his cool, wet hands on the back of his neck for a while. It was OK, he reassured himself, trying to calm himself down. He had tried, and it just hadn't worked out. He wanted to do right by his friends, but the kid had gotten in the way. He took a deep breath. It was comforting to realize there were some depths he wasn't able to sink to.

He checked his watch—12:49.

"Busy morning," he told his ragged reflection.

He returned the key and bought a quart of

orange juice, some coffeecakes, and a pack of Marlboros. He took the Newports out of his pocket and placed them on the counter.

"These are for you," he told the cashier.

He sat in the car with the AC on high and ate his breakfast. He lit a cigarette and watched trucks whip past on the crumbling roadway of the Major Deegan. He considered his options. Of all that were left to him, Tara seemed the most positive bet. She'd been pissed, but he could explain things to her. He took out his wallet and checked that he still had the key to the safety deposit box. All that money in the bank probably wouldn't hamper the discussion. He'd waited for this moment a long time, when he would be able to leave. Now that it was here, he didn't seem to want to do it alone. He took a quarter out of his pocket and got out and went to the pay phone. He got Tara's job number from information, but when they answered, they said she had called in sick.

"Not the first time either," said the asshole on the other end. Farrell hung up. He'd have to swing by her sister's apartment.

He drove south on the Major Deegan along the Harlem River beneath the cracked, vaulting ramps for the George Washington and Throgs Neck bridges, past Yankee Stadium and the Bronx Courthouse up on the hill behind it. He passed over the 116th Street Bridge into Manhattan and came up Fifth Avenue through Harlem. Older and more intricate architecture was interspersed with lots so long empty that Mother Nature had reclaimed them with grass so green, tall, and thick that it hid the garbage.

He double-parked behind a truck in front of Tara's sister's East End Avenue apartment and got out. The sidewalk burned beneath the sun. He went into the alcove and pressed the buzzer. There was no answer, so he pressed again. A workman came down the stairs and out the door. Farrell stopped the inner door from closing as the man passed. He took a step into the lobby before he realized that the man had stopped. He felt something hard and cold behind his ear.

"Move and I'll blow yer fuckin brains out," the man said with a thick Irish accent. The inflection in it made it seem like he was asking a question. Durkin had had a brogue just like it. Farrell put his hands up while the man patted him down. He took Farrell's keys and his wallet. When he saw the wad of money, he whistled loudly. Farrell turned and recognized the man with the blond crewcut from Reilly's, where he'd met Tara the night before.

"We meet again," said the man with a stiff smile. "Me name's Brian. Tom, is it? You're a dead man, Tom. Ya know that, don ya? Any more of yer fucking tricks for me or anything now? No? I didn't think so. Come on."

There were people on the sidewalk. Brian put the gun beneath Farrell's shirt as they left the building and walked to an old delivery truck that had "Three Gaels Demo" painted on its double back doors. Brian opened the doors, pushed Farrell inside, came in after him, and closed them. He took out some handcuffs, shackled Farrell's wrists behind his back, and shackled his feet with another pair.

"We could work this out," Farrell told him calmly.

Brian was bent over, looking for something, and he stopped at Farrell's voice. Farrell tucked in his chin a second before he kicked him. The blow caught him high on the head, and he banged loudly off the metal wall of the truck.

"You keep yer fuckin mouth shut!" he screamed.

Flecks of spittle landed on Farrell"s cheek. "Shut," he said, and then he popped a bag over Farrell's head.

Farrell lay on something hard that dug into his back. He could feel blood blotting up on his temple from where the laces had split skin. He listened to his captor talking in the front of the van.

"Got 'im!" he called triumphantly. "He came to see his little bitch just like I told you he would. We musta just missed him last night. Didn I tell ya it was worth it to tail her?"

There was a pause.

"There was a little on 'im, no bagful or nothin. He's probably got it stashed," the Irishman said. "No, I have him right here in the van. I'm only fuckin lookin at him while we're talkin. He told me we could work somethin out. Just me and him. Wasn tha nice?" Another pause.

"OK. Gimme half an hour. See you then. Right-o."

"Wha ya say last night? No trouble at all?" Brian said. "Well, you got yourself some trouble now, Tom. Ya fucked with the wrong crowd," he called to the back of the truck.

Farrell didn't say a word. He listened as Brian opened the door and got out of the truck. He could hear him opening Marvin's car outside. After a moment, he rushed back into the truck. The metal clack of the Heckler & Koch being unloaded was distinct.

"You're full of fuckin surprises, aren't cha," he said, starting the van.

They drove down East End for a while and then made a right and a few more turns, pausing every few seconds with the city traffic. Farrell lay sweating, listening to the blaring horns, the rough diesel growl of buses and trucks. When they sped up and he heard a metal hum beneath the tires, he knew they were on a grated bridge, the Fifty-ninth Street, most likely. He couldn't decide which he wanted more, a hit of coke or a shot of whiskey. Something—anything—to stop the panic. The fuckin IRA, he thought. Too fuckin much. He thought Mullen had been just talking, but he'd been right about Durkin, after all. These cocksuckers were going to kill him for what he did to their friend. He lay paralyzed. It took everything he had not to break down sobbing. There was some cleaning polish or something in the cloth of the bag over his head, and it was giving him a headache. After a while, he calmed down a little. The fact that he was still alive was promising, he finally convinced himself. If they had truly known about what he had done to Durkin, they wouldn't be going to all this trouble. They'd just have put a bullet in his head in Tara's hallway, right?

An idea came into his head, a story he could tell them. He worked on it as they drove along, trying to convince himself that it was true.

The truck slowed and turned in somewhere to the right. A slow crunch of gravel beneath the wheels. They stopped, and Brian got out. Farrell heard the clacking slide of a garage door. Brian came back, drove the truck in, and killed the engine. Farrell heard him close the garage and open a door. In the truck's hot silence, Farrell listened to the ticking of the old motor.

When the truck's rear finally opened, two sets of hands grabbed at him. His arms were slippery with sweat, so they had to hold his shirt to get a grip. They dragged him out of the van, carried him in through a doorway, and sat him in a hard-backed chair.

A door slammed. He heard some murmuring behind him. Heavy footsteps approached.

When they took the bag off, he closed his eyes at the bright light. After a while, he was able to squint. He sat in a room with cement-block walls and a cement floor with no windows or furniture. A large man in a button-down shirt and a black ski mask stood before him holding his wallet. Farrell thought he could detect a smile behind the mouth hole.

"Thomas," said the big man benevolently. He had an Irish accent, but it was different from Durkin's and Brian's. Less harsh, more musical. More like his mother's and father's had been.

"Hello, Thomas. My name is Gallagher. We have a mutual friend. A gentleman by the name of Durkin. We'll get back to that, but first I want to ask you a couple of questions about yourself as a way of getting acquainted, you might say. You're not lookin well, I'm sad to say, Thomas."

Farrell squinted up at him.

"I've had a long couple of days," he said.

The big man chuckled.

"I'm sure you've had. Well, I will say one thing. You Westies are a resilient bunch. As resilient, I would say, as you are hard to locate."

"I'm not a Westie," Farrell said.

"No?" the big man said with surprise. "I thought you were. Where are you from then?"

"Inwood."

"Ah, Inwood. Up near the Bronx there, right?

Fine Irish country up there. And your parents?"

"Your side."

"Ah, a narrowback. I knew it. What part of the old sod are your ma and da from?"

Narrowback, Farrell thought. That's what his father had called him and Terry when they were kids. He'd yell it whenever they did something wrong. "Goddamn narrowbacks." Like some type of original sin. As if they were somehow no part of him.

"My father was from Galway," Farrell said. "And my mother from Sligo."

"Sligo? I'm from Kerry, right next door. How do you like that? Small world. Maybe I banged her in a bog when she was a wee lass. What was her name?"

Farrell could hear laughing off behind him.

"Sweet Molly Malone," Farrell said.

The punch came from nowhere. The big man just stepped forward and brought down his big right fist. Farrell landed on his back on the floor, his face in agony, blood from his now broken nose dribbling off his lips and chin all over his shirt. Hands grasped him from behind and sat him back in the chair. He pressed his nose into his collar as his eyes teared up.

"That's a no-no," the big man said soberly. "You

can be cute, but not too cute. Now, I must say, that's one thing about you Irish Americans—you narrowbacks—that really gets me going. All this bullshit about the old sod and the leprechauns and St. Paddy's Day. As if we gave a fuck about where your parents are from, your fucking roots."

Farrell looked up at him. He shook the handcuffs at his back and spit out a gout of blood.

"Well, you're curin me of it real fast," he said, his voice giving off a whining nasal twang.

"Not by half," the big man yelled at him. "Not by fucking half! Where is Mr. Durkin?"

Farrell held the big man's eyes.

"He's dead," Farrell told him sincerely.

A boot caught him in the side of the head, and he went to the floor. Hands pried open his mouth, and a gun was put in it, the taste of metal and oil making him gag. He closed his eyes, waiting.

"Didn't I tell ya?" Brian said excitedly.

"I din do id," Farrell said around the barrel.

Brian took out the gun and looked at him.

"It was these Albanians. They killed everybody except for me," Farrell said.

"This is bullshit. Let's just do him and be done."

"No," the big man said. "Let's see what kinda shit he's gonna spout."

They sat him back up. Farrell explained it to them. He told them everything except with one important revision. He stressed Durkin's presence in the bar where Mullen and the Sideburns had been slain. The Irishmen stared at him throughout. Farrell could feel the skepticism burning behind Gallagher's mask.

"What about this?" said Gallagher, walking off behind him and then returning with the Heckler & Koch.

"I went after them."

"The Albanians?"

Farrell nodded his head.

"How?"

"Got the gun off an old friend of mine and cut into the roof of their club. I would have taken them, too, if some kid hadn't walked in. Can you believe it? I told them I was coming, and they let a kid hang around."

"I don't believe any of it," said the big man, folding his arms, "but go on."

"That's all there is. I popped by Tara's, and your friend was there."

"Where's the money?"

"It's still in the safety deposit box at that bank."

The big man looked off somewhere behind

Farrell and nodded his head. Brian came behind him and undid the cuffs. Then he suddenly put a knee in his back, bringing him face forward to the cement. A gun was jammed in his ear painfully.

"Put out your hand."

"What . . . "

Gallagher came forward and pulled Farrell's hand out upon the cement. A boot crunched down tight on the wrist.

"Have you ever heard of breezeblocking?" Gallagher said.

"Please," Farrell said, struggling.

The cinderblock that struck his hand didn't make any noise. His flesh and bone cushioned it completely from the floor. Farrell screamed. It felt as if his hand had been set on fire. He couldn't feel his pinky or his ring finger. He struggled up to his knees, panicked, looking to see if they'd been severed. They were still there, but barely. His hand was mangled as if caught in an industrial press. The young terrorist Brian, now holding his wrist, seemed like some benevolent coworker trying to tend to the wound.

"Now you have," said the big man merrily. "It's not kissing the Blarney Stone, but I thought you might be interested in experiencing one of our more recent ancestral rituals."

Brian sat Farrell back up. Farrell held his wounded hand between his legs.

"WHERE IS OUR FRIEND?" Gallagher screamed.

Farrell told them again. He went slower this time, went over the pertinent points rationally, repeatedly. He broke down once, came close to admitting his guilt, but managed to control himself. It took some time. When he was done, the big man didn't speak but suddenly wrapped his huge hands around Farrell's throat.

"Stop lying to me," he said.

"HOW DID IT HAPPEN THEN?" Farrell sobbed. "YOU TELL ME!"

The big man slapped him with a huge, hardened palm. It was like getting hit with a skillet. Farrell's head snapped violently sideward, his eyes rolling.

He teetered on the edge of consciousness. For a moment, he was five again in his pajamas, splayed on the floor in the hallway of his apartment, his old man swaying above, telling him if he wanted some more, he knew damn well where he could get it. His mother running out from the bedroom, scoop-

ing him up, and locking them in the bathroom,
rocking him with the soft, wailing mantra, "Jesus
Mary and Joseph Jesus Mary and Joseph Jesus
Mary and Joseph." Then afterwards, the crash of
glass, the sound of which was more violent than
anything he would ever witness—even in prison,
even in the last few days. The china cabinet coming down, the crystal and the glass and plates
exploding in the hallway in an impossibly loud
continuous screeching that would not end.

Then he is drunk, stumbling, and there's pink
neon and lights flashing on and off, on and off, and
this ugly little man directs him through a door
where he's supposed to meet his brother and he
sees things he doesn't understand.

"Terry, is that you?" Farrell called out.

"No," Gallagher said as Farrell came around,
"Terry isn't here at the moment."

They had him down again—his uninjured hand
set out. The big Irishman was above him again,
holding a hammer of some sort. He was gripping
something long and thin and black between his
teeth. He plucked it out and held it in his fingers
for Farrell to see. A common six-inch wood nail.
Then Farrell noticed the block of wood that was

braced underneath his uninjured hand and the rope that was lashed about his wrist.

"Before we continue," Gallagher said, his voice lower now, almost calming, "I want you to help me imagine something, all right? Are you a religious man, Thomas? You look like one to me. I bet you were an altar boy, am I right? Sweet Molly of Inwood chasin ya to church every Sunday. I'm much the same. I was gonna be a priest, if ya can believe that. They came by recruiting when I was twelve, but me da finally talked me out of it. I was the only boy, you see, and he wanted to see the family jewels passed on, I suppose. It's always fascinated me, though." Gallagher was staring at the nail as he spoke, thumbing the head, squeezing it. Softly, he pressed its tip to the middle of Farrell's palm. Farrell closed his eyes. He would have clapped his ears shut, had he access to his hands.

"Haven't you ever wondered what it felt like— for Him? The iron through the flesh. Now, I know what the skeptics say—that he was tied or nailed through the wrists—but you know what? I'm a purist. I mean, if he could fuckin walk on water and make the blind see, he could support his body through his palms on the cross. Ah, that's me own theory. Where was I? Oh, I remember." Gallagher raised the hammer behind his head.

The severity of his beating had distanced Farrell, put him someplace else. He looked into his captor's eyes through the holes of the ski mask with neither anger nor reproach nor even acceptance— something akin to kindness perhaps, maybe even forgiveness. The big man paused at this new placidness in Farrell's features. He placed the hammer on the floor.

"Terry?" Farrell asked, smiling, delirious.

"What are ya waitin for?" said Brian.

"We're up to the inch, I think," said the big man. "Sit him up again."

"Aw, for fuck's sake. What inch?"

"The last one within his life. Now sit him up," Gallagher commanded.

Brian tssked as he lifted Farrell into the chair. Gallagher took out a handkerchief and dropped it in Farrell's lap. He came around somewhat after a few minutes, the room still spinning. His breath burned from his chest in grating, injured bursts. Then he lifted the cloth to his nose.

"Well, either you're telling the truth," the big man concluded, "or you take a nice beating. Now, from what I've gathered on you narrowbacks, I'd have to go with the former. We have to keep you around a bit longer, for you to get the money out of that bank. Let me tell you something, though. If you're lying to me, we'll be actin out some more dramas before you'll be going down a hole."

Farrell raised his head with effort, found Gallagher's eyes, and nodded with slow and great understanding.

They brought him into a windowless bathroom, left him there, and locked the door. The water he ran over his mashed hand was like acid. He found a first-aid kit in the medicine cabinet, and he wrapped his hand in gauze, taking care in taping up the two last fingers. They were completely numb. He didn't even bother trying to move them. With some Q-tips, he tended to his blood-clogged nose, and when he was done, he looked in the mirror. He had had a straight nose, and he refused to acknowledge the one he found mashed into the side of his face. These bastards had really tuned him up, hadn't they? He grasped the cool porcelain of the sink to keep himself from falling. He sat on the toilet stifling his sobs.

He managed to calm down after a minute or two and drink some water from the sink. He still had his cigarettes in his pocket, but they were broken from the blows he'd sustained. He selected a larger piece and lit the filterless stub with his lighter. He turned off the light and sat in the darkness smoking. Better. All right. Still alive was something.

After a while, Brian opened the door and threw him a T-shirt and some jeans. Farrell stripped off his bloody clothes and changed. His nine-hundred-dollar pants were stained with blood and tar and sweat. His three-hundred-dollar shirt was indistinguishable from a butcher's apron. Brian was there when he came out, and he led him up some rickety basement stairs.

In the kitchen Gallagher sat at a wooden table, a steaming cup of tea before him. He had his mask off and was wearing glasses. He seemed kindly in the bright sunlight, an overgrown child. He smiled at Farrell as if he might have been a friend come on a social call.

"Tea?" the big man offered.

"Coffee, if you got it," Farrell said, playing along.

Brian went to a shelf.

"Those fellas who killed our friend—you have their address?"

"On my key ring," Farrell said.

The big man picked up Farrell's keys off the table next to his wallet.

"Albanians," the big man said to himself. "They're like gypsies, right?"

Farrell nodded.

"We have them in Ireland, or relatives of them, anyway. Have you ever heard your ma or da talk about the tinkers?"

Farrell shook his head.

"They sound like the same bunch—tricksters and con men the lot. Well, don't you worry about your missing them. We'll pay them a visit ourselves soon enough. Where did you say you got that gun again?" the big man asked.

"My old partner."

"You've dabbled in the trade?"

Farrell nodded.

"Do you think this old partner has any more?"

Couldn't hurt at this point, Farrell thought.

"Only a crateful," he lied.

"Bullshit," said Brian, setting a mug of coffee before him. He turned to the big man. "The SAS squadies have the same armament. Ya think they sell them in sweet shops?"

"It's easier than you might think," said Farrell. "Whatever."

"I don't buy it," Brian continued.

"Whatever," Farrell said again. He sipped at the

coffee. The big man looked at his watch and slid out his chair with a screech.

"We better get going if we want to make the bank," he said.

They took the truck again. This time Farrell got to ride in the back without handcuffs. The big man sat in front while Brian drove. He had been right about the Fifty-ninth Street Bridge. They were in Woodside, Queens. They drove up to Queens Boulevard and turned left beneath the number seven el, following it to the bridge. Farrell lit another cigarette. He wanted to inquire about how they'd split the money, but he didn't think that would go over well. He did not like the fact that the big man had taken off his mask. He did seem interested in the gun angle, though. Perhaps it was his way out of this. He sucked hard on his cigarette. He'd just have to see.

It was ten to three when they got to the bank. It was in the fifties on Madison, and Brian went in to make sure that the front door was the only entrance. Gallagher gave Farrell back his wallet.

"No tricks now," the big man cautioned him. "We just want to do what's fair and right. You'll still get your share, OK? The rest we'll take— Durkin's rightful share and the other shares—as a donation to a memorial fund in his name. If you told the truth, you have nothing more to fear from us. After this, maybe we can go to your old partner and do some business, and then maybe we can all go back to take care of those fucking tinkers. Be a good lad now."

The big Irishman held out the hand that had previously done so much damage to him. Farrell didn't want to, but he took it.

"My name is Seamus," the big man said.

Farrell got out of the truck. He crossed the street and walked into the bank and through the silent hum of the AC to the courtesy desk. The young, well-dressed woman behind it was the same one who'd rented him the box. She tried hard but couldn't disguise her shock.

"I know what I must look like," Farrell said, smiling sheepishly. "I was in an accident yesterday."

The girl's shock morphed into concern.

"What happened?" she asked.

"Uh, I got hit by a motorcycle out in front of the St. Regis hotel," Farrell said, making it up on the spot.

"That's horrible," she said. "Are you going to be OK?"

"I hope so," Farrell said, handing over his key.

He followed her through the bullet-proof security door into the vault. In the room of safety deposit boxes she turned her key simultaneously with his, and the door to his box opened. He'd rented out the largest box available. He slid out the laundry-basket-sized container and waited until he was alone in the private viewing room before he opened it. They'd fit all the money into a knapsack. He pulled the knapsack out, put it on the table, unzipped the top, and peeked inside. All that money. It would have been enough for a chance at some kind of life. That he had been able to get it in the first place was something, right? He zipped the knapsack up and put it on his back. He wasn't too sure anymore.

When he came out, the girl wasn't at the desk. The guard at the door had it locked so no other customers could come in, and he smiled at Farrell and told him to take it easy as he opened the door and let him out.

Farrell stood for a moment. He looked up the side street to the west. There was a slight rise in the receding distance that gave him a view of people and cars that were passing along the parallel avenues. Their forms made odd silhouettes in the late-afternoon sun. Like strange targets in some immense shooting gallery. He watched the people packed tight on the sidewalks and pouring out of the buildings. They let them out early on summer Fridays, he remembered. He watched as they streamed by. Men and women of every description, every color, every age. Even in the summer sunlight, their faces held downcast eyes, dreary expressions. In their somber business clothes it seemed as if they'd all just come from a funeral. As if perhaps a great man had died and his loss had caused a grief so acute that it had set each one bewildered and wandering in the shadows at the feet of the buildings.

Gallagher gestured to him from the truck across the street. When he stepped off the curb, another van screeched before him. The man in the passenger seat had a thick mustache and black hair. The world began to slow. When the side door of the van slid open before him, Farrell suddenly realized that he was about to die. What he saw in the back of the van was difficult to immediately assimilate. An Albanian in a suit had a machete in one hand, and he held down a long-haired man with the other. When he pulled his captive's hair back, Farrell's jaw dropped open. Mullen stared out at him from behind a map of bruises. The blade was put to his throat. Three steps behind, the concealing crowd walked on, but Farrell didn't even turn around. He took two steps forward and was grasped roughly by the Albanian and thrown down on the floor of the van. The side door slid shut with the sound of a tomb being sealed, and the van pulled forward as Farrell put out his good hand, reaching for his friend.

14

RYAN WAS IN A COFFEE SHOP ON KATONAH AVENUE
when his beeper went off. He barely needed to
glance at the number. He knew who it was. The
only other customer in the place was a bus driver
on his break, and Joe, the owner, was busily cooking him a hamburger at the grill. Ryan stood, went
to the pay phone in the back, and dialed a number.

"Ryan?" Gallagher answered on the first ring.

"Good afternoon, Seamus," Ryan said.

"We need you. A man is on his way to pick you
up."

"What's the story?" Ryan asked.

"In due time," said Gallagher. "Just get here."

Ryan hung up, went back to his stool at the end
of the faded linoleum counter, and sat down. He
was about a block away from the gas station. He
had time to finish his coffee. The bus driver in one
of the two booths turned the page of his newspaper.

Ryan liked coming here for lunch weekdays when he wasn't working. It was dead in the afternoons, and sometimes he and the owner would play a game of chess. Ryan had taught the game to the man years ago, and he hadn't really improved much with time, but that didn't matter. Ryan just liked the company and the quiet and looking out the glass to the street. It was an OK life, he knew. There wasn't much in it, and that was fine. Simple and quiet was all right when you'd known the alternative. He sipped his coffee. Exactly why he was so compelled to wreck it, he wasn't sure. Old habits die hard, he thought. Maybe that was it.

He finished his coffee, put a five dollar bill on the counter, and stood.

"Good-bye, Joe," he called over his shoulder.

The bell on the door jingled when he opened it.

"Good-bye, Pat," he heard as he went out.

Gallagher's station wagon was waiting for him as he came across the oil-stained cement. As it idled, blue smoke billowed noisily from its tailpipe. There was a wiry, nervous-looking man with short, blond hair in the driver's seat. Ryan opened the passenger door and got in.

"Are you Patrick Ryan?" the man asked with an

accent that conjured up damp, gray skies, black-booted soldiers, pints, cigarettes, and songs.

"No," said Ryan, "I'm J. Edgar Hoover, and you're under arrest."

The man looked at him in shock.

"Lighten up, lad," Ryan said with a smile. "Let's go."

They pulled out and made a left on 233rd and drove down the hill. At Webster they turned right along the cemetery wall. When they turned left at Fordham Road, Ryan's interest was piqued. He'd assumed they were heading for Gallagher's bar. He would have asked where they were headed, but the kid looked like a good soldier and they probably had told him not to say shit. The rank discipline was pretty strict. At least it had been when he was in it. He leaned his elbow on the window, enjoying the breeze.

They got on Pelham Parkway heading east. They passed Jacobi Hospital, where his father had died. He'd had a stroke while Ryan was at work, and they hadn't been able to contact him. His father held on for six hours until Ryan arrived. He couldn't speak, but the old eyes had burned with intensity. Ryan remembered the way he'd grasped his hand. That huge nimble hand, not clinging in its last act, but passing something on—forgiveness, love, and strength. Ryan looked out. There were people on the grass between the two roads of the parkway, on picnic blankets, with strollers, a kid playing frisbee with a dog. He turned to the young driver.

"Is it much farther?" he asked.

The man said nothing, his eyes steady, concentrating on the road.

They pulled off and drove down a street so quiet it reminded him of Woodlawn. They made a right and drove up behind a parked utility truck that said "Three Gaels Demo" on its back doors and stopped. They got out, and he followed the driver into the back of the truck. Gallagher was in the front looking through binoculars somewhere down the block to the left. After a minute he put them down and came back.

They squatted in the rear of the truck.

"Paddy, this is Brian. Brian, Paddy."

Ryan met those hard eyes. Neither man even nodded.

"This is the story, Paddy," Gallagher said, looking at him intently. "We found our boy, Durkin. He's being held by some lowlifes down the block here."

"How'd you find this out?" Ryan asked.

"We got word that the Westies are associates of these Albanians who have a social club down this block and that Durkin is being held there."

"Why are they holding him?" Ryan asked, confused.

"That we don't know," Gallagher said.

"How accurate is this information?" Ryan asked.

"Very reliable."

"Albanians?" Ryan asked.

"I wouldn't be here if I didn't believe it in my heart. Our man is in there."

"I take it you're going to try to get him back out," Ryan said to Gallagher.

"Yeah," said Gallagher. "And I was kind of hoping you could give us a hand."

Ryan glared at him.

"Maybe you were drunk when I spoke to you the other night. I said I'd help you find him, that's it. What? You just want me to maybe kill a couple of people? What's a few more on my list?"

"Need I remind you of Mr. Clancy?" Gallagher barked at him.

"Fuck Clancy," Ryan said. "I knew Clancy, but I don't see him here now. I ain't goin to prison."

Gallagher's face reddened.

"Why did you come out here then? To waste my time? Get lost then if you don't want to live up to your responsibilities. You want a ride back, take a bus."

Ryan held Gallagher's glance.

"Fuckin bullshit," Ryan said finally. "All right, what's your plan?"

Ten minutes later Ryan got out of the station wagon, and Brian drove off. He wore coveralls that Gallagher had given him. The duffel bag he carried was not overly large, but it was heavy. He went around the side of the building he'd selected into the cement backyard. There was a ramp leading up to an open doorway. Water was drying on the floor inside, and he could hear someone whistling down the corridor to the left. He went right. He came into the clean, empty lobby, passed by the elevator, and opened the door to the stairs. It was nine flights up to the roof.

There was no alarm on the roof door, and he went out and closed it behind him. The housing of the elevator was on the right, and he climbed up its black paint-chipped ladder to the mechanic's room. There was just a rag stuck in the jamb to wedge the door shut, and he pushed it open. He set the bag down in the cramped, oily space. After a moment, the elevator kicked on with a deafening snap, and then it hummed loudly, its huge wheel spooling cable.

He left the door open, lay down on his belly, and looked out. The clubhouse stood unobstructed in the distance about six hundred yards away. Not an impossible length, but not an easy one either. He zipped open the bag. Perfect, he thought. He took out the Armalite and folded the stock into place. Other rifles would have been better, he knew. They could have bought a deer rifle from a Yonkers gun shop that would have been more accurate, but they wanted to work on him, wanted to suck him in, bring back the memories. He took out the tripod and screwed it into place. The movements came back to him naturally, the preparation ritual as calming as the last time he'd done it two decades before.

He found the scope and held it to his eye, peering down at the clubhouse. A man at a front table appeared behind the glass. What was that he was drinking? Espresso? Ryan put the scope to the rifle, screwed it down, and calibrated it, adjusting it downward with tiny clicks for the distance. There was no wind to speak of, so he didn't have to worry about that. He had chosen the location for the elevation and also to put the sun at his back. He upended the bag, and a full clip tumbled out. He loaded the gun and chambered a bullet. There was a thermos with some coffee in it and a pack of Majors cigarettes. He'd smoked them like a fiend when he'd been in Belfast, going through a pack or more on some godforsaken cobblestone roof in the rain waiting for his shot. That goddamn bastard. He'd thought of everything, hadn't he?

They liked to string you along and play to your vulnerabilities. He had let them when he was in his twenties because he had another agenda, some personal demons to work through—demons he'd brought back from Vietnam. He opened the coffee and took a sip. Even at this late date they didn't all seem to have been exorcised.

He remembered the day he'd walked into the Sinn Fein office in Belfast. He just waltzed in off Kevin Street and asked the man behind the desk where he could sign up. When the man asked, "For what?" Ryan had replied, "The IRA. What else?" After he'd been thrown out, he tried to get a drink in a Provo bar. A twenty-year-old Yank who didn't know a soul. A group dragged him out in the back, and someone put a gun to his head. They first thought he was some type of policeman. Then they didn't know what to think. CIA, somebody suggested. What they finally decided was that he was some Yank who had escaped from a mental home and didn't know what he was doing. Then he started talking, telling them of the things they had taught him in sniper school, some other things he had picked up on his own in Vietnam. He wanted to help. He said it wouldn't cost them anything, he was just doing his part to get the Brits out.

They gave him a tryout at a training camp in Leitrim. At first they'd been skeptical, but what he showed gave them pause. High-wind head shots at targets nearly half a mile away. He demonstrated how to do it for a few months, and then one night they took him up to Belfast and asked him to do it for real. The target was a British patrol known for its great efficiency and its even greater abject hatred of Catholics. Detention and beatings of young, male Catholics were commonplace. This, even though the official line was that British soldiers were a peacekeeping force. What had happened, though, was that one of their number had raped a Provo captain's daughter, and the sanction of extreme prejudice had come down.

Ryan was on a frozen rooftop over a quarter mile away when he drilled the point man of their squad in the head. He watched the others scurrying around, swinging their SLRs at the close rooftops. It was obvious that they weren't prepared for a world-class distance marksman. He didn't blame them—neither were the Vietcong. He shot three British soldiers dead and wounded another, and they still weren't too sure about the direction. They had to bring in a PIG tank to get their men out. The boyos had been impressed then, he remembered.

It had been a whole new ballgame after that. They wanted him for training purposes mostly, tucked him away down south and used him sparingly.

After a year he started getting bored. The longer he kept at it, the more likely he'd get caught. He didn't feel like spending the rest of his life in an Irish prison cell. The food you could buy in restaurants was bad enough. Besides, the sociopathic effect from the trauma of Vietnam seemed to have begun to wane. He started feeling guilty, having nightmares. He asked out, but they were reluctant to grant it. He'd killed nearly ten soldiers by that time, a few RUC constables. They had five or six near world-class shooters that he had trained. Still they were balking. "Once in, never out" was the motto. Besides, he'd come to them an outsider, and they'd let him in.

But the captain named Clancy, whose daughter's rapist Ryan had made a quadriplegic, had swayed the board finally, and he was let go. At the airport Clancy had asked that Ryan make just one promise; if Clancy ever sent him someone, Ryan would give him a hand. Ryan agreed, and a signal was arranged.

He had been living in Boston when the two men came to kill him. It was the winter Of '79, and he had been working a forklift in a warehouse under a different name for the better part of that year. He knew that the British probably knew about him and accepted the possibility of some retribution, but he thought it would come in the form of an arrest. He thought the British might arrange for him to be extradited for trial. That the British were capable of covert retaliation he was well aware— the Special Air Service, the crackerjack antiterrorist unit of the English military, was not beyond cornering and killing terrorists its government did not particularly like. Ryan just did not believe they would act on U.S. soil.

It happened as he came out of a bar by the harbor. It had been a cold night, he remembered. Dustings of snow swirling against the high curbs in the street. He saw the first one almost immediately as he exited the place, a face uplit for a split second in the process of lighting a cigarette in a parked car across the usually empty street. There was a scrape of shoe on cement immediately to his right, and he had thrown himself back as a gunshot deafened his ears. He had drawn the .38 that he carried for that express eventuality, and the man came in front of him, and they exchanged shots almost simultaneously. The man's second bullet whipped through the thick cloth of Ryan's peacoat above his shoulder, missing him, and the man sat hard on the cobblestones with a look of pained remorse on his face. Then Ryan shot him again.

The car across the street was revving insanely, and the driver had his gun out in his hand upon the wheel and looked perplexed. Ryan stood then, crouching on the balls of his feet, and marked the man along the barrel sights of his revolver and shot him directly behind the ear. The man slumped back in the car. Ryan closed the distance quickly and pulled the ruined driver from the car. He dropped his body to the street, put the idling car into gear, and tore away from the place, as the bartender and some horrified patrons looked on from the sidewalk.

He tossed the .38 in the Charles and drove out to Logan Airport. He left the car in the parking lot and at a pay phone got the number for the FBI from the operator. He informed the woman who answered the phone that there were two dead British soldiers on McDougal Street, and she asked politely if he'd like to leave his name. He had laughed genuinely at the absurdity of her tone and her question and asked, "Why? Would you like to reserve a prison cell for me?" He then took a cab to the bus station and was back in New York by the next morning. After two days of nothing in the newspapers, he returned home to Woodlawn after almost seven years away. The British might try to kill him again, but at least he wouldn't be arrested, because officially no crime had been committed.

That was a long time ago. Besides the black he'd hit with the pipe at the work site yesterday morning, those soldiers were the last of God's children he'd visited violence upon. He checked his watch. Up till now, he thought.

He got into his shooting crouch. He was able to wedge a boot against the railing behind him. He got the butt of the rifle in tight against his shoulder and put his eye to the scope. It wasn't the gift of sight, he knew, but the gift of stillness that made a great shooter. The paradox of squeezing the trigger without disturbing the gun.

The last time he fired a rifle was in Belfast over twenty years ago, but like a lot of things, it was just like riding a bike. He flicked off the safety with his thumb. There were a number of men down there. Ryan passed the crosshair over the hearts of three standing in front of the plate glass, then over the heads of three at a table within, like a silent distant benediction. Something wasn't right, he thought. He looked around with the scope. He saw a hole was cut into the roof. Strange. He brought the gun down and sighted the first man. But for some reason he couldn't do it. Nope, he thought, laying the gun down on the tar paper, he didn't have it in him anymore.

Well, fuck it, he thought, searching for the cigarettes. He opened them up and took one out and put the short, fat cigarette between his lips. Just as well, he thought, flicking the cigarette off his perch. He'd only quit about fifteen years ago.

15

FARRELL GAPED OVER AT MULLEN AS THE VAN SPED down Madison.

"How the fuck?" he said, smiling, raising himself. Then something hard struck him over the top of the head. Brass knuckles or a pipe. It didn't knock him out—just hurt him. The Albanian was swinging the pommel of the machete again when Farrell pulled out his ankles and knocked him down. The man's legs were spread before him, and Farrell drove a fist into his groin, putting as much weight behind it as he could. The man lay paralyzed, holding himself, a stunted gargle escaping his lips.

Farrell was rising when he heard the over-and-under clack of a shotgun being racked from the passenger seat. He stopped without turning around and moved over next to Mullen, who lay curled like a bundle of rags in the back corner of the van. He looked at the man who pointed the shotgun at him. He dabbed the blood on the top of his head, stiff in the stubble of his hair. After a while the man he had struck rose, and the man in the passenger seat barked some orders at him in their harsh language. The injured man went up to the front of the van, glaring back at Farrell.

Farrell turned to Mullen. "Mulls, talk to me."

Mullen stared up at him, his eyes milky, glazed.

"Tommy?" Mullen asked. They had beaten him badly. His left eye was purple. His face had been scratched badly, and his lips were split. His shirt was torn, and there were yellow bruises along his ribs. The deep red line of a welt encircled his throat like a burn.

"It's me, buddy," Farrell said soothingly.

"They came in with shotguns, Tommy," Mullen sobbed. "Roy was coming back with drinks and one of 'em just came in through the door and shot him in the back of the head. Billy tried to get his gun out, but they just opened up on 'im. I had a beer in my hand when they shot Roy, and I was still holding it when they grabbed me and dragged me out. You understand, Tommy? I didn't do shit. They shot Roy down, and I just froze up."

Mullen looked up at him, a pall of utter despair cast in his features. "What does that make me,

Tommy? What does that make me?" he asked in an urgent whisper.

Farrell shook his head. What had they done to him?

"How do you think I feel?" Farrell said. "I left you guys there, and I was the one who pistol-whipped the motherfucker. When I heard what was happening upstairs, I ran like a pussy. I'm the one responsible, not you."

"They would have killed you if you came up. These are some cruel bastards. They shot that old lady I was dancin with just to shut her up. They made me tell them about the bank," Mullen said. "Sorry about that. I didn't have nothing else to work with."

"Fuck all that sorry shit," Farrell said. "We keep apologizing to each other, they're gonna think we're a couple of fags."

Mullen gave him a thin smile.

"Maybe you," he said. "Not me."

"Where'd they take you?" Farrell asked.

"It was some type of social club or something in the Bronx."

Farrell shook his head disgustedly.

"Get the fuck out of here. I was there!"

"When!?"

"This morning. Fuck. I could have gotten you out!"

"Damn," Mullen said. "What happened?"

Farrell told him about the kid in the hallway.

Mullen smiled and shook his head amazed. "That took some fuckin balls, my man. Cut into the fuckin roof. Played their favorite trick on them, the fuckin cocksuckers."

Farrell shook his head. He paused solemnly.

"What did they do to you?"

Mullen took a deep breath, his smile departing slowly. "They took me into the basement. First they were beating on me. Then they started playing this crazy fuckin music." Mullen's breath came in rapid gasps. "A couple of dudes came in showing me knives and shit, tellin me how they . . . "

"Forget it, dude," Farrell said, patting him on the back.

"No, I'm all right. Then there was a whole bunch of them—like thirty of these motherfuckers—and they dragged me into some place—I thought it was a dance hall or something. There was guys drinking. There might have been a few women, some kids. A fuckin dinner dance. And they brought me up on a little stage and a guy puts a gun to my head and . . . " Mullen started to cry. "They're smiling up at me, these people, like me gettin killed is the entertainment. Then they made me get up on a chair . . . "

"It's all right man. Don't worry," Farrell said. "I'm gonna get you out of here."

"How are you gonna do that, Tommy?"

When Farrell looked up, all the Albanians but the driver were looking back silently, smirking.

"I'll think of something," he said.

"What about you?" Mullen asked.

"Oh, this," Farrell touched his swollen nose with his bandaged hand. "You were right about Durkin. Couple of his buddies paid me a visit. Lookin around for their friend."

"Get the fuck out of here? Donkeys?" Mullen asked.

"Yep. We got piggybacked by the fuckin IRA or whoever the fuck these two fuckin maniacs were. Can you believe that shit?"

"What happened?" Mullen asked.

"I left them back there."

"Back where?"

"At the bank."

Mullen laughed loudly.

"Jesus, look at us, will you?" Mullen laughed. "We'll have to knock over the fucking Plaza if either of us wants to get laid again."

Farrell smiled.

"It's good to see you, dude," he said.

Mullen smiled and nodded his head.

"You, too, man. You, too."

They drove down one of the avenues and then went over the Willis Avenue Bridge and got back on the Major Deegan. Heading to their club, Farrell figured. There was a little bubble window on the side of the van, and he and Mullen stared out. By the time they pulled onto Pelham Parkway, the day's light had changed. Even those low, dusty buildings were bathed for a moment in gold. The faultless sky splendidly paling. He had been planning to appreciate these things once this whole thing had been over, but it just hadn't worked out. It was the story of his life, but so fuckin be it. As the van rolled closer to its destination, he felt oddly calm, as if he'd already participated in these odd events, had been secretly expecting them all his life. Only one more thing to do, he thought. He closed his eyes. One more thing.

When they pulled up at the club, Mullen sat up.

"This is it. The place these fuckers kept me!"

They ran them into the club. An angry crowd of men was gathered. They jeered loudly as Mullen was pushed in. They were spitting at him. Farrell stumbled through the doorway into a stinging slap that brought tears to his eyes. Somebody booted him in the ass. He fell against them, and they pushed him up and sent him reeling half blind with pain and confusion. The money bag was grabbed, but he had wrapped the strap so many times around his arm that he was dragged down to the floor. When someone caught him a good boot in his armpit, he let go involuntarily, the violent catching of a nerve releasing the clenched muscles of his good hand. They were brought through the same corridor Farrell had come down not five hours earlier and were shoved into a windowless room. The door was locked.

Mullen was breathing rapidly.

"What are we gonna do, Tommy?" he asked.

Farrell wiped spit from his face.

"See what happens," he said. He had to fight to keep the steadiness in his voice. He went into his pocket and felt around for his cigarettes. He fished out a couple of filterless larger pieces and handed one to Mullen. He still had his lighter, too, and he lit them both. They smoked in silence. Mullen breathed in deeply.

"Oh, man," Mullen said to himself. "Oh, man."

Farrell could hear heated talking from the hallway, some type of debate. When the door opened, it was Frank, George's nephew, the locksmith Farrell had originally agreed to deal with. He came in, and some men stepped behind him, but the young Albanian said something to them, and they left reluctantly.

"I need to speak to you very quickly. My uncle is on his way. That was a very stupid thing you did to my uncle, very foolish. My uncle is a man of respect. Have you ever heard of vendetta?"

Mullen stumbled up from where he'd been sitting on the floor.

"I'm gonna kill this motherfucker," he said.

Farrell grabbed his friend.

"Was he at the bar?" Farrell asked.

Mullen looked at the Albanian. "I don't think so, but what does . . . "

"It's all right," Farrell said, sitting him back down. He looked at the young Albanian earnestly. "What's that, Frank?" he asked. "What's a vendetta?"

"Our vendetta is not like—what do you say— eye for an eye—more as head for an eye, you see.

Because you hurt my uncle, he must kill you. It is very bad situation."

"Why the fuck you in here then, Frank?" Farrell said loudly.

"There is one thing. It was you who came in through our roof this afternoon, yes?"

Farrell nodded his head quickly.

"Well, the father of that boy you did not shoot, he has some power within our group. He says he does not wish you to die."

"Add it up for me, Frank," Farrell said. "What does it mean?"

"With the money you provided, maybe because I feel somewhat responsible, I can try to get for one of you to go."

"One of us!" Mullen exclaimed. "Jesus Christ. Why just one of us?"

"Because you were at my uncle's home and you injured him and you threatened to murder the men beneath his protection. This has never been done to him. Never. You do not understand."

Farrell stared at Frank for a long beat. Then he looked over at Mullen.

"Do it," he said, turning back to Frank.

"Hold on, Tommy. You . . . "

"I did it," Farrell said. "I'm the one."

"You're sure?" Frank asked. "For the release of your friend?"

Farrell nodded.

The Albanian stood saddened, searching for words.

"Again I just wanted to say that . . . "

"GO!" Farrell screamed at him.

The door opened immediately at this outcry. Some men glared in; one held an automatic pistol. Frank stared at Farrell as if pained. Then he left, and the door was closed again.

"Tommy," Mullen said.

"Don't," Farrell said. "Don't."

Soon they could hear more commotion behind the door. As it was opened, Farrell yelled, "Just don't fuck it up, Mulls!"

They were handcuffed behind their backs and brought out into the hallway and into another room. George sat behind a big wooden desk. He wore a bandage on his cheek. The black thread ends of some stitches poked out from his temple like an unruly eyebrow. Mullen and Farrell were sat down before him in straight-backed chairs. Sitting together with the crowd all around them, the three injured men looked like they belonged together. Survivors of the same accident or some type of support group.

Farrell looked at George. The stocky Albanian smiled at him, his pale blue eyes twinkling. He pulled out a drawer and retrieved an old, long-barreled .38 with a polished wood grip. When he stood, it seemed to weigh heavily in his hand. Frank came out from the crowd, went to his uncle, and said something in his ear. George's pale blue eyes scanned the room. Out of that crowd Farrell watched one man step forward with a black-haired boy holding his hand. George's forehead knitted, and then he said something and nodded his head. He looked at Farrell. Then he said something else and began laughing.

When hands grasped at Farrell, he wanted to remain calm but couldn't. He came out of the chair struggling, crying. Someone grabbed the back of his shirt and ripped it away. He was tackled to the floor. A heavy boot was placed on the back of his neck, and a cloth was tied around his eyes. Then he was raised to his feet and led away. After a few steps he was pushed to the left and led down a narrow flight of stairs. He was brought across a rough cement floor and walked until he was against a wall. He could hear them swarming in behind, a crowd to a spectacle. He held complete breakdown an inch away. He thought of his brother, and that gave him some courage. Some pain, and that would be the end of it. He remembered Terry coming to the father's funeral. He'd been living on the street, but he'd shown up wearing an old but clean suit. It had been years since they'd seen him. He was emaciated, eaten up by the drugs, but he'd said hello to everyone with an unquenchable sense of dignity. He remembered how Terry'd spoken to him, telling him not to end up like him—to get out of there, go into the service. After what Farrell had done to him.

Farrell dug his head against the brick, trembling. The crowd went silent. With every ounce of strength he had, he raised himself up straight, and he waited. Metal clicked loudly. The crowd hushed.

"TOMMY!" Mullen cried out.

There was an explosion then. A concussive detonation from upstairs shook the room. Glass shattered. Someone yelled. Machine-gun fire trilled loudly. The crowd screamed and rushed for the stairs. Farrell thought quickly. As he got on the floor, he yelled out to Mullen, "Get down!"

Farrell listened to the gunfire. It went on for

some time. Then heavy footsteps came down the stairs.

A hand took off his blindfold. He stared up at Gallagher, wearing his ski mask. He had Farrell's money over one shoulder and held the Heckler & Koch in his hand. He popped out the clip as Farrell watched and put a new one in with a clack.

"Fuckin Germans are brilliant. Come if you're comin," he told Farrell with a wink.

As Gallagher turned, he raised the gun at Mullen on the floor.

"No, he's with me," Farrell said quickly. Farrell went over, helped Mullen up, and they walked for the stairs behind Gallagher.

Men were moaning in the hallway. They passed bullet-riddled bodies beneath tables, blood pooling on the linoleum floor. Shattered glass crunched beneath their feet, while a slight breeze blew in through empty window frames. Someone screamed out a name far down the block. They came out into an eerie silence in the street. An Albanian with a face full of blood stumbled past blindly with a pistol in his hand. It was the boy's father, and Farrell was about to call out to him, but Gallagher had already raised his gun almost casually and put a quick burst of rounds into the man's head. The Albanian fell to the sidewalk; the spent shells from the bullets that had taken his life bounced off the cement and landed in the folds of his fancy suit coat.

They went to an old station wagon parked on the other side of the street. Gallagher got in the front seat. Farrell and Mullen got in the back. Brian took off his mask and drove down the block unhurriedly and made a right at the corner. Gallagher took his mask off, too, and turned around, offering a hand to Mullen. Mullen took it.

"Seamus Gallagher," he said.

"Bobby Mullen," Mullen said. "Thank you."

Gallagher laid the gun on the floor, put the bag in his lap, and opened it up.

"No. Thank you," he said.

"What was that? A car bomb?" Mullen asked.

"Ya hear him?" Gallagher laughed to Brian. "A car bomb would have left a fuckin crater. It was a nail bomb. Nice work, too, Brian," Gallagher said to the driver.

"A nail bomb?"

"Yeah," Gallagher said. "You just get a little C_4, put it in a box, and add some nails. Great for a crowd. Doesn't kill too many, but gets 'em bloody and bloody confused. Tinkers were pretty surprised."

Farrell shook his head. All that carnage had been caused by two men.

They stopped on a corner. A man in coveralls got in quickly, sitting next to Farrell.

"This here's Patrick," Gallagher said.

Farrell looked at the man. He was older, middle-aged at least. He looked Irish, but when he spoke, Farrell realized that he was American.

"Which one of you is Durkin?" Ryan said.

Farrell shook his head quickly at the name. So did Mullen.

"He wasn't there," Gallagher said, turning around. "After all that. What happened to you?"

"I had some trouble getting set up," Ryan said. "Didn't seem like you needed me all that much anyway from where I was sitting."

Gallagher turned back around.

"All's well that ends well," he said. Ryan stared hard at Gallagher for a moment and then looked out the window. Farrell took his broken cigarettes out. Ryan shrugged them off and took out his own. He put one between his lips and gave one each to Mullen and Farrell.

Farrell lit Mullen's cigarette with the Zippo and then his own. He held the flame as Ryan lit his.

"Isn't it bad luck?" said Gallagher from the front. "Third light off the same flame?"

Ryan rolled his eyes to Farrell.

"That's right," Ryan answered. "Where it comes from was, supposedly, in World War I a soldier would light up in a trench at night, and a sniper'd get his location. Then with the second light he'd figure out the windage, and by the time the third unlucky bastard was gettin lit, it was his last cigarette. But I'm not that superstitious."

Ryan looked out the window as a cop car came screaming by in the opposite direction on the other side of Pelham Parkway.

"Besides," he said with a smile, "we're all Irishmen here, right? All our luck is good."

16

MCCARRY TOOK THE CAR OUT OF THE LOT WHERE
he'd hid it down the street from 26 Federal Plaza
and headed back up the FDR for the Bronx. It was
about three o'clock, and the traffic was stop-and-
go the whole way. He felt like putting the portable
light on the dashboard but figured he'd had
enough of that for one day. It was incredible how
fast things could turn on you. One moment you're
on top of everything; the next it's on top of you.

He had planned to be jovial and cool for his pre-
sentation, but when he got up there and saw the
crowd of professionals before him, his mouth went
dry as paste, sweat beading up on his forehead.
He'd given hundreds of presentations since his
debating club days in high school, and he'd never
flipped out like that. And if his delivery was bad,
the reaction to his recommendation was worse.
"What? More time?" someone had called from the
back. One of the big cheeses up from Washington.

"What are you doing? A study on bar culture?"

"It's, ah, inconclusive at this point," McCarry had said, sounding like a fucking idiot. The guy from Washington had looked at his friend and shook his head.

McCarry took a deep breath. It was that god-damn stupid story about Wallace that had rattled him. Who gave a fuck about his goddamn combat cross? Lots of people had them, he was sure. If he'd been dumb enough to join the NYPD, he'd have one himself. To top it off, while he was look-ing over his files to match the surveillance picture, a grievance had been made to the office. A man asserted that an agent had crashed into his daugh-ter's car. The complainant was a state circuit court judge, the Woodpecker had informed him confi-dentially, and he was pissed off. "If it's true," the carrottop had told him, "that'll mean someone's job." The only thing that was promising was the description: white male in a dark suit, thirty to forty years old, black hair, five-ten to six feet tall, driving a dark, late-model sedan. Fitting into the FBI mold could come in handy in the most unex-pected ways, McCarry thought.

He pulled off the completely jammed FDR at

61st and drove slowly to Third. There was traffic there, too, so he went over to Park and made a right. He came by the old, majestic Upper East Side residences, their white-gloved, bow-tied doormen out in front. They were probably all empty by this time, he thought. The rich and famous already out in the Hamptons chomping down foie gras and champagne out on the back deck, the money-green Atlantic in the background.

McCarry stomped on the accelerator. As he crossed the Willis Avenue Bridge, he could see the cars all but parked on the Deegan. TEN TEN WINS told him it was a jackknifed trailer, and he made a left on a side street. It wasn't a pretty ride, but it would be quicker than the highway.

He drove past windowless, burnt-out buildings and buildings that had false windows—curtains and vases with bright flowers painted on plywood stuck in the frames. McCarry wasn't sure whom these were supposed to fool, because even from the highway, they looked ridiculous. Why stop at curtains, he thought. Why not take the ruse to the end and paint a pretend mother and father saying grace at a table with a bunch of pretend smiling, happy kids? Maybe they could make people forget about the real people who squatted in these condemned hovels—the ones sucking on crack pipes and beating each other to death.

He pulled onto Jerome Avenue and stopped at a light next to Yankee Stadium. There was a group of youths in baggy shorts and sideways caps on the corner. One spotted him and started going "Woop, Woop," twirling a finger in the air. Another held out all the fingers of his left hand exaggeratedly, then made a circle with the thumb and forefinger of his right. He did it again and again. Five O, five O. Police, he was signaling. McCarry'd been made. He clapped at them.

He got onto University Avenue, and two blocks before Fordham Road he passed the building he'd grown up in. A dog was ripping at a newspaper in the front, cement courtyard, while on the corner of the sidewalk a fat man in a chair—not a beach chair, mind you, but an actual fucking chair, a recliner—sipped a forty-ounce bottle of malt liquor and scratched at the roll of ample belly that peeked out beneath his tank top. "Comfy?" McCarry yelled out the window as he passed.

He couldn't believe his mother had actually still lived here less than three years ago. It had taken the old man's death to get her out. It was a rent-controlled apartment, and he just couldn't let it go.

"Two hundred and twenty-six dollars and twenty-three cents," he'd say to any argument posed to him. "Two hundred and twenty-six dollars and twenty-three cents." His face would beam at the words. The only time the super painted any part of the building was when a kid bombed his name in the lobby with a spray can, but the old man wouldn't move.

"You find me a three-bedroom apartment for the same money, and I'll gladly go," he'd say. "If you could get me a deal like that, not only would I go, I'd hire ye myself, ya fancy lawyer, ya."

Any more talking would yield only his father's patented mien of menacing obduration. How many generations of Queens schoolchildren had that face made walk rather than attempt excuses about lost bus passes, he wondered.

McCarry turned left, drove past his old grammar school, and then went right onto Bailey. It ran parallel to the Deegan here, and he passed by the jammed-up cars. There were some houses off to the right overlooking the highway. He'd known a girl from one of them. She'd been real pretty and a couple of years ahead of him at Tolentine. He'd pretended he lived down here just to follow her home. He'd gotten into a fight over her on the night after his eighth-grade graduation. Someone had a party, and it was the first time he ever drank. He started dancing with her, and then her boyfriend, who was about five or six years older than him, kicked his ass in front of everybody. He wondered what happened to her.

Wow, this was just a trip down memory lane, wasn't it, he thought. He got to 238th, made a left, passed under the Broadway el, and stopped up the block. He never should have agreed to do the surveillance. His return to his old neighborhood kept disinterring all the stuff that he had buried so neatly. He looked at himself in the rearview mirror. Pull yourself together, he told himself. In the corner of the mirror, green neon caught his eye. It was a shamrock beer sign for a gin mill under the tracks. Could he stop in for one? He checked his watch. Four-fifteen. He sure could use a beer. Why the fuck not, he thought finally. What else could go wrong?

What struck him first about the place was its surreal darkness, the walls and bar and floor all a shiny black. It was like entering a cave. The beefy bartender stared as McCarry came through the door, as if he had been waiting. He came over and dropped a square, cardboard coaster before McCarry and asked, "What can I do ya, lad?"

McCarry looked at him. He made an order he'd heard his father make a thousand times, getting stuck with him in bars when he was a kid.

"Some Teachers and a draft to knock it back," he said.

The bartender poured his drinks and brought them over. McCarry paid him, and the man left him alone. He threw back the shot and sipped at his beer. There was a sound outside, probably the train rattling overhead, but you could hardly hear it over the AC. After a while, the bartender put on the Irish music station from Fordham U. There were some rows of bottled beer in the small, darkened fridge behind the bar, and McCarry stared at them behind the slightly fogged glass. What was that girl's name again, he thought. Tierney, that was it. He drained his beer. What had that cocksucker said at the meeting about him doing a study? McCarry called the bartender over.

"Line me up again, will ya?" McCarry said. "I've got a thesis to do here."

17

BRIAN DROVE THE STATION WAGON THROUGH THE
Bronx up Fordham Road and turned onto the
Grand Concourse. Farrell sat silent, staring at the
passing streets. People were crowded on the
neighborhood sidewalks and sat leisurely in the
wide windowsills. Some kids ran through a
hydrant sprinkler. He looked for the Marine
recruiting booth where at the age of seventeen he
had forged his mother's signature on the papers,
but it was nowhere to be found. Much like everything else in his life of late, it had moved on. He
thought they might head over toward Bainbridge,
where Durkin had lived, but they got on the
Mosholu Parkway instead, driving west. After
they passed the stark, black-stone cylinders of
Tracy Towers, they turned off at the exit and came
down past Clinton High School on Kingsbridge
Road along the reservoir.

Farrell flicked the end of his cigarette out the

half-drawn window. He stole a glance up at Gallagher. He studied the deep striations on the reddened back of the immense Irishman's neck and the big sunburned forearm resting heavily on his money. That madman sat oblivious, almost certainly pleased by the bloody episode just past. Farrell wrote off the money as he sat there. He looked over at Mullen, who seemed newly invigorated by their unlikely rescue. Mullen cocked a chin at the big Irishman and rolled his eyes, smiling confidently. Farrell took a deep breath. Maybe with Mullen here they had a shot at getting out with their lives.

An orange sun burned low over the black building tops as they passed over the Major Deegan Expressway and drove over to Broadway. They crossed under the elevated track and turned into a gravel parking lot beneath it. Farrell looked up into the underside of that dark hull. Rust stains bled like faded sores out of the tea-saucer-sized rivets in those sheets of ancient metal. Roosting pigeons cooed among the raw iron buttresses. He looked up through the trestles barred black against the blue sky beyond. Then he turned and looked off into the distance underneath the actual railyard where the out-of-service trains were parked, into the thick copse of dirty steel beams that bore that untold tonnage, forever dim and lifeless. He realized then that he had been here before.

Brian pulled up to a warped chain-link fence and got out of the car. Beyond, a one-story, gray ramshackle building was practically nestled beneath the raised subway line. Then it came to him: Gaelic Park. He'd played Irish football here when he was what? Twelve, thirteen? There had been a league. Good Shepherd was his team from Inwood. There were the Rangers from Kingsbridge, St. Barnabas from Woodlawn. There was even a team from Rockland County and a few from Jersey. The building housed a bar and dance hall; the field was on its opposite side. He shook his head in amazement as he got out of the car.

They went through a hole in the chain-link fence. Gallagher pounded on a door, the corrugated steel rattling under his fist. When the door opened, Farrell looked over his shoulder. Sunlight beating down between the trestles threw a line of gold bars on the oil-stained gravel. Motes of dust hung in the light, floating softly, like snowfall.

Farrell turned to the dim threshold and stepped in. The smell of the place hit him hard. Beer, pine cleaner, and smoke. The smell of men, of his father.

The wooden walls were faded, but the bar wood was still a shiny shillelagh black. The place had a stamped-tin ceiling, and the floor was worn black-and-red tile. Dim memories came to him of rough laughter and playing in sawdust, reeling music, too sweet cokes drank from thin red straws.

There was a middle-aged, white-haired man in an apron and rolled-up shirtsleeves before the bar.

"Ho, Timmy," said Gallagher, strolling across to him. "Set us up in here now, won't cha?" Gallagher held the bagged money in one hand. The Heckler & Koch was draped casually over the other shoulder.

The bartender jogged over to the window by the street and pulled the blinds. Then he threw the heavy lock on the door loudly and hung his bar rag on the nail above the square glass.

"Are ya nuts, Seamus?" he said, a look of pained perplexity crossing his worn visage. "I got the fuckin caterer comin in an hour."

"Hour's plenty, Tim," Gallagher said, opening a swinging door off to the side. He beckoned them into a dark room. They followed him into a large, low-ceilinged chamber as someone turned on the lights.

It was the dance hall. A little plywood stage was

set on some milk crates in a corner. Aluminum folding chairs were stacked along the cheap paneled walls. There had been team dances in here, Farrell remembered vividly. There'd be a band (always seemed like the same bunch of forty year olds singing "Proud Mary" with thick Irish accents), step dancers, a fifty-fifty raffle, and their coach ending the night singing a drunken "Four Green Fields" or "Danny Boy." Maybe a bagpiper or two if there were trophies to hand out. Long nights of eating potato chips and soda bread, drinking gallons of soda or maybe a beer on the sly, dreaming about how once you were older you could get up there and cut a rug with one of the finer-lookin ladies or maybe just how you couldn't wait to get the fuck out of your shitty little neighborhood, your shitty little life.

But you come back, Farrell thought, sitting at the round, splintered plywood table with the others. You always come back.

Cigarettes were lit. Outside a train clattered faintly, then stopped, then started again. Gallagher sat across from Farrell. Here in his domain the Celt smiled unabashedly at his companions, all pretense of displeasure in his barbarous activity dropped clean. Farrell studied him closely.

Gallagher passed this self-satisfied gaze on Mullen, on Ryan, and then, finally, rested it on Farrell.

"Why the long faces, lads?" he said. "We paid back the bleedin tinkers. We even got the money back. That's what I don't get about you narrowbacks. You can't see a good thing when it's right in front of your nose."

He winked at Farrell and looked over toward Brian as he spoke.

"Or in your case, Tommy-boy, your broken nose."

"Narrowback?" Mullen asked. "I've heard that before. What the hell is it supposed to mean again?"

"That's what they call Irish Americans," Ryan said. "Either because we tend to be taller or they think we're less tough, I don't know which. Both maybe."

"It's the latter," Gallagher assured them with a wide smile at Farrell. "The latter."

The bartender came in, bearing a tray of beer bottles, a labelless bottle of a clear liquid, and a neat stack of shot glasses. He placed it all in the middle of the table and went back out through the swinging door without a word.

Gallagher dispensed the glasses, clinking them down on the table in front of each man. Farrell ran his thumb over the dings in the aluminum rim of the old table from where it had been rolled for untold years to untold weddings, untold dances, untold wakes. Gallagher poured measures round, then raised his glass. Farrell stood, leaving his drink untouched on the table before him.

"Mind your manners, Tommy," Gallagher said. "I'm about to make a toast here."

Farrell's hand had started bleeding again at some point, he couldn't remember exactly when, and he held up the crimson bandage.

"I'm gonna go clean this off," he said. He walked toward the swinging door, waiting for an outcry from Gallagher, but none came.

"Good luck," he heard Gallagher call out, but whether it was his toast or advice, Farrell didn't know.

18

RYAN KNOCKED BACK HIS SHOT WITH THE OTHERS. IT was strong, like rubbing alcohol. He looked at Gallagher. The big Irishman smiled at him.

He'd been double-crossed big time, Ryan knew. Used, lied to. He had tried to repay a favor, tried not to welch, tried to be a man, and what did he get? An earful of shit and an opportunity to hold a bag. Butchery in broad daylight over what? Over money, it seemed. Maybe drugs. He'd believe anything at this point. Maybe that was the way they were doing things now. Who knew? Not him, that was for sure. It was wrong from the word go, and yet he'd let himself get in the middle. There was shit going on here that he had no idea about, but he did know one thing: It was about to stop. One way or another. He sipped cold beer, waiting.

"Ack!" Mullen gasped, putting his glass down. "What is this shit?"

"Putcheen," Ryan told him. "Irish moonshine."

He'd drunk it once or twice before. Ryan took out his cigarettes, lifted Farrell's lighter off the table, and lit one.

"I'm sorry, Patrick." Gallagher smiled benevolently, ever the genteel host. "This is Mullen, right?" Gallagher motioned to the scraggly Irish American.

"Mulls," Mullen said, extending a hand.

Ryan shook it.

"You ran into a little trouble, I see," Ryan said.

Mullen shrugged his shoulders.

"I got a tendency to land on my feet."

"You're from the city, right?" Ryan asked calmly.

"Eleventh Avenue," he said. "My great-grandfather jumped a Galway steerage ship off pier 86 during the Civil War, and we've been livin around there ever since. You ever been to the Kitchen?"

"I can't say I've had the pleasure," Ryan said.

"It's a little on the rough side, but tight. You got good people. Neighbors who look out for each other, which works out OK. Especially if you're lookin for somethin hard to locate. Like that item you got there." He indicated the machine gun on the table before Gallagher. "I could probably come in handy with somethin like that."

Gallagher turned to Mullen, raising an eyebrow.

"Isn't that intrestin. Your friend Thomas alluded to a similar opportunity he might be able to present to us when we had a little talk this afternoon." Gallagher turned to his stone-faced companion. "Looks like we'll be having more than one offer to weigh, won't we, Brian?" The Irish gunman just sat there, staring at Mullen.

Gallagher's expression turned more serious. He took a drink from his bottle before speaking. "There's one thing I'd like you to tell me, Mulls, if you can remember. You were there when our comrade Durkin met his death, were you not?"

"Yeah," Mullen said, taking a cigarette from Ryan's pack and lighting it. Ryan watched him blow out twin streams of smoke through his nose; swirls of blue and yellow floated in the weird light.

Gallagher continued.

"You didn't happen to notice in the confusion if the ones who were responsible for that were at the club just now?"

"Yeah, he was there," Mullen said, looking Gallagher solidly in the eye.

"Was he among the ones I took care of, the older man with the pistol?"

Ryan watched Mullen drag at the cigarette deeply, its orange ash glowing bright.

"Oh, no," he said matter-of-factly, looking off the way Farrell had left. "Tommy did it. Tommy did your friend."

There was complete silence in the hall. Gallagher looked at his companion and then at Mullen in wide-eyed shock.

"Thomas?" he asked, stunned. "Thomas?"

"I was there," Mullen said.

"The others also?"

"No," Mullen said. "Those Albanians killed Roy and Billy."

The short-haired Irishman reached behind his back and brought out a flat black pistol. He stood up.

"Oh, and ya weren't involved?" Brian asked bitterly.

"Yeah. If I was involved," Mullen said, sitting up, "I'd fuckin bring it up."

"I thought you two were friends," Gallagher said.

"We are," Mullen said. "But I don't want anything he mighta done getting mistaken with me. Better you know what's up."

Gallagher was looking out at the door where Farrell had left.

Ryan stood. He pointed at Mullen.

"I believe him," he said. "Like he said, why would he bring it up?"

Gallagher looked at Ryan skeptically.

"Well, I'd say your opinion has less weight than it might, Patrick, due to your disappointing performance," he said. "I forgot to mention it, but I don't like when I get stuck out in the breeze."

"All right, I apologize for that. I'll admit it," he told Gallagher confidingly. "I got stage fright. It's been quite some time, you know. Plus the way you dropped it in my lap. I wouldn't exactly call that fair."

Gallagher seemed to weigh the matter, then nodded.

"I hadn't thought of that, Patrick. They talk of you with awe back home. I just assumed you would take it up. I overestimated you."

"No," Ryan continued. "You're right. I almost got you killed out there. Let me make it up to you," he said. He took a deep breath. "Let me take care of this kid who did your friend. I mean, I don't want it getting back to Clancy that I fucked up on you." Ryan walked over to Brian and held out his hand. "Let me take care of it."

Gallagher gauged Ryan and after a moment nodded to his companion. Ryan took the gun. It was a big Sig Sauer nine millimeter. Ten rounds minimum, he surmised as he put the heavy pistol in his belt. He looked over at Gallagher.

"Just like old times," he said with a smile.

19

THE BARTENDER HAD HIS HEAD DOWN, GOING through notes on a page, when Farrell came out of the dance hall, and he went straight into the bathroom on the left. The urinals were massive, chest-high hunks of sculpted porcelain. Like much in that place, they were from another time. When good meant big and heavy and well made. There was also a small blacked-out window, Farrell saw, but it was nailed shut—probably decades ago from the look of the rusting nailheads that poked up from the green, chipped paint. He went to a sink and undid the bandage and in doing so reopened some of the cuts. The swollen, purple pinky and ring finger were welded together with black blood.

He looked in the mirror, and he told himself that he would walk back in that room and set up something with Gallagher. A bullshit gun buy or something, and then he and Mullen would be gone.

Let Gallagher just keep the fuckin money. He

could have it. He realized that he'd been insane to believe that he'd be able to pull it off. No, not insane. Worse. If his life had ever tried to tell him anything, it was that nothing would ever work out for him. Never had. Never would. He rewrapped the dirty bandage and left the bathroom.

The bartender glanced at him as he passed, disdain naked in his craggy face. When Farrell entered the dance hall, all sets of eyes were upon him. He sat down slowly and returned each man's glance until he came to his friend, who looked off toward the empty stage, as if waiting for a band to come on.

"What?" Farrell asked.

"Murdering a soldier of the Irish Republican Army," Gallagher said with a heavy solemnity, "carries the penalty of death. Do you have anything to say for yourself at this time?"

Farrell looked up, astonished. His face paled. He thought he might pass out. "What the fuck are you talking about?" he finally said, mustering up indignation.

Ryan lifted the gun. "Your friend let us in on everything."

Farrell turned slowly to Mullen, who still looked away.

"What are they saying, Mulls?" he asked.

Gallagher stood. Then Brian. Mullen rose with them.

"What are they saying?" Farrell pleaded.

"Let's adjourn to the bar," Gallagher said. "Mr. Ryan has some business to attend to." Gallagher looked down at Farrell, shaking his head. He bent down and leaned in to Farrell's ear.

"What did I tell you?" he whispered. "Down a hole you go."

Farrell was silent. He watched as his friend followed Gallagher and Brian to the door. He tried to call out, but nothing came. The only sound in the room was the door swinging loudly back and forth in its frame. Then it stopped completely and a slide was thrown home behind him.

20

MCCARRY WALKED DOWN THE EMPTY HALLWAY TO the cubicle with a large brown paper sack in his arms. He had a little trouble getting the key in the lock, but he finally managed it. Wallace had his feet propped up next to the console as he came in. "Hey, Francis. What you got in the bag?" he asked.

McCarry took out a sandwich wrapped in white paper and handed it to him.

"Turkey, provolone, and mayo, right?"

"Way to go," Wallace said, smiling.

McCarry took the items out of the bag. "Another sandwich for me, some chips. Hey," he said. He took out a six pack. "How'd these get in here?"

Wallace leaned in and looked at McCarry, confused.

"Francis. You've been drinkin, haven't you?"

"The FBI has trained you well," McCarry said, popping open two cans and handing one over to his partner. "Now we both are."

"The meeting went that bad?" said Wallace.

"Worse," said McCarry.

"That sucks."

"Tell me about it."

"Well, fuck it, man. I'm proud of you."

"For fucking up the meeting?"

"No, man. For bringing these beers. For lightening the fuck up. I was having my doubts, you know."

McCarry tilted up his beer, chugged it dry, and belched loudly.

"You can put those to rest, my friend," he said as Wallace laughed. "Tuck those fuckers right in."

McCarry looked over on the surveillance console at a car parked in the lot.

"Whose piece-of-shit station wagon is that?" he asked.

Wallace looked at it, shocked.

"I must have closed my eyes for a second."

McCarry laughed.

"We're just a steel wall of defense for democracy today, aren't we? One of us will have to get those plates. You're eating. I'll do it." McCarry reached into the bag, came out with another beer, and opened it up.

"Right after I finish this sucker."

21

RYAN CAME AROUND THE TABLE WITH THE PISTOL. Farrell glanced up. His features were void, petrified. Eyes of desolation, a face of stone. When Ryan raised the gun, Farrell didn't even flinch. He just stared into Ryan's eyes.

Ryan lifted Farrell's untouched drink off the stained wood and offered it to him. Farrell moved as if he was going to take it, but then he smacked it out of Ryan's hand. It flew, chinked off a wall, and then rolled off loudly in the dimness beyond. Outside a train sounded its horn.

"You're real tough," Ryan said. "I'll make sure they put it in your epitaph."

Farrell kept staring. "You're worse than him," he said finally.

"Who?"

Farrell shook his head. The smile that creased his lips was a bitter one. He said nothing.

"Gallagher? Why do you say that?" Ryan asked.

"That cocksucker's insane. He'll kill you, too."

"What do you think you know about me?"

Farrell wiped his face with his hands and rubbed his eyes. "Aww, enough," he said weakly, wearily. He looked up into the low cracked ceiling as if an answer to his predicament might be writ there.

"Just do it. Do it."

Ryan sighted down the barrel. This wretched kid before him. He looked at the blood caked on Farrell's face and his blackened hands. He looked closer and saw it was tar, and then he remembered the hole in the roof of the club. He shook his head. He'd probably gone to save that piece of garbage who'd just sold him out. He looked over at the diamond of glass in the swinging door. He couldn't tell if anybody was watching them. He pointed with his gun to a chair between him and the door.

"Sit there," he said.

Farrell cocked his head to the side, disgusted.

"I ain't gonna do that."

"You don't want to live?" Ryan asked.

Farrell looked up warily.

"What do you mean?"

"I mean, do you want to live or do you want to die?"

Farrell paused.

"I'm waiting," Ryan said.

Farrell stood up, walked two chairs over, and sat back down. He looked to the bar and then at Ryan.

"Why?" Farrell asked.

"Does it matter?" Ryan said. "There's a window back there. I'm gonna shoot right next to you, and you're gonna fall down like you're dead, and when you hear me go into the next room, you're gonna go out it and get the fuck out of here."

"What about you?" Farrell said.

"Don't you worry about me," Ryan said, putting his eye to the sight. "You ready?"

"Who are you?"

"I'm Patrick," Ryan said.

Farrell looked at him and smiled weakly.

"Thanks, Patrick," he said.

"You ready?"

Farrell nodded.

Then Ryan put the gun up to his eye and pulled the trigger.

22

WHEN RYAN SHOT, FARRELL KICKED HIMSELF BACK off the table, the bullet passing beneath his arm, tugging at his shirt. He hit the floor hard, the chair banging into his back. He lay still with his eyes closed as Ryan's footsteps went away.

When he heard Ryan pass into the bar, he lay still for another count of two, then sat up. He turned and saw the window at the back end of the hall. A soft breeze blew in, the playing field beyond still verdant in the darkening light.

He closed his eyes.

He remembered.

It was the winter after the Marines, and he was very drunk, walking around Chelsea, and he had gone into a tawdry parlor off the sidewalk. He had been oddly compelled by the flashing lights, the pink neon glow against the black-painted plywood in the window. He remembered the pocked nose of the barker who'd directed him in, the bells on the door ringing, and the aisles of shelved videos blindingly lit to better show the degradation, the disgust. The repulsive paraphernalia displayed on the walls like toys in a toy store. The counter was elevated on a pedestal, and the dusky proprietor had to lean down to hand Farrell the coins for the booth in back, as if he was separating himself from what occurred in the store beneath him. The first video was straight sex; after a while the moans became more incessant than arousing. The second one was gay men, and he was about to leave when he realized in horror that he knew one of the participants. Even those ten hard years couldn't completely mask his looks.

Terry, who had split open an older kid's skull with a hurley stick after he'd threatened Farrell. Terry, who had protected him, loved him, when nobody else gave a fuck. Who had been kicked out by their father because of him and whom the city had swallowed up. His brother: shirtless, emaciated, tortured, gone. God, he'd tried to get over it, tried to forget the cries that followed him as he ran sick out the door. Tried. But he couldn't. There wasn't any way.

He could hear muffled voices from the bar, those who wanted to see him dead, divvying up what was his. He could go now, couldn't he? He was done with, now that he'd been stripped clean, been taken for everything. As he was getting up, he noticed that the bag Ryan had brought with him into the wagon after the fircfight was under the table. He reached down and hauled it up. He zipped it open quickly and saw the folded rifle. It took him a moment to decide that it was loaded. And he saw it. Even after everything that had happened to him. Even after what Gallagher had done. Even after his father and Terry and the goddamn city. He saw it there as a choice, before him vivid as a conscious decision. And he savored it. Savored it for the bitterness, for the lifetime he had spent holding it off. And he chose it.

He put the stock of the rifle in his ruined hand and came across the dusty floor, his voided eyes cutting through the gloom, the hopelessness in his face replaced by a terrible focus.

23

WHEN RYAN STEPPED IN FROM THE DANCE HALL, Gallagher, his accomplice, and Mullen were already set up at the bar with drinks. The bartender was washing a glass in the sink. Although Gallagher was gazing away toward the field, the rest of the group looked at Ryan the way his fellow workers had looked at him at the site after yesterday's fight. The same way that men had always looked at him whenever he did things that they talked about and said they'd do but never did. A mix of fear, respect, and relief.

He walked off a little to the left of them and nodded to the bartender. A glass was produced, a tap opened. As his drink was prepared, he looked over at the long rows of bottles that receded down along the wall toward the window by the park, the fading light reflecting like votive candles in the dark-colored glass. He took the glass from the bartender and brought it to his lips and drank, closing his eyes. When he placed it down on the bar, half of it was gone. He wiped the back of a hand across his mouth and looked to Farrell's friend, Mullen, who stared back blankly, none the worse for the wear.

"Thirsty work?" Gallagher asked.

"You know it," Ryan said. "I hope this makes us even here."

"Clancy will know that you've gone above and beyond," Gallagher said.

"What's it about, Seamus?" he asked Gallagher. "What's it really about?"

"Ya know that's not the way it works, Paddy. Even I don't know exactly. It's all need-to-know," Gallagher informed him deliberately, instructions to a slow child. There was a sound from the dance hall, but nobody noticed it except Ryan. Come on, kid. Get out of here.

"Well, I hope it was important," Ryan said.

"You're an asset to the Cause," Gallagher assured him. "You always have been. Here you've shown it again. The work you have done here today, Patrick, will be reflected on occupied Irish soil tomorrow, I can assure you. We regard you as a patriot."

Ryan took a sip of his pint.

"Thank you," he said modestly.

It was confirmed. They thought he was a complete idiot, didn't they? Some NORAID nut job they could grease with patriotic sentiments, a whacked-out loser they could lead about like a puppet on a string. He looked over at Gallagher sincerely, as if he actually appreciated the flattery. He'd leave peacefully if he could, but if it had to be the other way, so be it. He was acutely aware of the gun still on his hip. He felt comforted in a way. He just hoped the kid was gone, that he'd given him enough time.

There was a distinctive footstep, then a loud wooden creak behind the dance hall door. Unmistakable. Gallagher snapped his head toward it. There was an elongated moment when everything was still, the beads of sweat standing on Mullen's forehead, the bartender's open mouth, Gallagher's eyes darting into Ryan's in surprise, the enclosed air heavy as water. Then the door swung open.

24

THE SOUND AND THE ECHO OF RIFLE SHOT IN THAT cramped area were overwhelming. In one motion Farrell just swung through and shot. Gallagher was maybe seven feet away, and the top of his head was sheared off—the thick gore wavering in the air behind him for a moment like thrown paint, then hitting the rows of liquor bottles behind with a wet splatter. Brian threw up a hand and Farrell shot him. The man stumbled for footing. Farrell shot him again, and he dropped. The bartender had his hands down going for something behind the bar, and Farrell shot, the bullet passing through his neck. The front window blinds behind him wavered, and the bartender fell, his lifeblood pouring out of him quickly and cleanly through the rubber mats behind the bar and down the drain. Mullen had curled up into a fetal ball beside the tarnished foot rail. Farrell surveyed the carnage blankly.

"I thought I told you to go," Ryan said, coming over.

Mullen had stood by this time.

"Tommy," Mullen said. He made a motion for the money on the bar. Farrell raised the gun and shot again, the wood beside Mullen's hand splintering.

"Next one goes in your heart," Farrell said. "You got ten seconds."

Mullen looked at him, pained.

"You don't understand . . . "

"Eight," Farrell said. "I understand, all right. Seven."

Farrell aimed the rifle at him and stared down its barrel. Mullen went quickly for the side door and bolted through it.

Farrell dropped the gun to the faded tile. He went over to the bar and took the money bag. He took it into the dance hall and came out a moment later with the bag the rifle had been in. He roughly divided the money in half and slid it over to Ryan.

"What's that?" Ryan asked.

Farrell picked up the rifle. He swung it by the barrel smashing at the bottles behind the bar.

"That's yours."

"Oh, no. You earned all of it, my friend," Ryan said.

Farrell smashed at the bottles again.

"Then leave it there, Patrick," Farrell said. "Let it burn."

25

MCCARRY FINISHED HIS BEER AND TOOK OFF HIS suit jacket and his tie.

"Going undercover?" asked Wallace. He took a huge bite out of his sandwich.

McCarry took his Glock off his belt and strapped it into the velcro holster at his ankle.

"Yeah," said McCarry. "If anyone feels the need to talk to me, I'll just ask them if the jitney stops around here."

Wallace laughed as McCarry went out the door.

As he stepped outside, McCarry thought he heard a muffled crack. Fuckin fireworks, he thought. Kids couldn't wait to blow their fingers off. He came around the front of the vacant building where they'd been doing the surveillance and walked down the empty street across from the bar. He noticed that the shades were drawn. First time he'd seen that. Interesting, he thought.

He went to the corner, waited on the light, and

crossed. He walked along the rust-blackened fence of the parking lot beneath the elevated track. He got 427 off the plate as he passed and glanced casually the first time. He read the rest—Charlie Charlie Alpha—as he came back. He was on the corner, about to cross, when he heard a tremendous blast from inside the bar. Then another. Oh my god, he thought. No doubt about it—shooting. He reached for his radio, but he hadn't brought it. Fuck. He took the Glock from its ankle holster and ran for the bar. As he passed its low window, there was another shot, and the bullet came out, almost hit his ankle, and ricocheted off the granite curb with a metal whine.

He jumped back and jogged down the street, away from the bar. There was another blast from inside the bar. He stood on the sidewalk fifty feet from the entrance. What had they trained them to do at Hogan's Alley? He was drawing an absolute blank. Cover, he remembered. Find cover. No parked cars on either side of the street. No help there. He remembered the station wagon, and he ran for it.

He got behind the car. He held the gun up, looking over toward the door. Where the fuck was Wallace, he thought, sweat making his shirt stick to his back. Wallace was old-hat at this shit, wasn't he? As he stood there, an old door they thought had been sealed opened at the side of the building, and a figure emerged. Five-ten, 160, unshaven, McCarry computed. Long, black, scraggly hair, marked-up face. McCarry got down on the other side of the station wagon as the man scrabbled through a hole in the fence. As he passed the wagon, McCarry tackled him. The man folded beneath him onto the gravel with no fight whatsoever.

"Don't kill me," he pleaded.

"FBI," McCarry said. He had his cuffs, and he shackled the man's wrists behind him. "You're under arrest."

The man looked at him and laughed.

McCarry got him up, brought him over to the station wagon, and sat him down with his back against a bald tire.

"What's goin on in there?"

The filthy man just sat there laughing.

He split his attention between the two doorways. Where the fuck was Wallace? A minute passed, and then another man emerged from the side door. This one was older and cleaner. He carried a bag, and when he spotted McCarry behind the car, McCarry came out with his gun trained.

"Freeze! FBI!" McCarry yelled, but the man didn't even slow his stride. He acted as if he hadn't heard him at all—as if he were deaf perhaps—and just kept coming. When he was three feet away, McCarry yelled "Freeze!" again and pulled the trigger, but nothing happened. Then the man grabbed the gun.

McCarry felt the man ripping at his fingers, but he knew to let go was to die, so he held on. He looked into the man's blue eyes as they struggled. They didn't seem dangerous; if anything, they were somehow gentle. Then he felt excruciating pain as the man kneed him in the balls. The gun went off. The man was trying to pull him down. They swung around. He pulled the trigger again. The third time he fired, the gun was facing the ground. The man let go of the gun, and McCarry was raising it when a blow caught him in the throat. He went down to his knees, gasping. When he looked up, the man was quickly hobbling across the street to a city park. McCarry sighted and fired twice and thought he hit the man, but then he was in the park and gone.

Wallace finally showed up on the run, his gun drawn.

"I'm fine," McCarry rasped. "Middle-aged,
white male on the path across the street. I hit him.
Go get him."

"I called it in!" Wallace screamed. "Stay put.
They're coming."

McCarry turned to check on his prisoner. The
man was still. There was a little blue-black hole in
the man's temple, and McCarry took a step back
and saw the brains in the gravel beside the car. He
had killed the man in the struggle, he realized, and
he was just able to crouch down along the bumper
of the car for cover when he began to vomit.

26

RYAN HEARD FOOTSTEPS POUNDING BEHIND HIM ON the path he'd just come off. They'd catch up to him in a second. That young fuckin cop or whoever he was. He was just trying to get away. He'd been surprised when the cop had pulled the trigger. Thank god, the idiot had left the safety on, or he'd be dead right now.

He looked down at the bloody mess of his foot. He looked down at his side where the second bullet had passed through. Maybe it didn't matter much now anyway.

The money was slowing him down, so he threw it into the trees. He came over the rise to the old Putnam Line tracks. There was tall grass on the opposite side—elephant grass, they'd called it in Vietnam. He dove into it, crawled through the tall stalks quickly, and then lay still.

He heard the person chasing him lumber down the hill, his footsteps loud on the gravel of the raised roadbed. Then he heard the rasping of the long stems as the man crashed through the grass. Ryan waited. When the man passed where he was crouched, he lunged out silently and grabbed him. He held the man's gun down with one hand and snapped back his thumb with the other. The cop screamed and went down. Ryan picked up his revolver and showed him that he had it.

"Don't make that mistake again," Ryan told him, putting the gun into his waistband.

Ryan disappeared into the trees. After a few minutes he came to a rusting fence protecting the black face of a polluted lake. He tossed the gun over and went on, moving deeper into the woods.

He passed out once with the pain and the blood loss. When he came to, he moved farther east, crawling through the dark undergrowth. The crickets were deafening. He wanted to make it to the Woodlawn Cemetery, where he could die upon sanctified ground. When he awoke the second time, it was much later. He could see faint stars winking in the darkness. He lay there, cherishing those last moments, and then he saw the candles along the grass and the rimmed trees of the clearing and cloaked men walking up in a procession. Only when they started chanting did he scream.

Then he died.

27

WHEN HE FELT IT WAS SAFE, MCCARRY PULLED HIM-
self up. He'd have to check out the inside. He
couldn't just sit and wait when there could be others dead or in danger. He stumbled across the lot
and went through the fence and in through the
open side entrance. The bar top was in flames, two
bloody bodies on the floor beneath it. On his right,
he thought he saw a swinging door move, and he
raised his pistol and approached. He looked
through the glass pane, but it was dark beyond.

He entered the dance hall. It was empty, but
there was an open window in the back, and he
went to it. There was a dark figure in the field,
walking away. There was another door in that back
wall. He opened it up and went out.

This door was beneath the stands, and he was
looking for a way to get out from beneath the
planks when he heard the first low growl. He
made out the pack of guard dogs: multiple

bristling forms in the blackness. They had probably been riled by the smoke, and when he took a step back for the door, the first one struck his thigh. The dogs attacked then, their savage barking drowning out his cries. He raised the gun once, but a German shepherd bit through his wrist to the bone, and he dropped it. They were in a frenzy. "No" was his only thought as he felt the tearing of his flesh, teeth snapping in his ears as the warm, foul mongrel breath overtook him.

28

FARRELL STOPPED AND LOOKED DOWN AT THE PARK
from the hill above. The entire roof of the bar was
in flames, and then the stands caught and flared
across. The roar of those impossibly dry boards
being consumed by the conflagration reached him
even there. An audience of orange flames illumi-
nated the field. Black smoke billowed out, darkening the sky. Then a siren went off somewhere in the
train yard, and he turned away.

He walked west through a quiet community of
big dark houses, not passing one person. He came
out by a bridge, headlights beneath him streaming
south for the city. He turned left down a small, narrow road, and when he reached a steep, downward incline, he could see the Hudson flowing
black and wide between the branches of the trees.

He went through the empty train station at the
bottom of the hill. He stood out on an opening at
the top of the stairs and watched the water. He'd

drank here years ago when he used to cut school. The huge river rolled dark and silent. The rusting telegraph poles along the tracks stood like huge dark grave markers on the shore. He stood there in the still darkness thinking no longer of his dead brother or his father or his drawing, but of the money at his side and the bottle he had taken from the bar and how far he might get before they caught him.

A train horn sounded as a tiny cone of light appeared in the distance. He picked up his heavy bag and went down the steps, the bottle already open by the time he made the platform.

He bought a ticket for the last stop and sat backward to the train's northbound direction on the river side of the car, staring out with his face pressed to the glass like a kid. He had to change trains at Croton-Harmon, and when he reached Poughkeepsie, he was barely awake. He got into the first cab he saw at the curb of the station and told the driver to take him to the nearest motel. He got a tiny, clean room, locked the door, and piled furniture in front of it. He put the money under the bed, stripped naked, turned on the air conditioner, and slept.

He woke once to the sound of rain drumrolling

on top of the air conditioner. He went to the window, peered through the blinds, and saw nothing but rain and dark. He checked the bag, and then he slept like a man in a coma for the next twelve hours. When he awoke, it was almost evening, and out in the parking lot there were no puddles to show the rain of the night before. He took the bag out from under the bed, opened it, and just stared at the piled money. He took it into the bathroom and put it on top of the toilet before he hopped in the shower.

Even though he saw the headline, he waited until he was in the booth of the diner before he read the story. The Albanian firefight had made the front page, the torched park, page three. The paper said that an FBI agent had been killed at the park, and Farrell sat stunned, forcing himself to finish. He spilled half of his coffee just trying to take a sip.

He saw the car on his way back to the motel. It was a gold '68 Chevelle with rusting mags and a FOR SALE sign in the gun turret of its back window. He paid three thousand to the dazed, middle-aged woman owner without even turning it over. She told him he could turn in the plates himself.

"You look trustworthy," she said.

It was the first car he'd ever owned.

He crossed the Hudson at the Bear Mountain Bridge at sundown and pointed the car west on the curving roads in the early blue shadows of the mountains. The whizzing road in his headlights was pale, and the wild grass and flowers choking its edges bent and swayed at his passing. He didn't know where he was headed, nor did he care. And for a moment, looking out on that foreign landscape, he felt a loneliness that stunned him, that coursed through his veins like something he'd injected. But it passed, and he rolled down the windows and let in the night air, and the amplified liquid throb of the car roared in his ears and spilled out into the night like a cry, a warning.

POCKET BOOKS
PROUDLY PRESENTS

BAD CONNECTION

MICHAEL LEDWIDGE

Available in Hardcover
from
Pocket Books

Turn the page for a preview of
Bad Connection. . . .

CHAPTER
ONE

Sean Macklin pulled his phone truck over to the corner of Forty-second and Lexington only after the third time Control had beeped him. The first summons, he knew, could've been just an all-points beep-out for some crappy job for the first sucker who called in. The second beep he could deny ever getting. But the third time his Motorola buzzed, and his boss's number appeared in the display box with the disheartening suffix 911, he was forced to pay it some heed.

He put the truck in park and got out, leaving it running. He stepped to the pay phone. He had a cell phone in his bag in the truck, but he knew not to use it. If his foreman learned he had a cell, he'd never have peace again. He dropped a quarter and dialed.

"Frank?" he said when it was picked up.

"He's in the can," a voice said. "You wanna call back or wait?"

Macklin took a breath.

"Hold, here I come," he said.

He looked up Forty-second. It was almost eight, and rich business types from Westchester and Connecticut were spilling out of Grand Central, their watches and shoes and brass briefcase clasps glinting in the sun.

Macklin looked at their new clothes and tans, their intent steps. Most seemed happy this late-summer morning, as if each were the star of his own show and turn-of-the-century Manhattan was the thrilling backdrop. Their bemused eyes went right through him as they walked past. Of course, he thought, he didn't warrant a glance. He just worked on the scenery. He was one of the key grips.

Macklin dug the plastic pay phone receiver into the crook of his neck and fished out a well-thumbed paperback from the side pocket of his coveralls.

He opened it at random.

Every person is given at least one opportunity to become successful, he read. *The object is to be ready to capitalize when that opportunity presents itself.*

"I'm ready," he said.

"Sean?" a voice said on the line.

"I don't want to work overtime, Frank," Macklin said. "I'm late as it is."

"Jesus, Sean. Relax yourself," said his boss. "Where the fuck you been anyway? I been beeping you for an hour."

"Over on Lex. You know how signals bounce around these glass canyons."

"'Bounce around,' my ass," Frank said.

"As tempting as that sounds, Frank," Macklin said, smiling, "I gotta get out of here. I'm already running late."

"Take you five minutes. Run by Eleven ninety-two Sixth and find out if cable twenty-two thirty-four terminates there. Griffin got some kind of fucked-up loop goin' on. I don't know what the hell he's done."

Macklin took out a pen and scribbled on the inside cover of the book.

"One-one-nine-two and two-two-three-four?"

"Uh-huh."

"You're the boss," Macklin said.

It took two minutes to drive to the building three blocks up and three over on Sixth and Forty-fifth. It was a fifty-story office tower of glass and steel set back from the avenue behind two half-block-long fountains. He parked in front, reached beneath his seat, and lifted out what looked like a telephone receiver. Clipping the dial set to his belt loop, he opened the truck door and got out.

More suits were on the sidewalk. They eyed Macklin and his dusty lead-splattered coveralls skeptically as he walked with them between the still fountains to the revolving door. Inside, the lobby was thirty feet high and encased in green marble. The rumble of shoes on polished stone, mixed with the dinging of the elevator doors, echoed out loudly in the high-ceilinged chamber like the sound of a massive cash register. He walked up to the security desk, took out his wallet, and showed his ID.

"Gotta get down to your phone room," he said.

He signed his name in a book, and the guard pointed to a door. It opened into a descending puke green stairwell that was thick with hot air. Macklin hadn't been in this particular building before, but he knew the drill. They stood on less ceremony in the back rooms and basements. He wiped his forehead and dropped his eyes, scanning for rats.

The phone room was better than he'd expected. The wall-to-wall steel frame that held the posts of all the building's phone lines was clear. Some high-speed data muxing consoles blinked along a wall. At least they didn't use it as a storeroom, he thought. There was nothing like trying to get a hundred customers back in service cramped between clothing racks or squeezed on top of boxes.

He took out his paperback and checked the 2234 cable number he'd written against the "CABLE 2234" written in marker along the top of the frame.

Well, what do you know, he thought. One of the records up in the control center actually matched something in the field.

He held his dial set in the crook of his neck and clipped its leads across the random twin posts of a line to call back his foreman.

"So how does it feel being twenty-six and about to become a multimillionaire?" said a voice.

"Well, it feels—" a young voice said in reply. "It, um, it feels real good, Speed. Real good."

Macklin became very still. He could feel his

heartbeat very distinctly. Relax and contract. Relax and contract.

"Now, you guys literally started this company out of your garage?" the first, smooth voice was saying.

"Well, um, it was a barn actually. We were renting this farmhouse outside of Syracuse after we graduated and there was this barn and we worked out of there."

It was okay to use a line when you were working on it, Macklin knew, but if someone was on it, you were supposed to disengage. He glanced at his book.

Every person is given at least one opportunity to become successful.

A bead of sweat dripped off the ridge of his temple and made a small dark circle in the dust of the cement floor.

The object is to be ready to capitalize when that opportunity presents itself.

He held his breath and pressed the receiver in closer to his ear.

"What are you guys trading at right now?"

"Right now, eight and a quarter," the younger man said. "Yeah, eight and a quarter."

"Do you know what American Internet is trading at?"

"Close to two hundred, isn't it?"

"One ninety-seven and a third."

"Jeez," the kid said.

"After the takeover, your stake will translate somewhere in the neighborhood of two hundred and seventy million, Tim."

Macklin felt like he'd just been zapped with an electric charge. Tim whistled.

"I don't know what to say."

Macklin's knee began bobbing up and down.

The name of your company, he thought.

Please God, say the name of your company.

"How did you guys come up with 'Palomino' anyway? There were horses on the farm?"

Palomino, Macklin mouthed. His hand was shaking as he wrote it in the back of his book. Palomino. Palomino.

"Nah, it was a joke. The landlord's wife had this long face, bucked teeth, and a ponytail. We called her the Palomino."

"Boys will be boys," Speed said. "Well, congratulations, Tim. You deserve it. So that's Tuesday at nine at the Waldorf. Suite eleven-oh-six. I'll see you then, okay? Oh, and remember, don't purchase any Palomino stock between now and Tuesday, okay? Last thing we want is to make the SEC nervous, all right? Again, congratulations, Mr. Truman."

"Gee thanks, Mr. Ang . . . I mean, Speed. Thanks a lot. See you then."

"Bye-bye," Speed said.

They both hung up.

Macklin listened to dial tone for a while. Then he pulled the leads of his dial set off the posts of the line with a double snip. He looked down at the battleship gray floor.

Too good to be true, he thought. No way. It'll be some type of practical joke or something.

Palomino, he thought.

He'd have to find out.

He quickly wrapped up the dial set, clipped it back to the belt of his coveralls, and jogged out the phone room door. He jogged up the stairs and took out his notebook as he approached the security desk. The white-haired guard looked up.

"What's up, guy?" Macklin said. He looked at his notebook. "Does a Speed somebody or other got an office in this building?"

"Speed Angstrom?" the guard said.

"Maybe. Is he an investment banker?"

The guard hit some keys on the terminal in front of him.

"Uh," the guard said, reading, "he's the head of Mergers and Akwa—akwa—"

"Acquisitions?"

"That's it."

"Which company?"

The guard gestured with his chin at the marble wall. Macklin turned to the golden bull hanging there. Huge muscles stood out in the bull's neck as if it had just busted through the majestic stone from the street. Even he knew it was the logo of one of the most prestigious investment firms in the country.

"First Investment," the guard said.

Macklin felt light suddenly, helium filled, as if he'd start to float.

"Why? Something wrong with his phone?" the guard said.

Macklin looked with effort at his blank page.

"Ah, I don't even know. The information my boss gave me is all fucked up. I work nights for christsake. I'm supposed to be outta here already."

The guard rubbed at his own tired eyes.

"Tell me about it, brother," he said. "I'm working a double right now myself."

Macklin nodded sympathetically with fierce effort. He needed to be on the Internet right now.

"Ah, I think I'll just let the day crew pick it up," Macklin said, taking a measuredly casual step toward the revolving doors.

"That's what I'd do," the guard replied.

Macklin didn't start running until he got past the fountains. He left the truck where it was and ran down Sixth toward the library, where there was public Internet access. He'd gone two blocks when he remembered the library didn't open until eleven. Out of the corner of his eye, he spotted the CYBER LATTE sign across the street. Horns wailed as he ran into the rush-hour traffic.

It was dark inside, and there was some weird New Age music playing. A line of impatient-looking executives with metallically textured shirts and ties waited by the counter. There were tables in the back with monitors on top of them. He stepped to an empty table, cleared the screen, and typed in the address of his stock-trading Web site. He'd just typed "Palomino.com" into the research section when he felt a presence at his elbow.

It was a short, odd-looking humanoid, possibly female in origin, with severely cut black hair and thick, square eyeglasses. He watched her nose wrinkle. He knew what she smelled. He'd been ladling molten lead on a damaged telephone cable in a dank Fifth Avenue manhole all night long.

He leaned toward her. She took a step back.

"Hi," he said.

"Only customers are allowed access to our terminals," she said.

"I'll take a coffee," he said.

The side of her mouth twitched down.

"Fine," she said. "We have Moroccan Tradewinds, Kili-manjaro Supreme . . ."

He looked back as the screen changed. Palomino was a two-year-old book-and-CD Web company that was considered culturally savvy, he read. It was hip, upscale, another Amazon.com.

"Sir?"

He thought the last thing she'd said sounded like "la monde" or something. He would've asked her if it was French for "chock full of nuts," but he didn't have time.

"What?" he said

"Which coffee?"

"First one sounds great," he said, without looking at her.

"For sizes, we have short, small, medium—"

"Supersize it," he said.

He brought up his trading account. There was five grand there from his retirement savings. All the stories he'd heard and read about people getting rich by doing their own investing had appealed to him. He'd taken some money out of his mutual fund and been screwing around with it. He'd been trading for a month, and his account was up a couple of hundred bucks. He wasn't sure if that was better or worse than what the pros managed. But what he had learned was that when one company took over another, the stockholders in the company getting taken over made a bundle of money.

He typed up a five-thousand-dollar purchase order of Palomino stock at the opening price. Then he crossed his fingers and clicked *submit.*

The waitress brought his coffee and the check as he was clearing the screen. Even though it was $4.79, he didn't say a thing. He put a five on the table, picked up the coffee, and left.

Outside the sun was full up. Light flooded down the side streets and lay in white stripes across the avenue. He could feel the temperature rising already, the night cool long gone. He crossed the crowded street and walked to his truck. He opened its door and sat. Errant executives and pretty sneaker-clad secretaries scurried quickly in the buildings' shadows like actors heading for their places before the curtain's rise. He looked out at the building he'd just been under. Most of it was still a stark, shadowed glass form, but when he craned his neck, he could see the dazzling sparkle of the sunlight that licked its upper floors.

He winced at the first sip of the expensive coffee. It tasted like hot perfume. He got out and chucked it into the trash can on the corner. He ordered another coffee from the doughnut cart there. The Arab behind the shiny aluminum counter smiled widely as he handed it over to him.

"You look happy, my friend," he said. "Just hit Lotto?"

Macklin gazed out at the brand-new day and grinned.

"Something like that," he said.

Look for
Bad Connection
Wherever Hardcover Books Are Sold

BOSTON PUBLIC LIBRARY

3 9999 04098 011 0

PS
3562
.E316
N37
2001

Ledwidge, Michael

The narrowback

0401   6.99

DUE DATE			